Magwitch

Magwitch

Michael Noonan

HODDER AND STOUGHTON
LONDON SYDNEY AUCKLAND TORONTO

A Special Purposes Grant from the Literature Board of the
Australia Council to complete the research for this novel is
gratefully acknowledged.

British Library Cataloguing in Publication Data

Noonan, Michael
  Magwitch.
  I. Title
  823 [F]   PR9639.3.N6

ISBN 0 340 28362 9

Foreword

The manuscript of this novel was found in the loft of what had been a coach house on a property in the Blue Mountains, New South Wales. It was tied in a bundle with the three volumes of a rebound 1861 first edition of *Great Expectations* by Charles Dickens, each volume being well thumbed and heavily annotated. It continues the narrative of the protagonist of *Great Expectations*, Philip Pirrip (or 'Pip'), and fills a gap left in the earlier work in that it tells how Abel Magwitch occupied himself during his long years in Australia when he was spurred on to make a fortune by a highly romantic motive, which was secretly to reward the boy who had been kind to him when he was a convict on the run.

CHAPTER 1

When I, Philip Pirrip, related the story of my 'great expectations' and the disappointment, soul-searching and self-
discovery to which I was ultimately (but, nevertheless, fortunately) led, you will recall that I stated I was absent from
England for a period of eleven years following the death of Abel
Magwitch.

If, on the other hand, you know nothing of that story, so be it:
the narrative that I now commence is one that stands entirely
in its own right.

In those long eleven years (during which I led myself to
believe that I had forgotten for ever the Estella I had so
hopelessly adored), I worked for the most part contentedly –
and, I trust, in the eyes of my partners, industriously – at the
Eastern Branch of Clarriker and Co., merchants and shipping
brokers, in Cairo. As the years went by, when my leaves fell
due, I devoted them in the main to archaeological pursuits,
being reluctant to return to England for fear that I might be
confronted with some aspect of the past which might involve me
in further heartache. For instance, a meeting with Estella in the
company of her husband. That would have been more than I
could endure.

Meanwhile, I nursed a secret desire to make a journey of an
altogether different kind, in another direction of the compass.
My interest in that mysterious and still largely unexplored
continent south of the equator led my good friend and partner,
Herbert Pocket, to divine something of what was in my mind.
And so it was that one morning, when I was in my tenth year in
Egypt, he came to me at my desk and suggested that I might
like to consider taking a leisurely voyage at the Firm's expense
to India and the East Indies to explore the possibilities of our
operations being extended to parts of that area. The enterprise
already had our senior partner's approval.

'Furthermore,' he went on, 'since regular trade has now been established between the old world and the new, why not take in the colony of New South Wales and investigate our business prospects there, too?'

'My dear Herbert,' I said, masking as best I could a sudden surge of expectations (although, let me hasten to add, of a vastly different kind than those which had been my ill-fated guiding stars), 'I will think it over.'

'Do,' he urged in his lightly-spoken way, and there was a sparkle in his eyes which hinted that he could already see that I had instantly committed myself to taking up the offer.

This I do not deny. Such a voyage might enable me to see with my own bodily eyes the scene of the labours of Abel Magwitch and perhaps something of the properties he had bequeathed to me. However, my curiosity went beyond this.

Abel Magwitch, or 'Magwitch, chrisen'd Abel' as he once chose to name himself, had never provided me or Herbert – or anyone else who might have been in a position to pass on any enlightenment to me – with anything more than a very sketchy account of how he had managed to come by his fortune. The reason for his wanting to amass that fortune, yes. That had been impressed on me to the point of intense embarrassment by the man himself. I was, and was to be, the sole beneficiary of his ambitions; ambitions of such a romantic turn for a man in whom such violence was embodied that I have never ceased to wonder at the conflicting sides of human nature nor seen them in such extremes of contrast in the one being.

The voyage I now contemplated could mean an absence of over a year by the time I left Egypt by ship and made the journey around the Cape and then returned by the same route. But, as Herbert pointed out to me, some thousands of miles and many weeks would be saved were I to sail from Suez. Things have a way of fitting into place when you least expect the possibility of their doing so and within twenty-four hours of my approaching an acquaintance who dealt with cargoes in and out of Suez I was informed that a ship was due to weigh from that port in five days and sail down the Red Sea and across to Bombay.

'Splendid!' Herbert declared when I told him of this. 'From Bombay you'll surely be able to board some other vessel going to New South Wales by way of Ceylon, Batavia or Timor.' He called in Clara to share his delight at my having come to a decision. 'Waste no time, Pip,' she said. 'Get your packing done at once. I'll help you.' It was as if husband and wife could not launch me on my way swiftly enough.

'Please remember,' Herbert reminded me, 'this is to be as much a long-deserved holiday as a business expedition.'

What he did not say . . . yet I saw the understanding of it in his eyes . . . was that this would also be a pilgrimage.

The ship turned out to be a dilapidated schooner loaded with dates and cotton with accommodation for a passenger or two. The quarters were of such dimensions that there was scarce room for a cat to swing a mouse let alone a human animal to swing one of the feline species. Never mind, it sufficed to get me started. With winds ranging from nothing whatsoever to a little more than absolutely nothing, and seas from mirrored mill-ponds to very slightly blurred millponds, we made slow time down the Red Sea and, after a short stay at Aden, across the Arabian Sea to Bombay. Here I sought out a number of agents and discussed how we might handle certain lines of merchandise for them in Egypt and they for us in India.

After a week or so I secured a passage on a second ship, one that had more claim to the title: a three-masted vessel from which a company of British soldiers and wives had disembarked, leaving it to continue to New South Wales with close on two hundred emigrants, and a handful of Dutch officials picked up at the Cape and due to be dropped off en route. We sailed in the company of a crowded convict transport.

As you may imagine, I had time on my hands now to plan where I might begin once I reached Sydney and who I might seek out. In doing so, my mind went back to my seventh year when I first encountered Magwitch in the churchyard near my boyhood home. I describe him now in much the same way as I did then. A fearful man, all in coarse grey, with a great iron on his leg. A man with no hat, with broken shoes, and with an old rag tied round his head. A man who had been soaked in water, and lamed by stones, and cut by flints, and stung by nettles, and torn by briars; who limped and shivered, and glared and growled; and whose teeth chattered in his head as he seized me by the chin and demanded that I tell him my name. And then, after turning me upside down and thus emptying my pockets, and firing many questions at me, and making dire threats, he commanded me to bring him a file and food – '*vittles*', as he called our bodily sustenance – and to mention no word of our meeting, nor of his presence on the marshes, or I would have my heart and liver '*tore out, roasted and ate*'.

You may also recall the steps I took to oblige the escaped convict, by stealing some bread, some rind of cheese, some mincemeat, some brandy, a bone very nearly denuded of meat, a pork pie and, last of all, the file he had demanded; then my taking them to him at the agreed meeting place near the old battery.

My last boyhood glimpse of him was when he had been recaptured together with his fellow convict and mortal enemy Compeyson. I was fearful that he might think I had betrayed him, despite having brought him the file and the food; but the look he gave me – even if it lasted but a moment – told me that he realised I had not broken my trust with him. It was, of course, this encounter with me that caused him to reflect that his own child, a daughter, would have been about the same age as me – had she not, as he had incorrectly been led to believe, been killed. (And had she been killed, perhaps my life would have been very different indeed, for it was to transpire that she was none other than Estella. But it is not my intention to dwell on that.) It was this sentimental reminder of his personal loss, combined with his gratitude for my kindness to him (which was, let me admit it, predominantly the consequence of my terror of the man and his threats), that was to transform him from a hunted monster into a veritable archangel and to move him to reward me in a manner which few youthful daydreamers would ever dare envisage. From what he told me later – on his return in my twenty-fourth year – it was the spur that drove him on, his inspiration by day and night, in heat and cold, in loneliness and despair.

Yet precisely what did he tell me? What had it all amounted to when the bits and pieces had been gathered up and put together?

The first of these crumbs and morsels fell from his own cracked lips a week after I had celebrated – unknowingly at his expense – my twenty-third birthday. I was there in my elegant chambers in the Temple down by London River living the life of a gentleman – again unknowingly at Abel Magwitch's expense – when Saint Paul's and all the many church-clocks in the city had just struck the hour of eleven at night. Then came that first fateful footstep on the stairs. I took my reading lamp and went to the stair-head.

A deep voice from the darkness below inquired after me by name; and then the owner of the voice climbed the timbered steps until he came on slowly within the light. I made out that he was a man substantially dressed, but roughly; like a voyager by sea. That he had long iron-grey hair. That his age was about sixty. That he was a muscular man, strong on his legs, and that he was browned and hardened by exposure to the weather. I didn't recognise him then, and still failed to do so even when he was within my chambers and had pulled off his rough outer coat and his hat, revealing a head furrowed and bald with the iron-grey hair growing only on the sides. But the lightning was soon to loose its bolt at me. After seating himself in a chair by the fire and warming his large brown veinous hands, he reminded me that we had met on the misty marshes many years ago – and then I knew who he was.

My escaped convict!

Panic took possession of me and I wanted him gone. I made no effort to conceal this and remained standing while he sat. Even so, my feelings were mild in comparison with the outrage I felt, and the degree to which he repelled me, when he revealed what he had been doing on my behalf from the other side of the world, and that my good fortune was in every way thanks to his grotesque self.

Since I have described them in my previous narrative, there is no need for me to go into the wild vacillations of disgust on one hand and compassion on the other. My aim now is to assemble those fragments appertaining to his mode of life, as I did on my outward voyage to New South Wales, to try to obtain some picture of how he might have risen from a convict in chains to a man of money and property – even though he was still under the shadow of a 'conditional pardon', which meant that he was a free man so long as he remained within the confines of New South Wales; to break this condition and return to England was to incur death by hanging.

The fragments amounted to very little when all put together. On that night he climbed the stairs to my chambers in the Temple (which I was soon to feel were *his* chambers), he told me that he had been '*a sheep-farmer, stock-breeder, other trades besides, away in the new world.*' '*I've done wonderful well,*' he told me. '*There's others went out alonger me as done well too, but no man has done nigh as well as me. I'm famous for it.*' Some time later he said that he had '*spec'lated and got rich*'; but he failed to describe the nature of his speculations. He said that he had been '*a hired-out shepherd in a solitary hut*' and that '*from that there hut and that there hiring-out, I got money left me by my master (which died, and had been the same as me), and got my liberty and went for myself.*'

I racked my brains to think of any other remarks he had made, or any hints or clues he may have given; but apart from repeating himself on a number of the foregoing points, he failed to provide any other information.

What I did have, however, was a list of the extent of his fortune. My benefactor had supplied this while in prison after his recapture following his betrayal by the loathsome Compeyson. Mr Jaggers, the lawyer appointed as my guardian by Abel Magwitch, handed me a copy of this list, if only to admonish me by reminding me of the worldly possessions I had allowed to 'slip through my fingers', as he put it. I had kept this with me since arriving in the East, together with two keepsakes which Abel Magwitch had been permitted to keep in prison and which he had wanted me to have a few days before he died: the greasy little clasped black Testament that he had carried and the ragged pack of cards with which he played a game of Patience I had never seen before. These three items – the list, the Testament and the playing cards – accompanied me on my voyage.

The list told me first of all the name of the banking house in

Sydney where cash and stocks and shares totalling one hundred and twenty-seven thousand pounds, eleven shillings and ninepence had been held to his credit; it itemised the rings, candlesticks, watches, snuff-boxes and other silver and gold objects deposited by him; also bags of gemstones. All, alas, confiscated by the Crown. It gave the names, locations and areas of three score pieces of land ranging from a few roods to thousands of acres and, in several instances, square miles. All also confiscated by the Crown. It gave the numbers of sheep, cattle, horses, hogs, goats and other species of animals belonging to him; carriages, wagons and barrows; tools for tillage, tools for building; houses, huts, barns and sheds; boats, furnishings, stores and innumerable major and minor items. All of which in their entirety had shared the fate of Abel Magwitch's hard-won pounds, shillings, pence; his gold, silver, gemstones; his square miles, acres and roods.

I could never examine this list, nor think of it, without a sense of amazement at the extent of one man's accumulations from such lowly beginnings in a new and distant land, all the time lured on by the romantic vision of making a gentleman of a boy who had shown him no more than a passing kindness. Amazed also that, having accomplished so much in terms of material success, he allowed himself to become so obsessed with the desire to see with his own eyes this creation of his that he had risked not only the loss of all, to the very last coin and the very last handful of Antipodean earth, but also his life on the gallows by returning to England.

As to my attitude to what I might have possessed but had lost, I had no regret; I was well satisfied with what Clarriker and Co. had yielded to me and would provide for me in the future. I regarded this list primarily as a guide to help me in my investigations once I reached New South Wales. However, each time I looked at it or thought about it, I puzzled how Compeyson had come by certain of the information on it: the name of the banking house and the descriptions of some of the valuable properties. After his drowning in the struggle with Abel Magwitch, when he had frustrated the attempt by Herbert and myself to smuggle my benefactor out of England before he could be re-arrested, the notes containing this information

13

were found on Compeyson's body. They were in fact the only means of identifying his remains.

I wondered, thus, how this treacherous creature had come by such prior intelligence of Abel Magwitch's ill-advised return to England. Indeed, of all the unanswered questions which were to engage me during my quest this was to become the most intriguing and the most sinister.

CHAPTER 2

The usual outbound route for convict transports was eastward across the southern Indian Ocean from the Cape of Good Hope; but the ship in whose company we sailed had been diverted north to Bombay to pick up a hundred felons landed there after having been rescued from their original transport when it had foundered.

Once, when both becalmed, the two vessels – the emigrant ship and the transport – drifted beam to beam; and, before long boats could be lowered to tow the two apart, I glimpsed, as did others, a little (but more than enough) of the plight of those on board the floating dungeon opposite.

Over three hundred mortal beings, in the proportion of four men to one woman, were confined like caged animals and remained so in conditions which grew increasingly intolerable, with only stifling, fetid air to breathe, even at midnight. When we reached the latitude of the Doldrums, where for days at a stretch the two ships lay marooned a few chains apart under a pitiless sun on a sea of glass, both with their yards hanging limp and flat, the wretched souls across the water from us were kept battened below. A brave spirit there might venture to raise his voice with a fragment of song. But this was rare; and if it did occur, more often than not it was silenced by a military bark. Sometimes alone, sometimes in chorus, human voices would cry and moan. We were at times close enough to hear the whistle of the lash and the sound of leather thongs biting into human flesh. The horror that emanated from this hideous craft became physically nauseating as the odours and stench from human bodies in close and foul contact spread their evil tendrils across to where we lay. Thus, by day and by night, the presence of this dread vessel served to remind me of something of the hardship that Abel Magwitch had been obliged to endure on his enforced journey to the new world.

Many, of course, failed to survive the ordeal, as must have been the case on the transport carrying my benefactor. With precious little ceremony, the weighted bodies of the departed, crudely bundled in canvas and tied with rope, were dropped over the side. In the time the two ships were becalmed together, the peremptory disposal of this form of human slops took place almost every other day, and sometimes twice, between sunrise and sunset.

One night, along with some two score fellow passengers, I escaped from my airless cabin and took my bedding to the deck and tried to sleep under the stars. It was still suffocatingly hot. Around midnight, I rose and stood with my back against the deck-house. The moon had vanished and some five chains away the convict transport lay like a dark spectre. Extending from it, I perceived what appeared to be a widening ripple. The first explanation which came to mind was that the ripple was caused by a turtle swimming far out from land in the tropic sea – until I saw that the hairless cranium, which I had assumed to be that of a marine reptile, was in fact a closely-shaven human head. I shrank further back into the shadow of the deck-house, and from this vantage point I continued to observe the progress of the solitary swimmer, until he went out of my view because of the intervening gunwale of the ship.

Moments later, a rope that had been hanging loose over the gunwale suddenly grew taut and remained so, until a man all shiny wet and dressed only in breeches appeared over the railing with such a mastery of the art of stealth that it was as if he had discovered the secret of locomotion without sound.

Hollows showed between his ribs; indeed, he was mostly skin and bone; yet despite his emaciated appearance he exuded a powerful impression of defiance and strength. Until, as he glanced around about at the many sleeping forms stretched out on the deck, a cloud of bewilderment and hopelessness enveloped him as it was borne in on him that, having reached the only place to which it was possible to escape out here in an empty ocean, instead of achieving freedom he had done no more than land himself in another hostile camp. Albeit a floating one.

To draw his attention without unduly alarming him, I

extended my hand beyond the shadow in which I stood and raised it slowly. He was instantly aware of the movement, and reacted to it by freezing into a posture that was one of defence and one of attack at the same time.

As he stood like a panther ready to spring either at me or away from me, I had no fear of him – only a great feeling of sympathy for him in this predicament, recalling as I did a distant encounter with another fugitive on the run, my late benefactor, Abel Magwitch.

Stepping right out of the shadow, I put a forefinger to my lips to indicate that he could count on me to remain silent about his presence here. Beckoning him to follow me, I started along the deck in the direction of the galley, since I assumed that his first need, after the deprivations of the vessel from which he had effected his escape, would be food and drink. His eyes followed me as I stepped around one recumbent emigrant and then another, but otherwise he moved not a muscle. So I stopped and beckoned to him again.

Little by little he overcame his distrust of me and made a move towards me, only to become transfixed again when one of the slumbering passengers groaned and rolled over on the deck before falling back into the rhythmic breath of sleep.

Reassured that his presence still remained undetected by anyone other than myself, he moved for the second time, and continued to do so, as I proceeded towards the stern where the galley was situated and where refreshments were available should any passengers require them during the night.

He seized instantly upon my whispered invitation to him to partake, tearing a lump of bread apart and wolfing it down, together with hunks of cheese; then dates, raisins and nuts; after which he emptied a jug of tepid ale in one unbroken draught.

'Is there anything else I can get you?' I whispered to him, conscious that the one thing he undoubtedly desired above all else, his freedom, was something beyond me to grant.

At the same time I was thinking that it might be possible to provide him with some sort of sanctuary in my cabin, since I was the only occupant.

He gasped for breath and rasped his reply. 'God bless your kindness, sir – a potion.'

17

'A potion?' I repeated sharply, for it was a request for which I was altogether unprepared.

'Aye, sir. A potion against the disease that's taking toll of life on yonder ship.'

This was something I could provide. Ever since residing in Egypt I had kept a small chest of medicines at my side, one that could be made portable and carried when I moved about, and it contained a sort of universal remedy against diseases of all varieties.

It was down in my cabin, but just as I made ready to leave the galley to fetch some of this remedy, on board the convict transport there was a loud and sustained commotion, culminating in an alarm being sounded – as it was to transpire, by the sentry who had been knocked senseless by the nocturnal swimmer. Soldiers swarmed about the deck.

As I stood at our galley door, staring across the night water to this shadowy scene of confusion, the man at my side shot past me to the ship's railing, then up on to the top of it, whereupon he seized hold of the rigging and hauled himself upward at a lightning rate, quickly vanishing somewhere in the limp yards and the darkness.

Even so, he had not moved swiftly enough.

The shouting and the hammering of boots on the deck of the transport had roused a good many of the sleeping emigrants (who included one or two Dutch officials) in time to glimpse the escapee making his way aloft. They leapt to their feet in their night attire and began hollering across to the soldiers and marines to inform them that the quarry they were seeking on the transport was in fact somewhere in our shrouds.

This woke the rest of those passengers sleeping on the deck, and brought others from below, so that like a pack of hounds in full cry they stood around, shouting imprecations up at the hunted man who remained totally concealed.

Well before setting foot on the land of their choice, those voyagers bound for New South Wales were assuming a very superior attitude towards one of those unfortunates making their way to the same new land without having any say in the matter. From what I had observed of these emigrants, one of the perquisites that attracted them to a new life in a new home was the prospect of enlisting cheap convict labour to assist them in building their future fortunes; so therefore they were mutually outraged that an intended lackey should be in some way trying to avoid the service they had in store for him.

A long boat from the transport hit the water with a great splash and soon on our deck was a section of armed soldiers, each aiming a musket up towards the top of our rear mast while their officer, who carried a lantern, commanded the escapee to climb down or be shot down.

I think it was something of a disappointment to many of the migrant spectators that the man should have chosen the former course. He made the last stage of his descent at a much accelerated pace after having had his ankle grabbed by a soldier who dragged him the rest of the way down to the deck, whereupon he was seized by a dozen rough hands and quickly subjugated and manacled – just as I had seen happen on the marshes near by boyhood home when Abel Magwitch was re-arrested.

As the first moves were made to bundle the recaptured felon into the waiting long boat, I found myself quite involuntarily stepping forward to make a plea on the captive's behalf.

'Hold on!' I said. 'Now that he's here, surely we can allow him a few days' respite away from the horrors of that ghastly hell ship.'

The astonishment around me, signified by a general intake of breath, was so great that it might have been said to have very nearly emptied the surrounding atmosphere of its consumable air.

All eyes were fastened upon me, including those of our Captain, and when I ventured to look from one face to another for some kindly support to my proposal, I met the same surly and accusing expression which suggested that I might personally have been instrumental in somehow spiriting this convict from the transport to our ship. Moreover, my description of the convict vessel itself had obviously not endeared me to the members of the military detachment.

As for the prisoner himself, he gaped at me as if I must be trying my hand at some insane attempt to have myself forcibly transferred from one ship to another in mid-ocean.

The answer given me was a blunt one in that the removal of the prisoner was hurriedly resumed; and when I stepped further forward to try to give the departing convict a small plug of chewing tobacco, not so much in lieu of food but rather as a medicinal substitute for the potion I had been rendered unable to provide, the officer snatched it from my hand and threw it over the side.

I retained a stark image of the last lantern-lit glance received from the prisoner as he went over the side, one I think more of incredulity at my misplaced charity than of gratitude to me for what I had attempted to do on his behalf.

From that night I was treated with great suspicion by passengers and crew alike, and left to my own resources. The ship itself was soon without company; the convict transport set a course south east in order to reach New South Wales by sailing below the Australian continent, while we held a course for Java.

At Batavia, the Dutch officials were put ashore, and I disembarked and again investigated business prospects on behalf of Clarriker and Co. The migrant ship took on fresh water and provisions and was anchored in Batavia Roads only a few days. As I had no wish to voyage further with those on board – and in any event wanted more time here – I took my luggage to a hotel and was fully and pleasantly occupied for almost two weeks until I secured a berth on another ship bound for Sydney.

Once we came within sight of the west coast of the Australian continent, we sailed with the coastline frequently in sight, and I had my first introductions to a land that had been long wrapped in mystery and whose interior wonders had been unveiled only a matter of a few decades earlier.

Off-shore winds brought the tangy odour of eucalyptus, often so strong that it dissolved in the mouth to become a sharp taste on the tongue. The passage bristled with reefs, many still uncharted, so sometimes we anchored at night in the lee of an island. This gave us a number of opportunites to go ashore and examine the trees and shrubs from which the distinctive odours emanated, and so we found ourselves confronted with species of flora that were for the most part unknown in the old world, having curious and awkward shapes.

In close proximity it was no silent land, but one with an audible vibrancy which, with its choruses of furiously strident insects, had something in common with that heard in Cairo; yet here it seemed to penetrate into the very heart of each and every particle of the air around us, filling the day and the night with a sort of perpetual menace. The birds – when we began to see land rather than sea birds (which were of universal species) – were unique to these parts, some having harsh and unmelodious calls and songs, although the splendour of their rich plumages more than compensated for the ugly sounds they made. We also obtained our first glimpses of the animal life of this land – the kangaroo, the flying possum, the wombat – creatures for which there were no counterparts elsewhere in the world, except in the imaginations of those who created drawings and paintings of mythical creatures. We encountered several great whales, on one occasion being close enough to find myself eye to eye with a mammoth of the deep and receiving a stern if not warning look. Similar looks were directed at us from the indigenous inhabitants, dark-skinned and slender, mostly armed with spears held in readiness to hurl at us should we approach within range.

To me these looks were in keeping with what came from the land itself, a profound caution, and I became somewhat uneasy in its presence and was set to wondering how those tortured souls on the convict transport would have felt towards it, battened below – as my benefactor and his companions had been – and obliged to try to picture the appearance of their landfall on the evidence of what they could only smell and hear. Surely an unnerving way to make first contact with a new domicile on the far underside of the earth.

CHAPTER 3

Three and a half months after having taken my leave of Herbert and Clara Pocket in Cairo, I arrived in Port Jackson, New South Wales – the harbour on which the town of Sydney was situated.

From the crewmen on the ship bringing me from Batavia I had been informed that it was vast enough to shelter the entire fleets of all nations of the world. This I had very much doubted, but on sailing up to Sydney town and seeing the extent of the harbour's bays and inlets, I realised I had not, as I had suspected, been treated to any exaggeration. The presence of a hundred or so ships enabled me to visualise this. They were predominantly British – and among them at anchor I identified the convict transport which had accompanied me on part of my voyage – although a large number of whalers were flying American flags. This total could well have been multiplied a hundred fold, still without overcrowding the available anchorages.

A penal colony by its very name suggested a grim and forbidding outpost, so therefore I was greatly surprised with the open, orderly and bustling air of Sydney town. There were already many substantial and imposing buildings mainly constructed of the local sandstone which was of a most pleasing honey colour when freshly quarried. At the same time you did not have to look far to note that it was under military domination. Barracks and barrack squares occupied some prime sites on the tops of the low hills. There were fort-like buildings, also made of the local sandstone; large flags were conspicuous; but it was the people here rather than their habitations which interested me most. Having in my boyhood seen so many wretched and bedraggled men and women setting out to serve prison terms in the new world, I found it hard to link them with the vigorous, healthy and cheerful race of people now here.

Not that all was freedom. I was only just ashore when I spotted a gang of convicts at work cutting and trimming blocks of stone under the cold eyes of armed overseers. Perhaps, I thought, that nocturnal swimmer was already a member of such a gang. I noted that one particular prisoner had carved the letters P.O'M.E. on a block of stone. When I stopped and asked him the meaning of the letters, he promptly replied in an Irish brogue, 'The initials of me name, sorr. Patrick O'Malley Egan. We mark each block we cut. It's the rule, sorr.' (This struck me as being an amusing alternative to what I had been told by a ship's officer: that new arrivals from England were sometimes nicknamed because their freshly-coloured cheeks were like pomegranates; and sometimes after an abbreviation of 'Prisoner of Mother England'.)

Although I saw no blocks with the initials A.M., it was not necessary to look far for reminders of my benefactor. I thought about him and smiled to myself when in a whirl of yellow dust, two mounted colonists checked their horses and raised their hats to me, one saying loudly to the other, 'A gentleman from the other side.' How my late benefactor would have delighted to have overheard that.

Since I wanted to be near the commercial centre of the town, I looked for accommodation in this area and was offered an agreeable room in a small, well-kept hotel with a fine view out across the harbour. After bringing my luggage ashore, I unpacked some of the keepsakes I had brought with me – the Testament, the playing cards, and the list (to which were attached crude maps of the layouts of Sydney and New South Wales in general with those areas of land once belonging to Abel Magwitch marked on them).

Using the combination of the list and the maps, I found my way around the town and so was able to see some of the properties my benefactor had once owned. On one a cathedral was in the course of construction; on another, which had become a cemetery, a funeral service was being conducted; on a third stood a military hospital; and the fourth area I inspected, the largest in the town itself, was now a horse-race track. These plots of land alone would have made me a rich man by any standards in the colony. However, I still felt no sense of having lost out or even of having been unfairly deprived of my legacy – although, to be honest, I did begin to wonder whether Abel Magwitch had in fact listed all his possessions and if perhaps something did remain which the Crown had failed to confiscate.

On that first day in Sydney, I made a number of calls, the first to the *Sydney Clarion*, simply because I happened to find myself outside the newspaper offices. It occurred to me that it might well assist me in my quest if I were to insert an advertisement stating where I was staying and that I would welcome communications from any person or persons who could furnish me with information about Abel Magwitch who had resided in the colony for some fifteen years prior to his unauthorised return to England. This I did. The details were taken down by an elderly clerk who also wrote out a receipt after I had paid him. As he told me that my insertion would appear in the next day's edition, I was conscious of being subjected to a veiled but searching scrutiny. I was about to ask this man whether the name Abel Magwitch had meant anything to him when he thanked me, bade me goodday and turned to attend to another customer, leaving me with no alternative but to go.

My next calls were to merchants with a view to coming to trading arrangements on behalf of Clarriker and Co. The last of these was eager to interest me in handling wool. He claimed that the very best merino strain passed through his warehouse.

'Ask anyone,' he said, 'and they'll tell you. "Magwitch".'

The name came out so totally unexpectedly that all I could do was repeat it in the form of a question.

'Magwitch?'

'The man who produced the cross-strain. Fortunately, for the sakes of many of us, he has long since departed from these shores. And as far as I'm concerned, it was the only other worthwhile thing that murderous scoundrel ever did.'

After this vehement outburst I deemed it prudent to forgo any further form of questioning, let alone disclose my connection with the alleged scoundrel referred to. Except that I asked for directions to a certain banking house – refraining, of course, from mentioning that it was the one where Abel Magwitch's money and valuables had at one time been deposited.

24

The manager of the bank saw me at once. I explained how I was on an exploratory business trip and told him that I would like to make tentative arrangements for his bank to handle any future financial transactions for Clarriker and Co. After this had been attended to, I related something of what had transpired in the course of my visits to local merchants: for instance, that it had been suggested I might handle consignments of wool. Thus I gave myself the opportunity to mention the vaunted Magwitch strain of merino wool. I noted how the manager betrayed immediate unease at the mere mention of that name before confirming what I had already been told. 'Yes, indeed – Magwitch wool is probably much the best the colony has produced to date.'

Taking care to probe gently, I said, 'I rather gathered that it was named after the original breeder of the sheep from which the wool is shorn.'

'That is so. Abel Magwitch. He was at one time a client of this house, but is now dead. If I may be so bold, Mr Pirrip, I shouldn't inquire too far into his background. He left some sore memories behind him.'

Now thoroughly on my guard, I took leave of the manager and hastened back to the offices of the *Sydney Clarion*, telling myself that I should have remembered what my unwelcome patron had said to me on his return: '*I don't intend to advertise myself in the newspapers by the name of A.M. come back from Botany Bay.*'

A youth came to the counter. I asked to see the elderly clerk who had accepted my advertisement and was told that he had left the premises for the remainder of the day. I then asked if I might have my advertisement back. The youth hesitated: he had no authority to do as I requested. I realised he had to abide by instructions, but I had to get my hands on that advertisement and prevent it appearing in the newspaper lest it bring unwelcome attention to myself. I said I wanted to alter a word or two in it. On the basis of this reason, the youth extracted the advertisement from a file on a nail and handed it to me to amend, whereupon I tore it into pieces which I slipped into my pocket as I thanked the young man and departed, leaving him too astonished to move or murmur. In the circumstances I

25

counted the forfeiture of my original payment as no loss.

On the way back to my hotel, I located another plot of land that had belonged to my benefactor, a plot on which a grog-shop had been erected – if such an appellation could be claimed by such a rickety-looking structure.

Seated outside on a tree stump was a lean wrinkled man who might have been pickled in a cask of vinegar and then hung out like a herring and smoked. He was crouched over a long board suspended between another two tree stumps on which he was playing a game of Patience. The pack of cards which he used were not as old and ragged as those used by Abel Magwitch to while away the time, but the game this man played was identical – a game of Patience which I have never seen played by anyone else, except this once. And then, as Magwitch had done, this man used a jack-knife to mark the score in the board.

The jack-knife still quivered upright after being plunged into the wood as I said, 'There was only one man I ever knew who played Patience the way you do.'

The shrivelled man's eyes rolled up to meet mine. His voice was a dry somewhat disembodied croak. He said: 'There were only ever one other man wot played it – him wot invented it an' tort me.'

'Was his name perchance Abel Magwitch?'

Like some human form of a chameleon, capable of changing in size rather than in hue, the solitary card-player seemed to shrink perceptibly, his eyelids coming closer together so that his eyes were glints in narrow slits. 'Wot do 'ee know concernin' 'im?' he asked.

By way of reply, I slipped a hand into the inner pocket of my jacket and produced credentials in the form of my late bene-factor's black Testament.

The man twitched at the sight of it and drew himself well back from it. I opened out the cover to reveal its late owner's name printed on the inside in the rough hand that had been taught him by a travelling giant who had signed his name for a penny a time. The man's prolonged silence was set against the babble of coarse talk and raucous laughter that came from within the grog-shop. At length he spoke.

'That be the very book on which I once swore my life away. How'd 'ee come by it?'

How had he sworn his life away? Before I could ask him this or answer his question – and yet at the same time disclose nothing of my true identity – it was as if he possessed psychic powers, for he said, 'I knows who 'ee are! You be 'im!'

'Him?' I repeated.

''Im wot 'e kept seein' an' talkin' to. 'Is young gennelmin. When 'e was all by 'isself, 'e was allus atalkin' to 'ee.'

The possibility that I should ever be identified in New South Wales, let alone on the very first day I set foot in the colony, had not entered into any of my planning. Masking my inner panic, I claimed that I did not know what this man was talking about. But he persisted: I was Abel Magwitch's young gentleman.

'No mistake,' he said. 'You be 'im. I seen your pitcher.'

'*Pitcher?*' said I.

'That painted pitcher. Magwitch 'ad it 'angin' in 'is 'ouse.'

He meant my portrait. How was this possible? Some nine months before my twenty-first birthday, Mr Jaggers had informed me through Wemmick, his clerk, that he'd received instructions from my mysterious benefactor to the effect that my portrait was to be painted before I came of age. I had gone to the studio of a distinguished member of the Royal Academy in Soho Square for sittings. But that portrait, much approved, had been displayed in my chambers in the Temple and had been there until I was forced to vacate those premises after my allowances ceased. It had certainly not been in New South Wales while Magwitch was still here.

Gathering up his playing cards, the man rose from the tree stump. Once he had all the cards together, he used his cap to dust the top of the stump, after which he invited me to sit on it.

I preferred to stand and wasted no time in putting a question to him. 'So you knew Abel Magwitch?'

The smoked herring was not ready to talk, not yet. 'By your leave, sir – I'll be gettin' m'self a pot of ale. I'll be back presently.'

He slipped in through the open door of the grog-shop with a distinctly fish-like writhing movement.

A minute passed. Two. And then, after what I judged to be

close on ten minutes, when he had failed to reappear, I braced myself and stepped inside.

It was a boisterous scene – until, as one man nudged another, and the nudges ran around the entire interior, the imbibers fell silent and stared at me. There was no sign of the man who had come in to fetch out an ale for himself, so I spoke to the hulking red-faced landlord who presided behind the bar counter and asked him if he could help me. The red face swung from side to side as he shook his head. He claimed to have no recollection of either seeing or serving the man who had been playing Patience outside. Nor for that matter had anyone present, although their grins belied their denials of any knowledge of the person I sought. There was an open door to the rear of the shop, so I could only conclude that the man I had hoped to question about Abel Magwitch had wanted no part of it and had chosen a convenient way of giving me the slip.

In the face of so many mocking grins, in some of which I detected elements of hostility, I withdrew and continued on my way back to the hotel.

My room opened out on to the first floor balcony. Here, as the day came to a close and the activity of the town grew less, I sat in a cane chair and looked out over the scene and the harbour while I surveyed the progress I had made in my quest in a matter of a few short hours. Certainly more than I had anticipated. I seemed to have come up against a dark wall of antagonism to my late benefactor. And I remained unable to account for the presence of a portrait painting of myself in the colony at the time Abel Magwitch was still a resident here. Especially when I recalled the precipitate treatment to which I had subjected that particular artistic creation after the false world contrived for me by my benefactor had tumbled down around my ears. I had formed a violent aversion to the smug, snobbish image of myself; and on the day I had finally surrendered my chambers, I had torn the portrait from the wall, wrenched the canvas out of its frame; and then, after ripping the canvas into pieces and tossing them on the burning coals in the hearth, I had smashed the gilt frame and thrust the broken wood into the flames. So how, therefore, could anyone have possibly seen that portrait here in New South Wales?

As I pondered on this, a sort of audible black fire began to rage with increasing intensity the darker it became: deafening choruses of strident insects, creating wave upon ascending wave of sound, as if there were opposing legions of them deployed in the trees and shrubbery surrounding the hotel, one militant choir trying to outdo the other.

Through this uproar, bugles from barracks managed to be heard; and then, as darkness enveloped the dwellings and other buildings over which I looked, windows and doorways lit up with the glow of lanterns from within. Out on the waters of calm in-shore anchorages, similar illuminations appeared on deck-houses and through rounded portholes, repeating themselves in reflections on the water.

There were occasional lulls in the onslaught of the insects, as if they might have been remassing themselves for further attack and counter-attack. In these breaks, I heard snatches of the laughter of young people playing about in the dark – and also curious metallic rattling sounds which puzzled me until I peered over the balcony railing and perceived movement and made out the shadowy outlines of gangs of manacled felons shackled to one another by chains, shuffling past under an escort of armed military overseers. This led me to reflect that something of the harshness of this land, its climate and insect inhabitants, was being paralleled by man in his treatment of his fellow man.

These insects were, of course, species of the cicada found in Southern Europe and China. They started up again and reached such a pitch that they effectively drowned out all other sounds, so that I was unaware of the arrival of my host, the hotel landlord, until he was standing at the side of my chair and attracting my attention with a polite bow.

He and I both had to raise our voices to be heard by each other. Handing me a sealed envelope, he informed me that it had been delivered to him by a messenger. In an uncommonly elegant hand, it was addressed to me, Philip Pirrip Esquire. The landlord stood poised to go; at the same time I was aware that his curiosity was such that it would require little en- couragement on my part to persuade him to stay. A letter explicitly addressed to me here in a land where I had believed I was a total stranger, aroused in me a certain wariness and I felt I might well need someone to whom I could turn, so I said, 'Wait a moment if you will. I'll see what this is.'

After breaking the seal and extracting and opening out the folded letter, I glanced through it, leaning to one side in my chair to hold the sheet of paper so that it caught the light coming from the lantern on the table in my room. Embossed on the notepaper was the address: 'The Mansion', Potts Point, Sydney. And it read: 'Mrs Lucy Brewster requests the pleasure of your company at dinner at 8.30 pm this evening. In the expectation that you will be able to accept, a carriage will arrive at 8.15 pm to drive you here.'

That was all. It had the tone of a regal summons about it, a command. I read it aloud to the landlord, then eyed him for his reaction. I was glad that I had asked him to remain because he was able to furnish me with immediate information about the sender of the invitation – although his curiosity had switched from the letter and its contents to myself. Who might I be that I should receive such an unsolicited, if imperious, invitation?

'Mrs Brewster is by way of being one of the richest people in the colony,' he told me. 'And most influential.'

'Where abouts is this Potts Point?' I asked, referring to the embossed address on the notepaper.

The landlord raised his hand and indicated the dark shape of a headland on the south side of the harbour in the direction of the entrance.

' "The Mansion" is a fine house in extensive grounds,' he said.

'Does Mrs Brewster, to your knowledge, extend to complete strangers invitations to dine – and at short notice?'

'I shouldn't think so, sir. Unless, of course . . .' And with a deferential incline of his body towards me he petered out.

'Unless what?' I asked.

'You happen to be a person of consequence.'

'Of wealth, fame or notoriety? Is that what you mean?'

'More or less, sir,' he answered with a nod.

'On the contrary, I am but a junior partner in a firm of merchants – a person of little consequence in any respect whatsoever.'

The landlord made no comment but I was aware that he was not altogether disposed to accept such a modest self-assessment.

'How would this Mrs Brewster know my name?' I said. 'Or where to find me? I stepped ashore here only this morning.'

'Word about new arrivals gets around, sir.'

What he meant, but refrained from saying, was 'new arrivals *of consequence*'.

'Well,' I said, 'it's not as though my name or where I am staying are close secrets. In the course of the day so far, I have quite openly tendered this information to a number of citizens of Sydney. What else can you tell me about this lady? Who, for instance, is Mr Brewster?'

The landlord shrugged. 'He is believed to have passed on a good many years ago.'

'Leaving his widow richly provided for? Is that it?'

'No, sir,' the landlord replied, most positive on this particular point. 'What she has amassed, she has done on her own account.'

He hesitated, and I sensed that for him to continue might mean having to reveal something of a delicate or confidential nature which I might not care to hear.

I hastened to reassure him that there was no need for any such reticence on his part. 'I'd be most grateful for anything more you feel you can tell me. I have no reason to believe that this invitation is other than a simple gesture of hospitality from a resident to a new arrival. But it does no harm to be fore-warned.'

The landlord hesitated for some moments longer, but only to frame what he was to say. 'Sooner or later,' he said, 'and most likely very soon – someone wil! tell you her background. Running through the society here is a great dividing line: them who came of their own accord and them that had no choice in the matter.'

As well as making it clear that he himself was a free settler, it took me no time at all to catch on to what he was trying to tell me. 'What you are saying is that Mrs Brewster was transported?'

'Yes, sir. It's common knowledge. You were bound to find

31

out. Would the term "Conditional Pardon" have any meaning for you?'

'It would indeed,' I said, recalling what Abel Magwitch had hazarded by flouting the conditions of that pardon and returning to England.

'It's a stigma many live with – but why should she worry with all her money? Not that she does worry. If anything, she's proud of it!'

'Is it also common knowledge *why* she was transported?'

'Truth and rumour get all mixed in such matters. But it's generally accepted that when she wasn't behind bars, she was on the streets – and that she had a lot more to answer for as well.'

I looked at the letter, trying to link the character embodied in the graceful sweep and curve of its writing with the sort of person the landlord had described. 'She writes a good hand,' I observed.

'Mrs Brewster can neither read nor write. She takes pride in the fact.'

'Then who wrote this?' I asked, raising the letter to him for a closer inspection of its calligraphy.

'She has people around her to do such things for her.'

I was even more intrigued. If Mrs Brewster could neither read nor write, how then had she come to amass a fortune? And what did that fortune consist of? I asked the landlord about the latter and he pointed towards a totally black area in the middle of the main settlement.

'Property,' he said. 'Such as that.'

'I'm not yet sufficiently well acquainted with the layout to know what you're pointing at.'

'The race course.'

'The race course!' I repeated, startled because this was the largest area within the Sydney environs on the list of properties once owned by my benefactor before it had all been forfeited to the Crown. Calming myself, and relieved that the landlord did not appear to have attached any undue importance to my sharp reaction, I asked, 'Are there any other properties that you can point out?'

His hand swung in another direction and he said, 'There's

the ground on which the new cathedral is being erected.'

'Oh, yes,' I said, this time successfully concealing that it had any particular significance for me. 'So she owns that, too?'

'She did – until she gave it away.'

'Gave it away?'

The landlord permitted himself a mild chuckle. 'Feelings ran high among the dignitaries of the church as to whether it was morally right, in view of the donor's reputation, to accept the land. It was about the time when, among other things, she'd been charged with selling illicit spirits at one of her establishments – on the Sabbath. There was an outcry from certain of the clergy when the charges were dropped. But then, when one of the gaitered gentlemen got it into his head that the offer of land was the donor's way of trying to do public penitence for past wickedness, a vote was taken and the gift gratefully received.'

What if I asked about the other sites on my list? Would it transpire that they, too, were now in the hands of Mrs Lucy Brewster? This would surely set the landlord wondering how I should come to ask such questions when I was supposed to be a newcomer without any acquaintance at all of the area. And if I were to ask him whether the name Magwitch meant anything to him, whatever excuse I might fabricate for putting the question, would that not also risk bringing unwanted attention to myself? This very man could well have some cause to feel aggrieved towards my late benefactor.

And so I said nothing, but as soon as the landlord had withdrawn with a request to call me when the carriage arrived, I took out the list of lands once belonging to Abel Magwitch together with the crude map of Sydney on which those properties were marked. Among them was an area of ten acres with a water frontage on Potts Point.

Moth-like insects were being lured in over the balcony railing and through the open doorway to the lamp on the table behind me as I looked out to the darkened headland and wondered which of the lights gleaming there marked the residence called 'The Mansion'.

I have already said that I harboured no regrets at having lost a vast inheritance. Yet I had assumed that what might have

33

been mine had gone in its entirety to the Crown. No doubt that had been so in the first instance; but the Crown had disposed of these properties subsequently, and I already had evidence that some of them had passed into the hands of a private citizen. This was a different situation, and from being detached in my attitude towards the matter, I found myself bringing altogether different emotions to bear on it, and I began to have a curious sense of somehow having been cheated. Not so much by Fate as by the woman who was shortly to be my hostess at dinner.

With this feeling came a certain suspicion, and I returned to a question that had already risen in my mind: how had the odious Compeyson learnt that my benefactor had gone to England? If that intelligence had been relayed from Sydney to London, his betrayer could well have been someone who stood to gain much should Abel Magwitch be prevented from returning to Australia.

CHAPTER 4

The carriage, with driver and postillion both apparelled in smart livery, arrived punctually at the hotel and proved to be a handsome vehicle, very well-sprung to ride over the ragged surfaces of the roads, with polished leather trappings that reflected the lights from the dwellings we passed and then, when we were clear of the main settlement, the shine of a bold half moon.

Above the hoofbeats of the two horses and the rumble of the carriage wheels, the sound of the nocturnal warfare between insect factions of the settlement's cicada population continued to be heard, coming from dark and shadowy bluffs and promontories of bush and shrubbery, a sound that served to intensify the suspense that built up within me as I was carried towards Mrs Lucy Brewster's residence. The carriage swept down to run behind a sea wall before passing through ornate iron gates and ascending a driveway that wove through lawns and gardens.

From a moonlit hedge that appeared to be covered in small white knots came the scent of honeysuckle. Scents with which I have had strong associations possess the power to send my mind reeling back into the past, and so I was suddenly in Miss Havisham's garden with the young Estella provocatively at my side, as we walked together where the honeysuckle had been left to run wild among the weeds. (Did ever a single day pass without something reminding me of her?)

The carriage came to a stop under an airy portico with supporting columns made from the honey-coloured stone I had seen in buildings during the day. It was a solid, agreeable structure, of a style unique to the colony. A footman in the same dark blue livery as the driver and postillion assisted me from the carriage and escorted me up marble steps; then through a vestibule inlaid with stones of different subdued hues and into a spacious reception room where my boots sank into thick carpet as I glanced around under a blaze from lamps and chandeliers at a show of opulence crushing in its quantity and richness. The furnishings and magnificent *objets d'art* in this one room, this one salon, must surely have been as much as any one of those merchantmen anchored out in the harbour could have managed to carry here if loaded with nothing else. All in all, such a dazzling spectacle that it took my eyes some moments to recover from its impact. When they did so, I glanced around again, this time taking in one item at a time – tapestries, paintings and other ornamentations hung on the walls, until I came to one which was to deal me the first of many surprises that I was to experience before this night was out. Although surprise is too mild a word for the mind-shattering incredulity it engendered.

There on the wall opposite was what I had last seen in the form of black and grey ash in the hearth at my chambers in the Temple in London. The portrait commissioned by my benefactor in my twenty-first year. The same carved frame, the gilt a little darker perhaps and showing signs of peeling off; the same snobbish face in the same colours, these too perhaps darker, no doubt with the passage of the years since I had attended sittings in the studio of that Royal Academician in Soho.

What sorcery had resurrected ashes and restored them to their original form?

Or could it be that I had imagined ever destroying that smug image of myself and the frame within which it had been contained?

So transfixed was I that even though I heard a door quietly open on another side of the room, it was some moments before I was able to take my eyes away from the portrait and look around. I did so with the expectation of finding myself face to face with Mrs Brewster; but, instead, I was confronted by a much younger woman than my hostess could possibly be, one in whom I had never seen such contrasting hereditary strains – black and white, wild and tamed, bold and shy – brought together into such a stunning manifestation of feminine beauty.

She was in her early or middle twenties, with black tresses framing a wide brown forehead and well-spaced eyes of a vivid blue. I took her to be half-caste, having seen many of indigenous native and European blood in equal proportions in Egypt. One of my acquaintances there, an archaeologist at work on excavations, had theorised to me about the origin of the Australian aborigines, claiming that they could be descended from Egyptians who had sailed down the Red Sea and east to the west coast of the continent. This young woman could well by her appearance be living proof of that theory. On the other hand, in Bombay I had seen native Indians, and while sailing down the east coast of the continent I had seen native Australians, and between them noted a marked similarity in build, colouring and appearance. So therefore the young woman could also be half aborigine or half Indian.

After greeting me with a blinding smile, she spoke in the local accent, which I had found for the most part harsh and flat, although in her case enchantingly feminine. 'I see you're admiring yourself.'

'On the contrary,' I said, abruptly because I was barely coping with one surprise when I had another with which to contend, 'I would like to think that that person no longer exists.'

She seemed to react with quick delight at my unease and perplexity, teasingly looking at me and then at the portrait, cocking her head a little to one side as she did so. It was then that I had the impression that I had glimpsed her before and decided that perhaps the archaeologist's theory was the right one: in this young woman's appearance I had divined a similarity with half-caste women seen in Cairo.

Presently she said, her eyes coming back to mine, 'It is still you.'

There was a certain distaste in the tone she used; and while I could not be sure whether this was aimed at the portrait itself or its subject, my first concern was to disown this configuration of myself.

'It was done some thirteen years ago,' I said, 'and I have no idea whatsoever of how it comes to be here.'

From behind me came a rasping laugh and I turned to discover that Mrs Brewster had joined us. I cannot recall what picture I had built up in my mind of what she might look like, but only one of extreme vulgarity and ostentation would have done justice to what I now saw. A short, plump woman of fifty years, with a longish nose, swaddled in scarlet satin and laden with what appeared to be the contents of a dozen jewel cases, each piece big and brilliant – tiara, necklaces, ear-rings, pendants – and the fingers of the hand extended to me to grasp so thick with rings that they might have been diseased with gold and diamonds. At the same time, she introduced herself in raw Cockney. ' 'Ow are yer, Mr Pirrip? Lucy Brewster. Pleased ter meetcha.' She reached out and drew the young woman closer to her side. 'Charlotte, 'ere – she's my foster-daughter, that's if you're wonderin' about 'er.' And then, with a gesture of her hand that shot off sparkles in the direction of my portrait, she went on, 'An' that's you. Now did I hear you askin' 'ow it comes to be 'ere?'

'You did,' I said.

'It was left in my safe-keepin' by Abel Magwitch – an' 'e don't need no introdoocin' to us 'ere, does 'e now?'

'I don't understand,' I said, and I told her how I had destroyed the portrait in my chambers in London.

The raucous laugh again, her head thrown back, thus smoothing out the folds of flesh at her chin so that her features suddenly shed years and I discerned that at one time she must have been a pretty woman. 'I remember 'im tellin' me,' she said. ''Ad two of 'em painted.'

I was certain beyond all doubt that this could not have been so. On the easel in that Royal Acadamecian's studio there had been but one canvas. 'Two?' I said. 'Oh, no.'

'One painted, the other copied an' brought 'ere.'

It was an explanation so simple that I felt foolish for not having worked it out for myself.

'It arrived in time for your comin' of age. Magwitch threw a party an' we all gathered around – even Charlotte 'ere, an' she wos only a young girl then – and we all lifted up our glasses to you wot wos on the other side of the world an' drank your 'ealth. 'Appy twenty-first birfday to yer!'

Whatever else my late patron might have been capable of doing – and I was presently to hear things which I would sooner had been kept from my ears – when it came to sentiment there was something touchingly innocent in what he had done. My eyes misted and I could not speak. Not that there was much danger of any embarrassing intervals of silence when Lucy Brewster was present.

'We wos delighted to 'ear you'd arrived on a visit,' she said, and from the tone of the comment I knew that she was curious to know precisely why I had come.

My eyes cleared and I said, 'I've been wondering how you came to hear about that.'

'Oh, I've many interests in an' around Sydney town. One of 'em being the *Clarion*.'

She did not need to go further; she saw that I realised that the information had been conveyed to her from the newspaper offices. That would account for the absence of the elderly clerk when I returned to recover my advertisement about Abel Magwitch.

Now that my hostess knew who I was, there seemed no point in being anything other than frank with her as to why I had come to New South Wales. I told her about my work in Cairo and how a business trip to these parts would at the same time enable me to see at first hand the scene of Abel Magwitch's labours on my behalf. Making a joke of it, I added, 'It's going to be fun seeing what might have been mine.'

'If I wos in your boots,' she said, 'I think I would be resentful.'

'Not at all,' I said, but even in my own ears this sounded less convincing than it might have been before I started to link my late benefactor's former properties with those now owned by my hostess.

'This very land on which this 'ouse now stands wos 'is, yer know,' she said.

'Oh, yes,' said I, as if it were information new to me.

'Not the 'ouse itself, of course. That I 'ad built by m'own architek. Best in colony. One of the best in London before 'e come 'ere. Like m'self – on one of His Majesty's floatin' flea pits.'

As Mrs Brewster laughed, I stole a look at her foster-daughter and saw that the young half-caste woman was tense and preoccupied – until she sensed I was eyeing her and she

39

dazzled me with another smile. Although this time detecting a certain careless indifference, I again had the impression that I had glimpsed her before.

Mrs Brewster was speaking again. 'In that advert'ment which yer wanted inserted before yer changed yer mind, yer said you were seekin' information about Magwitch?'

'Yes,' I said. 'Naturally I'm interested to know what happened to him during his fifteen years here.'

'I can promise yer this, Mr Pirrip, there ain't no one better equipped than me to tell yer that. He confided in me, 'e did. Confided. We wos like big brother an' little sister, me an' Magwitch wos all them years. You'll be surprised wot I can tell yer – and after dinner I'll give it to yer, from start ter finish. From the day I first met 'im on the prison 'ulk at Chatham – after that time he'd been done such a great kindness by you, Mr Pirrip – until the sad day 'e took 'is life inta 'is 'ands and ignored all my pleas an' sailed away back to England just to see yer. I begged 'im not to go, I 'ad a present'mint wot could 'appen. An' it did. I begged 'im, but no use – 'e wouldn't lissen.'

Big tears, shiny and opulent, appeared in her eyes, as if, like her baubles, they were kept in safe custody and only displayed on special occasions. As she dabbed them away with a hankerchief, she might have been sopping up diamonds.

'Yer'll 'ave to excuse me, Mr Pirrip – I wos deeply fond of Magwitch. Big brother an' little sister, like I said. Confided in me. Everythin'. An' that's wot you'll 'ear – everythin'.'

She led the way through the side door into another vast room which had also been treated in terms of furnishings and other items to the best that money could buy. As a footman lit the candles in silver candelabras on the table, Mrs Brewster sat at the head, with me to her right and her foster-daughter on her left, opposite me.

As the candlelight settled into a steady luminosity, it spread over Charlotte's features and showed them up in such a way that I became more positive that I had seen them before. As this ghost passed again, and then again, the only explanation I could grasp was still that I was being reminded of half-caste women seen in Cairo. And then everything was solved for me – although with it came a shock greatly in excess of that of seeing my portrait on the wall in the adjoining salon.

It was there plain and unmistakable. In Charlotte I glimpsed Estella – the same high cheek bones, the same eyes, the same lips – and fleetingly the same expressions. For this there could be but one answer: Abel Magwitch had also been Charlotte's father.

CHAPTER 5

After having been so long at sea, I greatly relished the fresh meats and vegetables so appetisingly served at dinner. And I enjoyed the flow of talk provided by my hostess, even though she assiduously avoided as yet the subject of Abel Magwitch.

With mischievous delight, she entertained me with scandalous revelations about the bribery and corruption rife in the colony, making no attempt to correct any impression I might gather that she was one of the ring-leaders. And she left me in no doubt that she had access to so much that happened in and around Sydney town that, had I not brought myself to her attention so soon after arriving by making that call at the offices of the *Sydney Clarion*, she would still have learnt of my presence before long from some other source.

If she suffered from any sense of stigma because of how she had come to be a resident in New South Wales, she most certainly showed no sign of it. Indeed, she went out of her way to tell me that she had found freedom here. 'Believe me, Mr Pirrip,' she said, 'it were no picnic *gettin'* 'ere, but once I stepped ashore it were the 'appiest day of my life.'

I had never expected life in a penal colony to be viewed in this way but as time went on I was to discover that it was no uncommon attitude. The members of the new race here might have been self-appointed heirs to an old land, but there was undeniably something fresh and vital in the air, as I had discerned in the course of my perambulations during daylight hours.

Throughout the meal, Charlotte ventured nothing. Not that she had much opportunity to speak since Mrs Brewster seemed insistent on acquainting me with more of her own background. Yet from time to time I was conscious that the young woman was watching me attentively, her looks when I caught them being rather disturbing, as if she were deriding me with her eyes for giving a gentlemanly hearing to my hostess's story when I could not honestly have been that much interested in it were I to be frank about it. Nevertheless, I was genuinely intrigued by Lucy Brewster's account of her early years.

As she told me, 'I've as much idea 'oo wos my parents as I've got o' next week's wevver. From the earliest I can rec'lect I was a workin' member of a family of chimney sweeps, that item which wos just as important if not more so than all the brushes an' brooms – a climbin' boy. Don't be surprised, Mr Pirrip, there was many a girl wot wos a climbin' boy, clawin', gropin' and wrigglin' up an' down the ins an' outs of the darkest an' most tort'chuss chimneys in the whole o' London. Reg'lar mazes some of 'em were.' She glanced across at the marble chimney piece with a log in the grate and set of polished brass fire tools at one side, and I sensed her satisfaction that she had achieved what might have been a climbing boy's ultimate possession. 'That was valuable information I came by – the layouts of them houses, the ways in an' the ways out, and wot wos there for the takin'. It so 'appened a certain cat burglar of no mean 'complishment suggested I might impart that knowledge ter 'im for a penny or two. Which I done, even if it wos only to buy a piece of ribbon to wear after I dusted the soot outa me hair. Sad ter relate, the cat burglar got caught emergin' from a chimney piece wif more than just a bundle o' soot – and how 'e came to be there wos traced back to a particular sooty shrimp. After that, my fate was much the same as 'ow Magwitch used ter describe 'is: locked up as much as a silver tea-kettle. Wore out m'share of His Majesty's key-metal like 'im, too. One fing led to annuver and I found m'self bound for destination Botany Bay – an' infamy an' fortune.'

She detached a small but precious morsel of that fortune from one of the satin folds across her bosom, a brooch fashioned into a sunburst of diamonds, emeralds and rubies; then she leaned across to Charlotte to place the piece of jewellery like an exotic flower in the young woman's hair.

'Where else in the world would yer see anyfing lovelier,' Mrs Brewster said, looking back to me to concur.

'Nowhere, I'm sure,' I replied with fervour, reminded of a curiously similar occasion when Miss Havisham had set one of her jewels in Estella's hair. Indeed, it was so astonishingly similar that had I not been certain of detecting likenesses between Charlotte and Estella to the extent that I was already convinced that they were half-sisters I might even have been ready to believe that within Lucy Brewster, despite her having become gross, there was something of Miss Havisham. When the mind discerns one parallel, it runs away with itself and imagines others.

It was Estella's scorn that I saw in the eyes of the young half-caste woman as she pushed the sunburst of jewels aside and rose from the table.

'I'll bid you goodnight, Mr Pirrip,' Charlotte said; and with an undefinable smile playing on her lips, she added, 'it's a change to be able to say that to the person and not to the portrait.'

If she had wanted to leave me in mental turmoil, she could not have chosen a better way to do so than with this remark. Was I to conclude, I asked as I sought wildly for an explanation, that the configuration of myself in oil paints as a younger man had held some sort of fascination for her, one of a romantic turn?

With a rustle of skirts and a soft closing of the door, she departed, leaving me and my hostess alone together.

'Beautiful, ain't she?' Mrs Brewster said lightly, following the remark with a knowing chuckle.

'Very,' I agreed tightly, attempting to conceal the degree of my fascination by limiting what I said in reply, although probably only emphasising my true feeling all the more by doing so.

'And it's right wot she said about biddin' goodnight to yer portrait. Specially after it wos first left in my safe-keepin' by Magwitch. You wos 'er Prince 'Andsome, you wos.'

Already I was being tormented all over again, on the one hand being drawn on by the knowledge of Charlotte's girlish infatuation, yet in the midst of this being cautioned to hold back by that air of inaccessibility, which Estella had so often made plain to me, and which I had now detected in Charlotte's attitude towards me.

Lucy Brewster gave me no time to dwell on this dilemma.

'Why wos it I called 'er Charlotte?' she mused. 'It must have been a name wot took my fancy at the time. I've 'ad 'er since she wos just a few days old. A foundlin', she were. Brought to me after she were left stark naked on Magwitch's doorstep.'

If my hostess expected me to be startled, I certainly didn't disappoint her.

'On *his* doorstep!' I exclaimed.

A ripple of reflected light ran through the diamonds of her tiara as she dipped her head forward in a solemn nod.

'It wos my 'umble opinion that the child wos the outcome of Magwitch gettin' too closely acquainted wif a black gin, but 'e declared hisself insulted at the suggestion. No gins for 'im, 'e claimed. Well, there's no knowin' wot odd tastes men might 'ave – I'm a qualified expert on that, I can tell you. It appeared the mother died a short time after the birf, so there seemed no way of known' the truth one way or the uvver. Magwitch asked me, as an ole friend, if I'd look after the child. I said yes. Yet I couldn't 'elp wonderin' why 'e didn't get rid of 'is embarrass- ment. It were nothin' to 'im, if the occasion called for it, to 'ave a grown man bound an' gagged an' throw inta the 'arbour an' left to the sharks. So it's still my opinion 'e wos the farver – otherwise why else would 'e 'ave 'ad qualms like that, eh?'

I could have furnished a pertinent observation to back up my hostess's claim as to Charlotte's parentage, but something warned me to remain silent and not become involved. Besides, I had suffered a most disturbing chill of horror at Mrs Brewster's casual reference to the callous streak in my late benefactor's nature.

' 'Ad 'er eddicated,' Mrs Brewster went on. 'The best. She reads an' writes – does all m'letters for me. Plays the 'arp like an angel. Needlework so 'quisite it 'urts your eyes to look at it. A credit all round. But it's not Charlotte you wants to 'ear about, is it?'

I could have replied that while my main interest remained in hearing about Abel Magwitch, Charlotte ran a very close second; but Mrs Brewster gave me no chance. Having changed the subject, she kept it that way.

'If Magwitch tole me once, he tole me a 'undred times as 'ow 'e could never get you out of 'is mind. That time when you two first met up, 'e was low, a desperate man, very, very low. An 'unted animal, wifout a friend in the 'ole world, in dire need of 'uman kindness. An' it were you wot provided that, Mr Pirrip, young an' all as yer wos. You it were wot stood by 'im. You it were wot never failed 'im. An' let me tell you sumpin – it was on 'is conscience as 'ow 'e threatened yer. It tore at 'is 'eart to 'ave t'do it to you . . .'

It amazed me to hear this. My hostess saw that from my expression. She laughed. 'It could never be said of Magwitch that 'e 'ad an 'eart of gold. Though 'e could be a good friend – as you an' me both know. Oh, yes. But then 'e could also be a terrible enemy – an' there's many around about these parts as can vouch fer that. Oh, yes indeed. Friend or enemy there wos only one Magwitch. Will I ever forget that first time I set eyes on 'im – the day we wos all 'erded on board the transport for the voyage. Magwitch stood out, 'e did. 'E wos all power. Not just brute force, if you unnerstand – but it were sumpin' that came outa 'im.' She raised a hand and spread her plump ring-encrusted fingers, making the gems flash and dazzle. 'Like the sparkle from a diamond,' she said. ' 'E 'ad the power t'make others stand up an' take notice. On the ship wot brought us out 'ere, his word became law. He kep' order. There wos a Captain an' 'is officers an' crew; there wos a Major o' Marines wif 'is men; but there were only one Abel Magwitch durin' all them months we wallowed an' drifted our way souf. I doubt you could imagine wot misery that were, Mr Pirrip.'

'Up to a point,' I said, going on to tell her about the convict transport, now anchored out in the harbour, that had been such a sinister companion in the Indian Ocean to the ship on which I had travelled, and about the lone swimmer who had sought futile refuge on our deck.

Mrs Brewster conceded that perhaps I did have *some* under-standing of the misery she and others had endured.

'It would 'ave been worse for me, much, much worse, but for Magwitch,' she resumed. ' 'Ad a soft spot for me. Took me under 'is wing, so ter speak, an' saw I wosn't molested – 'cept when it suited 'im.' The lines on her face sharpened. 'While I 'ave allus been deeply grateful to 'im for what 'e 'ad me spared from on that voyage, I'm not so sure as 'ow I've ever forgiven

46

'im for 'anding me over to the ship's officers just so's 'e could protect the one real lady that wos wif us. Emma Beaumont, as she wos then. Emma Rushmore as she is terday. P'raps you've heard tell of 'er?'

No, I had not; so I shook my head.

'There wosn't too many of 'er type an' breedin' transported. Farver a wealthy landowner. Gentry. Surrey. She fell in love with a young 'ot-'ead, preachin' rebellion. Eddicated, too. Got 'isself transported, leavin' 'er 'eartbroken an' outcast, doomed to spinster'ood for the rest o' 'er natural life. She wos a good-lookin' young woman an' 'ad no shortage of proposals, but once 'er lover wos sentenced all she got was cold shoulders. Not that it worried 'er, because all that concerned 'er wos gettin' 'erself out 'ere wif 'er man. She took to breakin' inta poor boxes an' settin' alight ter barns an' 'ayricks, until wif all their influence 'er family could 'ush up matters no longer, an' she wos arrested, sent for trial, and wos delighted when she got sentenced to be transported to Noo Souf Wales for seven years. Magwitch couldn't see 'er anythin' but a lady – an' 'e wosn't content till 'e 'ad 'er in a proper cabin up top and wif a seat at the Captain's table for most of the voyage. To give 'er 'er doo, she never fergot wot Magwitch did, an' when the time come to offer 'im a 'elpin' 'and, it wos there.'

This time my hostess did not elaborate, but gave me a picture of what took place when a convict transport dropped anchor. First the Superintendent of Convicts came aboard to oversee proceedings. Then came would-be employers and agents. Emma Beaumont was allotted to a sheep farmer who was already employing her lover. This was no fortuitous coincidence. Through her family connections, she had been able to send word ahead, to her lover, Edward Rushmore, who was due to be granted a conditional pardon. When her transport arrived, he arranged to be in Sydney town with his Master, who was in need of a teacher. Lucy went to a Sydney family in need of a maid. Magwitch was much in demand by employers with an eye for a strong man, and his fate was decided by the simple expedient of drawing lots, and so he found himself assigned to a sheep farmer who later crossed the Blue Mountains, the range forming the barrier between the coastal plain and the rich

47

interior where Magwitch was later to extend his empire.

'Two fings 'appened to 'im there,' Mrs Brewster told me.
'First 'e 'ad 'is dream about 'elpin' you secretly an' makin' a
gennilman o' yer. Second wos the death of 'is Master, struck by
lightnin', after which it were discovered that accordin' to 'is
will, everythin' 'e possessed – land, sheep an' buildings – wos
left to 'is faithful servant, Abel Magwitch – even though it were
rumoured 'e 'ad a wife an' children back in England.'

To construe anything from this, either I would have needed
further details from my hostess or the opportunity to question
her; but neither were afforded me as she plunged on – unfortunately continuing to hint, however briefly, that much of what
Abel Magwitch had found himself driven to do on my ultimate
behalf had not been altogether above-board. And it was thus
that I began to experience the first intimations that I might
have been, quite unwittingly, a sort of evil influence on my
benefactor and the cause of distress, loss and unhappiness to
others.

'That gave 'im 'is start. A new superior strain of wool –
merino – wos bein' developed by cross-breedin'. Magwitch
made it 'is business to share the secrets of 'ow this wos done an'
to acquire the necessary rams an' ewes to get 'isself started.
Then came a giant flood, sweepin' away flocks that 'ad been
nursed along fer many years. But not Magwitch's flocks, 'e'd
driven 'is sheep up to 'igh ground before the deluge began. 'E'd
listened to what the natives 'ad told 'im – an' others, if they'd
cared to take heed – about wot 'ad 'appened in years gone by.
The result? Magwitch lost not one sheep, but 'is neighbours an'
rivals suffered appallin' losses. So in steps Magwitch. 'E sells
'em sheep so's they can build up their flocks agen – but when it
comes to payment, 'is price is so 'igh that they 'ave to 'and over
land in lieu of money. It wos a great calam'ty to many, that
flood – but Magwitch did well outa it. Must 'ave increased 'is
land 'oldin' by ten times over. Of course, 'e 'ad setbacks – fires,
disease – but for every step back there wos a dozen forward. 'E
wos four years wif' is first Master, but within a few years o' that
man's death 'e wos well on 'is way to 'is fortune – an' you were
on yours to bein' a gennilman. When Magwitch came to
Sydney, 'e'd pick up the latest letters from 'is lawyer, Jaggers,

an' Magwitch would read 'em aloud, sayin' 'ow you wos progressin'. It got that way that when he arrived at my establishment, I'd say to 'im, "Wot's new wif Pip"?'

I took this woman's use of my nickname to be a liberty and I bristled at it, but let it pass for fear of in any way damming the flood of information that had been released.

Mrs Brewster told me how all three of them – herself, Emma Beaumont (now Rushmore after marrying her rebel) and Abel Magwitch – had received conditional pardons.

She told me how Emma Rushmore's husband had also been a successful sheep and cattle farmer and how he had given Abel Magwitch valuable advice and assistance – at the same time somehow suggesting it was a kindness he had had reason to regret.

She told me about her main establishment in Sydney and how Magwitch was a regular visitor, and how through his influence he saw to it that its clandestine activities were in no way restricted by interference from troopers or other authorities.

She told me how the tentacles of Abel Magwitch's empire had extended in many directions: to buying up imported cargoes and creating shortages which enabled him to dispose of his speculative investments at huge gains; of his trading in arms with the Maoris in New Zealand; of his buying up of every square foot of available land and holding out for enormous profits; of how he was always ready to lend almost any sum of money, provided his terms were met – and they were terms which had to be met for he had desperate men standing by in readiness to carry out any order he cared to make; and of how his dealings in illicit spirits extended to every corner of the colony.

I had heard, as you will recall, about the celebration of my twenty-first birthday party: Lucy Brewster told me about that again, and this time went on to relate how Magwitch had hoped to see me in London. He had applied for an absolute pardon which would have meant that he was free to travel back to his homeland; but, alas, an enemy had spiked that plan so that his request, to his chagrin and fury, had been turned down.

She told me how, despite this, he had gone ahead with a plan to return by pretending to go to one of his distant properties on the other side of the Blue Mountains while in fact smuggling on board a ship sailing for England.

She told me what I already knew: that Abel Magwitch had been betrayed by someone with fore knowledge of his return to England. But she shed no light on who that person could have been – except to imply that there were many, even minor debtors, who would have been delighted to have done anything within their powers to prevent his return back to the scene of his labours and his fortune in New South Wales.

She told me about what happened when news of his death arrived in the colony, and Agents of the Crown moved in to confiscate his entire possessions; and how both she and Emma Rushmore, out of respect to his memory – or so she claimed – had endeavoured separately to purchase certain properties that had been his; and how the two women had come to an agreement in which Lucy Brewster bought from them what was available in and around Sydney, leaving country areas to Emma Rushmore.

She had told me, when the evening began, that she would tell me everything about Abel Magwitch's rise to fortune in New South Wales; and now, when it appeared that she had come to the end of her story, some of the candles were wasting out and spluttering in their holders. It was well past midnight and a vast silence was seeping in from the darkness outside. Had I, in less than twenty-four hours since landing in the colony, heard all that I had travelled so far to discover? Mrs Brewster had certainly given me a great deal to think about – especially when I considered how much had been done in the interests of my career as a gentleman – but she had told me considerably less than everything. In a way she had but erected a facade to account for Abel Magwitch's fifteen years here, a facade which I had to get behind if I were to discover the truth – however disturbing that might turn out to be.

She had paused, allowing me to ponder; and then, when she spoke again, I was to realise that the evening so far had been a prelude to her revelation of the real reason for inviting me to her house. In quite a different tone of voice, very softly, as if somehow sheathing her words in silk, she said, 'Of course, wot

50

wos confiscated wos only wot was known about.' And she interlaced her fingers and brought her clasped hands up in front of her face so that the lights in the cut gems matched the hard gleam in her eyes as she watched me.

'Do you mean,' I said, voicing something I had mused on during the preceding day, 'that not all of his fortune has been accounted for?'

'Far from it. In fact, 'e boasted that the greater part of wot 'e owned was 'idden.'

'Hidden?'

''Is very word for it.'

'Whatever could it be?'

'I wos 'opin' you might know.'

'Me?'

'Ain't that why you're 'ere?'

'I fear I don't follow,' I said, acutely aware of what she was getting at, but pleading ignorance to try to gain some time to sort out my thoughts.

'Are yer sure yer ain't 'ere t'collect it? Or t'try to?'

'No,' I said, better able now to cope with an answer. 'I have explained what brought me here. I know nothing whatsoever about any hidden fortune.'

She didn't say it, and she managed to mask any show of it, but I was quite sure that she disbelieved me. At the same time there was something I myself neither said nor showed: there and then I resolved – perhaps as a gesture on my part to Abel Magwitch's memory – to do my utmost to ensure that, if there was any hidden fortune remaining, I would get to it first – certainly before this grasping woman got her diamond-infested fingers on to it.

It did not occur to me that in adopting the role of the hunter I was also casting myself in that of the hunted.

51

CHAPTER 6

Lucy Brewster pressed me to stay for the rest of the night at
'The Mansion', endeavouring to persuade me by saying, 'I'm
very sure Charlotte would be delighted to find yer still 'ere in
the mornin'.'

I was certainly not in the least averse to seeing that beautiful
young woman again, but I had become most uncomfortable in
my hostess's presence. Under that jolly, self-effacing front she
put on, I was all too conscious of deviousness and cunning –
and that every word I said, every move or reaction, came under
her intense scrutiny. Besides, I wanted to be on my own to try to
digest what I had learnt in such a relatively short time. So the
driver and postillion were roused from where they were dozing,
and the carriage took me back to the hotel through a dark, silent
and empty-looking settlement. The warring legions of insects
had called a truce. Nevertheless, I sensed that danger might
lurk in the shadows and I was glad to see that both the driver
and the postillion carried firearms.

After waking the night porter to be let into the hotel, and
undressing swiftly when I reached my room, I fell into a deep
sleep the moment my head sank on the pillow. I recall awaken-
ing from a dream in which I had been in the company of a
dusky, blue-eyed Estella. The room was flooded with daylight
coming in through the open balcony doorway.

With the clear perception you sometimes have of things
immediately after waking from a refreshing sleep, it occurred to
me that if another Magwitch fortune were to be uncovered,
then, in the absence of further unknown Magwitch progeny, the
rightful heirs to it would be the two half-sisters, Estella and
Charlotte. That is assuming that my discernments and con-
clusions about the dark girl's ancestry were correct.

A servant brought me in some breakfast and a copy of the latest edition of the *Sydney Clarion*. A name jumped out at me, that of the ship which had brought me here from Batavia – and I saw that I had been listed among the new arrivals to the colony; but thankfully there was no mention of the reason for my visit.

After finishing my breakfast, I began to think about the day ahead. It seemed that my next move should be to see something of the outlying properties that Abel Magwitch had owned. I went to the dresser to get the list and the two sketch maps, one of which showed the country properties that had belonged to my benefactor – and it was then that I discovered that the black Testament and the pack of playing cards were absent from the drawer where I had left them. All other items were quickly accounted for, but the two Magwitch mementoes were definitely no longer there.

I called the landlord immediately. He was dismayed that such a theft should have occurred on his premises, and from the balcony he soon pointed out how the deed had been done. There were boot marks on the drain-pipe reaching up from the ground. Whether the burglary had been carried out when I was with Mrs Brewster or while I was asleep, the point was that two treasured keepsakes were missing.

The landlord sent urgently for a Constable.

While waiting for the officer to arrive, a number of matters which had occurred in the course of the intervening years, and hitherto regarded as of little consequence, began to take on a sinister significance.

Joe Gargery, who had been married to my sister Georgiana M'ria, and to whom I had been apprenticed as a blacksmith (God pardon me, I still find my inherent nature such that I tend to avoid any mention of this, if not actually taking steps to conceal it), had married again to my friend Biddy, after my sister, who was older than me, had died. Between them, Joe and Biddy wrote to me when I was in Cairo. In one such letter, Joe had informed me that a man visiting from Australia, and claiming to have been a close friend of my benefactor, had called at the forge and asked where in the world I might be found. 'Told him,' wrote faithful Joe, 'that we noo nothink, as neither me nor Biddy cared for his 'pearance nor his disposition.'

Another letter, from Wemmick, soldiering on as clerk in the service of Jaggers, the lawyer, had mentioned that a similar inquiry had been made at the legal offices in Little Britain; and as Wemmick had put it: 'Bearing your best interests in mind, I told the inquirer that to all intents and purposes the said Philip Pirrip Esquire had vanished into the blue.'

Had I, by coming here to New South Wales, conveniently delivered what in trying to trace me someone had been seeking? In other words, the black Testament and the pack of playing cards.

The Constable duly arrived, short of breath, but full of official zeal. I told him at once that only one person could have known about the presence of the stolen items here in the colony: the Patience player who had disappeared after I had spoken to him outside the grog-shop.

Of course, I should have thought of what this would lead to; but since I had not done so, I found myself obliged to answer a number of questions which were put to me by the Constable with all outward signs of courtesy, although he was unable to forgo a suspicious eyeing of the kaftan and tooled leather slippers from the East which I wore.

The Constable, who was flushed and seemed most uncomfortably – and unsuitably – attired in a heavy serge uniform, wished me to describe the Patience player to him. This I did, and while the Constable appeared to be giving some prolonged consideration to what I had told him, he went on to ask me other questions.

'At what sum would you value the two missing articles?'

'Oh, a matter of a few pence. The playing cards were near the end of their useful days – and as for the Testament, it was becoming ragged, too.'

'So it wasn't for their worth they were stolen?'

'I shouldn't think so.'

'Did you have any particular reason to show the book to this man you've described?'

I didn't want to raise a ghost by mentioning the name of Abel Magwitch if I could avoid it, so I replied, 'It was a way of trying to establish whether he might have known a person who lived here some time ago – someone I was interested to hear about – in an entirely personal way.'

As I was well aware, this sounded evasive. Which indeed it was. Coming back to an earlier question, the Constable asked me to repeat the description I had given of the Patience player, and when I had done so, he asked, 'Was he tattooed at all that you noticed, sir?'

'Come to think of it,' I said, 'he was. On his cheeks – and the back of his hands. I thought it looked rather odd.'

The Constable was already giving slow knowing nods. 'That's who it was, sir. Cannibal Jack. That's who.'

'*Cannibal* Jack? Then I'm lucky he didn't try to make a meal of me.'

'Oh, there's no record of him indulging his tastes here, sir. But it's said he was in with the Maoris in New Zealand – that's how he got them tattoos – and he helped them feast on American whalers and other unfortunate whites. He used to belong to the Magwitch push.'

With my late benefactor's name apparently determined to keep cropping up, I might just as well have saved myself the trouble of trying to avoid mention of it. But I didn't understand the word attached to it.

'Push?' I asked.

'It's a local term, sir,' the landlord explained. 'Gang . . . band . . . clique . . .'

The Constable agreed. 'I was only a new recruit at the time Magwitch left here, but I've heard plenty about him since.' And then a distant look came into the Constable's eyes, as if he had glimpsed something significant approaching from far off; and with the air of a man announcing a discovery, he continued, 'Magwitch had a very strong hold on anyone who joined up with him. It was said that he made them swear a terrible oath of allegiance to him. Some Gipsy oath. On a Bible . . .'

He did not need to continue further to make his meaning clear: was the Magwitch keepsake the Testament on which the Patience player had sworn his oath? The Constable looked to me for an explanation: how had I come to be in possession of

55

items that had once belonged to the nefarious Abel Magwitch?

I could have replied confirming that the black clasped Testament was indeed the Bible in question, for the man outside the grog-shop had recoiled from it, while at the same time claiming that it was the self-same book on which he had sworn his life away. The sight of it seemed to have occasioned great terror in the man – as if his only immediate concern was to place a healthy distance between himself and the book as swiftly as possible. Why, therefore, should he have wanted to take possession of it? To destroy it perhaps and so somehow release himself from a dark bond to which he was bound as long as it existed.

After hesitating while I pondered upon this, I decided that it would be injudicious for me to openly declare any link between Abel Magwitch and myself. So I shrugged and said nothing. The Constable then left no doubt that since I preferred not to venture any enlightenment, he chose not to be much concerned about tracing either the thief or the missing articles. He prepared to leave, saying, 'Cannibal Jack's not likely to be found around the town, not if there's any danger anyone might be looking for him.'

Once the Constable had gone, the landlord again apologised for what had happened on his premises. He seemed by his excessive deference to consider that he had confirmation of his assumption, despite my protestations to the contrary, that I was indeed a person of consequence. Furthermore, like almost everyone else I had met so far in the colony, he seemed to have another detail for me to add to the picture I was fast building up of the other face of my late benefactor.

'Magwitch, eh,' he said. 'Never set eyes on him myself, but my father did – said the big man couldn't go anywhere in the end without armed men on hand to protect him from attack.'

It appalled me to hear of this, although I betrayed nothing of it to the landlord as I made it clear that I wanted to be left on my own. The hatred Abel Magwitch had generated must have been intense. Yet what he had done had been for my benefit. When he came to my quarters in the Temple, London, and I saw from head to foot convict in the very grain of the man, had he not said: '*In every single thing I went for, I went for you. "Lord strike a blight upon it!" I says, wotever it was I went for, "if it ain't for him!"?*

What I had done in my mind then, I found myself doing again – loading Abel Magwitch with every crime in the calendar. At the same time I could not help but somehow hold myself to blame for his actions.

CHAPTER 7

The rough sketch maps of Sydney and New South Wales had not been stolen; so once the landlord had left me on my own, I examined them again.

Was the hidden fortune somehow secreted on one of the marked properties? Or spread around several of them?

All I did, I fear, by this examination was to convert the properties into places where parts of a gigantic Magwitch-made haystack had been deposited, with the search for the proverbial needle thus made infinitely more difficult.

If I was to abide my intention to look over what might have been mine, and learn more of how Abel Magwitch had made his original fortune, then one of the maps told me that I should explore beyond the environs of Sydney town in two main directions: north of Port Jackson to the Hawkesbury River, because an island in the stream was designated as a former Magwitch holding; and west, by way of a string of such holdings, across the coastal plain and over the mountain range to the valleys and the inland plain. By going west I could also try to meet Emma Rushmore and her husband.

Among the announcements in the morning newspaper were round trips by sailing barge to the Hawkesbury and coach departures to the Blue Mountains and points beyond. The office of the coach company was the nearer to the hotel, so I took myself there first, finding it in a yard behind a rambling inn.

The clerk, a small man who waved a quill pen to left and right under his nose, as if it were keeping time to some clockwork mechanism within him, acted as if he might have been expecting me. Which was precisely the case.

'You must be Mr Pirrip!' he exclaimed, making me feel as if I must be walking around carrying a placard with my name emblazoned on it. 'Mrs Brewster warned me to expect you.'

'*Warned* you?' I repeated, almost choking with surprise.

'Only so that I might be ready to assist in every way possible, sir.'

I knew what the answer would inevitably be, but I asked the question nevertheless. 'Has Mrs Brewster some connection with this coaching company?'

'She's part-owner, sir.'

'I guessed as much,' said I.

'It was her belief that you would be seeking a seat on a coach proceeding west.'

'That is what I had in mind,' I admitted, at the same time ready to declare that self-same and increasingly-bewildered mind an open book to all who cared to come and read.

'She was of the opinion that you would most likely want to travel as far as the staging-post after Hartley village.'

I nodded. This staging-post was the settlement nearest the Rushmore Estate.

The clerk held his pen motionless as he consulted a booking ledger; then he started the feather in a side to side movement in lieu of shaking his head.

'There's been a heavy demand these past few days. Much too crowded for comfort tomorrow. The day after perhaps?'

'Book me a place,' I said. I had the distinct feeling that he had been told to say that the next day would not be suitable so that I would travel when Lucy Brewster decided I should. Not that it mattered much.

This being Wednesday, and the coach booking having now been made for Friday, I decided to occupy the Thursday with a round trip to the Hawkesbury River; so I headed down to Sydney Cove where the sailing barge was already loading stores and the like to be delivered to settlements along the river the following day.

Here my reception was much less cordial. The sun-shrunk, peg-legged seaman who spoke to me, and the barge master who listened, certainly had not been forewarned to take good and polite care of me should I perchance seek a passage with them. It seemed that I had stumbled upon at least one local enterprise in which Mrs Lucy Brewster had no controlling interest.

'There an' back?' the peg-legged seaman repeated after me.

'The full round trip,' I said.

'Don't know as we'll 'ave room for passengers.'

This seemed a curious contradiction of the newspaper announcement. I told the seaman what I had read – and that the advertisement specifically mentioned passengers.

'Aye – "space permittin' ".'

That stipulation I hadn't noticed. Although it hardly seemed to have any relevance. 'You appear to have plenty of space,' I said, indicating the deck area with a sweep of my hand.

'Not when there's sheep an' pigs aboard.'

'Ah,' I said. 'So you expect to be taking sheep and pigs tomorrow?'

'Only if they arrive. Which they mightn't. Yer could try yer luck.'

The peg-legged seaman looked across to the barge master who gave an abrupt nod of his head and called to me, 'We sail on the mornin' tide, so be here by seven. Nothin' guaranteed, ye understand.'

'Quite so,' I said. 'I'll try my luck.'

Caring not a jot between them whether they had a paying passenger on the morrow or not, the barge master and the peg-legged seaman resumed their loading. Yet when I appeared well before seven next morning, expecting much the same attitude from them, I found them both eager to welcome me on board.

'No sheep, nor pigs,' said the barge master. 'Nor any other passengers so far, so you could have the deck to yerself.'

The peg-legged seaman was equally genial and took me to a place at the stern where I could sit. It had been a sultry night, difficult for sleep, so that I was hesitant to ascribe the good humour of the two men to sound slumber. More likely another explanation altogether – and it would have been naive of me to fail to wonder whether another party had not intervened. In other words, had Mrs Lucy Brewster been at work again after all?

The sun blazed down even at this early hour, so I was grateful for the shade the brown sail provided after it had been raised and allowed to fill with the wind. As that wind came up the harbour from the heads, it was necessary for the barge master to tack the vessel to the open sea. The end of a short tack brought the barge close to the point on which stood an imposing house which I recognised as 'The Mansion'.

All honey-coloured, with a sweep of green sward laying away from it down to a sea wall and a landing-stage, it stood wrapped in an elegant stillness, undisturbed by any sign of life. I imagined the dusky Charlotte and her foster-mother both asleep there, Antipodean versions of Beauty and the Beast. Having reminded myself of Charlotte, it was inevitable that my thoughts should be led to the one I believed to be her half-sister, the Estella I had yearned for yet lost. With it came a repetition of the ache for which it seemed time had either no cure or had chosen to deny me one. Had my coming to New South Wales but reawakened that pain?

Ours was but one of many sails already on the waters of this, the most beautiful of harbours. Added together, grey, brown, russet, white, patched and stained, their combined areas would have been all of several acres – sails supported by masts from the size of walking-sticks to former forest giants seventy or eighty feet high, and carried along by craft varying from what appeared to be mere water beetles to what certainly were fully-grown brigs. Half the vessels passed through the heads, some continuing on out to what the peg-legged seaman told me were good fishing grounds, others turning to the south, while the sailing barge and three or four others set courses to the north.

It was now that the seaman introduced me to what occupied the otherwise empty leg of his grubby white canvas trousers.

With the hob of his pipe he gave his exposed wooden leg a hearty thwack.

'I collected this at Trafalgar,' he told me.

'You mean you "lost" it at Trafalgar?' I suggested, remembering how I had been pestered on street corners by London destitutes claiming to have survived the great sea battle. The England I had left to go to Cairo had been overrun with begging, impecunious Trafalgar veterans giving eye-witness accounts of the engagement. And Waterloo, too.

'Lost an' collected both,' said the seaman, determined not to be put out. 'Blown off in the battle, replaced with a floatin' pole, solid oak.' He struck the wooden leg again. 'It was because of Trafalgar I was transported.'

I waited for him to elaborate, expecting him to claim that he had been the victim of some unfortunate circumstance but was of impeccable character otherwise. I was not disappointed.

'Aye. Struck a man for insultin' the name of m'old Admiral, Lord Nelson. I ought to 'ave killed the rogue. Up at the Assizes for causin' grevious bodily 'arm – an' given life. Just the same, I'd do it agen to anyone who insulted m'ole Lord Nelson.'

The seaman was presenting me with his credentials so that I would accept him as a person to be trusted – even the recipient of my confidences, for he threw out some big hints for me to explain my interest in making the round trip. I told him that while I was on a business expedition, I was also interested to see as much of the colony as possible during my stay, so he furnished me with a flow of information as to where we were and what we were passing. Places where ships had struck, for instance.

By now all the vessels that had turned north had fallen away, except a cutter which remained a steady half mile astern, apparently content to coast along at the same slow rate as the sailing barge.

The mouth of the Hawkesbury River where it emptied into the Pacific Ocean had the appearance of a deep inlet, being two miles across with a large island standing at its entrance (but not the one marked on the rough map). We passed south of this island with the wind now behind us.

Either side, the river banks were steep and densely-clothed in indigenous bush, except where gaunt rocks loomed alone or in aged clumps. Bird calls, including the maniacal laughter of unseen jackasses, came from the bush where the tops of trees occasionally shook or danced as birds and native possums moved about among them – or so my peg-legged guide informed me. A clutch of white cockatoos sped out of dark green shadow and raced their reflections across the surface of the water with such a rush of purity of colour and grace that they veritably took the breath away.

As we sailed further up the river, the gradual narrowing of its width seemed to bring a sort of intensification of the primaeval atmosphere that permeated this region. And to add to this impression, the waters of the river, which my Trafalgar veteran informed me were at this point still salt and tidal, became the setting for a phenomenon the like of which I had never imagined could be seen other than in a fanciful dream. From bank to bank and as far as the next bend, the river was choked with a dense shoal of opaque white jelly-fish, like some malign species of giant marine mushrooms. Immediately upon entering into this mass, the forward movement of the sailing barge was checked and its speed kept at a slower rate as it ploughed through the jelly-fish, leaving them heaving in its wake.

Turning to the rear to observe this, I saw that the cutter was still following us, although on reaching the jelly-fish, its speed was also reduced, so that any distance it might have gained upon us was now lost. Then the bend in the river intervened and the cutter could no longer be seen.

The barge master directed the man on the tiller to steer closer to the left bank where a large area of land had been cleared and was cultivated. Wattle and daub huts stood in the shade of trees around the open area. A rowing boat with a man and woman put out to meet us, the master allowing the mainsail to hang slack so that the barge slowly came to a stop.

After fresh stores had been exchanged for empty casks, flagons and crates, the mainsail filled out again and the barge proceeded further up the river, coming nearer to the point from which a strident sound originated, echoing up and down the high banks, a regular metallic hammering. Presently we saw the reason for this: a gang of twenty convicts under armed overseers at work with hammers and metal pickets as they cut more rock from the face of a sandstone quarry.

Two of the convicts dared to wave at us, only to be threatened by their overseers. The sound of the stone-cutting pursued us, even though we took a double bend in the river – and then the banks opened out one from the other to make room for the wooded island in the middle of the stream.

Pointing to the island with the stem of his pipe, the Trafalgar veteran told me what it was called – although at first I thought he had taken the liberty of calling me by my family name.

'Pirrip,' he said.

'Pirrip?' I repeated, sharply questioning his right to such familiarity.

'Pirrip Island,' he explained, and as I wondered what I would next find done by Abel Magwitch in my name, the peg-legged seaman went on, 'It's been deserted since it was discovered by Customs men as bein' a secret distillery.'

As I was confident that the date would have coincided with the confiscation of my late benefactor's properties, I did not ask when that discovery had been made.

Having given up one secret in the past, I was set to wondering whether the island might not yield another. As the barge was steered to pass the island on the starboard side, I saw that it had a small landing-stage, so I asked, 'Do you stop here at all?'

'Not as a regular matter,' the Trafalgar veteran told me. 'But if you'd care to go ashore we could pick you up on our way back.'

'If it's not too much trouble,' I said.

No sooner had I spoken than the Trafalgar veteran signalled the master who immediately gave quick instructions to the man on the tiller. I couldn't swear it, but I had the feeling that I was but merely making a request for what had in fact been pre-arranged: that it had been planned I should be put ashore here while the sailing barge completed its delivery run. Having sensed this, rather than its being a caution to me it became a challenge: why should anyone want me to go ashore?

The landing-stage had fallen into disrepair and creaked and swayed alarmingly as the sailing barge shouldered into it. Once upon it, I stepped quickly from one to another of the boards I judged to be more secure, until I was on solid ground, on a path heavily overgrown with weeds and long grasses.

Leaving the barge to get under way once more, I faced the interior of the island. The bush simmered with sounds of insects and muted the calls of birds, except when a flock of multi-coloured parakeets burst out above the tops of the trees and wove about, one chasing the other in scrolls of play, to the accompaniment of their calls which combined into a sound like that of many coins somehow being jingled furiously as they were carried unseen through the air.

The path on which I stood appeared to encircle the island; another, this one waist-deep in weeds and grasses, headed into the centre and led to what looked from a distance like some sort of habitation. So I set out along this path, but had gone only a short distance when I pulled up at what appeared to be a strange species of fine vines bearing small round fruit like black damsons. Just as well I did not succumb to the temptation to pluck one free – for what I took to be ripe fruit were plump spiders, some of which scurried for the shelter of the trees to which their webs were anchored. I hastened to retreat and followed the encircling path until I found another leading inward, one free of any such repelling obstructions.

The habitation I had glimpsed turned out to be the upside down hull of an old boat about the size of a sloop, with a doorway and a single window cut in the side. Standing at the doorway and peering inside, I saw crude furnishings all cob-webbed and grimed with dust; a fireplace of stones and brick, and beside it a rusting iron cauldron; also pieces of broken bottles and other receptacles. Were these remnants of vessels used in the illicit distilling of spirits? Spirits that had helped pay for my embroidered waistcoats and handmade boots; my accounts with wine merchants for port and Madeira; seats at the opera; coins to be airily tossed to gin-sodden destitutes of London's streets – and to veterans claiming to be survivors from the Battle of Trafalgar. I entered and looked around about under the inverted wooden ribs of the boat, and then searched the timbers that now made walls for markings that might tell me something. By calling this compact acre or two Pirrip Island, had Abel Magwitch perhaps been planting a clue as to the whereabouts of what he had hidden away?

At a sharp rustling sound outside, I turned to look out through the empty window and saw a sapling trembling in bush that was otherwise totally still. Probably a possum, I told myself, since the Trafalgar veteran had intimated that they were in large numbers in this area. Glancing about for a glimpse of such a creature, I saw a ladder attached to a high section of towering gum tree. To see where it began, I would have to go into the undergrowth and bush; and since it had become suffocatingly hot, I first removed my jacket and hung it over the back of a rickety chair.

As I had expected, this ladder began at ground level, the first part of it rising to a small platform about thirty feet overhead. The part I had seen started from this point; and from what I could make out from so far below, it was the second of three parts of about the same length.

Without further ado, I started my ascent, taking care to test each rung before putting any of my weight on it. The wooden planks on the first platform were warped, as were those on the second – and the third, which brought me to a point so high above the island and the land either side of the river that there were good views in all directions.

The sailing barge had stopped over half a mile upstream at a long, thin jetty that reached deep water over mud flats. Along this jetty, forming a chain, men, women and children stood a few yards apart and passed the stores ashore from the barge, doing so with a practised rhythm.

A rhythm of another sort came from the opposite direction: the hammering of the stone-cutting. From this height I had a very clear view downstream to the quarry, where the felons worked with the overseers standing by. I could see the blows struck, then seconds passed before the metallic sound of the blow reached my ears.

From this same height I located the shoal of jelly-fish, creating a pearl-like iridescence just under the surface of the water. And then, surprised at myself for having been so engrossed in other matters that I should have forgotten about it, I realised there was no sign of the cutter that had been following on the same course as us – until I sighted it moored close in to the trees on the opposite side of the island to where the landing-stage stood. The cutter was empty, so all who had been aboard it must now also be on the island. And so the possum I had assumed to have been responsible for leaving that sapling atremble was more likely to have been a two-legged creature of upright carriage.

Unless I got back down to the ground immediately, I was afraid I might be marooned on this tree-top eyrie, so I wasted

66

no time in descending the three ladders. After briefly pausing to listen, and hearing nothing more than the insects and birds, I made a swift dash through the undergrowth to the upside down boat to collect my jacket. It was still on the back of the chair in the same position, but around it on the bare earth floor I spotted footprints other than mine – boots considerably bigger; boots considerably smaller; and a set of bare footprints – so that I concluded that at least three persons from the moored cutter had been in this abandoned abode. I was about to slip my hands into the arm-holes of the jacket, fumbling nervously, when something flew in through the open doorway like an airborne serpent, ending its flight by impinging itself between the inverted ribs of the boat – a wooden spear of some four and a half feet in length that remained stuck fast, humming as it vibrated.

This was no place to be either, so jamming my hat tightly on my head and preparing to use my jacket in front of me as a shield, I raced out of the upside down boat, across the intervening open space to the path I had avoided because of the webs and spiders, sweeping those webs along with me in my rush, partly covering my jacket and myself with them – and with their fat residents, all of which curled up into balls with fright, so that I was able to brush most of them aside as I ran. At any moment I expected another airborne serpent to overtake me and impinge itself into my back, but somehow I reached the end of the path where, for some reason I cannot explain (it is as if the mind makes such decisions for you of its own accord in such situations) I took a slithering dive through the weeds and long grasses to where the landing-stage enjoined with the island; then swiftly scrambled under it, there to wedge myself among the cross-beams that helped support it, close below the planks of the decking.

In the course of my slither, my hat and I had parted company; and while I stopped, my hat continued in the direction I had been taking and was now floating out in the river.

With the thudding of my heart audible in my ears – indeed, so loud that it might have been echoing up and down the river and keeping company with the hammering from the quarry – I

67

strained to listen and heard the pounding of running feet and the breaking of undergrowth, until they came to a halt where the path from the centre of the island met the one that encircled it. My pursuers, from the voices I now heard, were three in number, all male.

One was dominant; he was not addressed by name. Another I judged to be of native blood, because he spoke English like one of the aborigines who had helped unload my baggage from the ship in Sydney when we arrived, and he was called Henry. The third was called Jack, and I recognised the voice of the solitary Patience player who had been outside the grog-shop – Cannibal Jack.

As they waited to see if I had tried to escape them by diving into the river and swimming underwater, that their prime aim was to capture me alive was evident beyond all doubt. From what they said to one another, it was apparent that they had bribed the barge master and the peg-legged seaman to inveigle me ashore alone on Pirrip Island; but their plan had gone astray after the spear had been thrown into the hut. They had assumed it would have struck such terror into me that I would have remained in the hut for shelter, instead of making a rush for freedom; and they had used a spear rather than a firearm as the sound of a shot would have travelled either way along the river and could have attracted unwelcome attention from troopers guarding convict working gangs.

' 'E'd 'ave come up by now if 'e'd took ter the water,' Cannibal Jack said.

'In that case he didn't take to the water. Only his hat did,' said the dominant member of the trio in abrupt stentorian tones. 'Henry, cut across the island and stand by the boat. We don't want him trying to use it to get away.' And once the native member had gone, the leader went on, 'Jack, you go that way around the island, I'll go the other.'

Who went to the right and who to the left, I could not determine as I was left to try to secure a firmer hold on the cross-beams, all too aware of the gaps between the boards close above me. It is curious what occupies the mind in times of crisis. On this occasion I found myself thinking how I was experiencing something of the hunted feeling that Abel Magwitch must

68

have undergone as he tried to hide in ditches on the marshes as the guards from the prison hulk searched for him. He had said, '*I wish I was a frog. Or a eel.*' I never thought I would come to appreciate what he really meant. It was this understanding of what he had suffered that made me less inclined to abhor his ruthlessness, but rather to discover excuses for it.

After their first circuits of the island, Cannibal Jack and the leader of the trio came back to where the landing-stage began. They made a second circuit, a third, returning each time to admit neither had glimpsed anything of me. Now for the first time they stepped on the landing-stage itself to peer around in the deeper water, just to make sure I had not dived into the river and failed to surface.

'Coulda bin took by a shark,' Cannibal Jack suggested. 'There's man-eaters gets up the river this far – bin knowed ter rear up an' take live dogs with one bite.'

The other grunted and paced about. It was as if he were walking on my back. I felt I must be exposed to their view, for could I not see the reflections of the two in the water, Cannibal Jack leaning over, the other upright and tall – both wearing dark neck-cloths as masks?

And then something happened which must surely give me away. A spider, which had been curled up in some of the web attached to my back, came to life and crawled on to my shoulder so that I was eye to eye with the creature. At first I was unable to move a muscle for fright; then, giving up one of my grips on the cross-beams, I used a hand to brush the creature away. It fell into the water with a faint plop. I listened. The sound had not been heard by either of the two above me; but then, just as I allowed myself a small measure of relief, the water swirled as a large silver-green fish rose from the depths at the swimming spider. A snap, swallow, and a thrust away.

Coming to the edge of the landing-stage to peer over just in time to catch a glimpse of the vanishing fish, Cannibal Jack said, 'Looked like a bream. A big 'un, whatever it was.'

The other grunted, stopped pacing, then headed back on to the island, saying to Cannibal Jack, 'We'll try the tracks across the island. When the barge returns, he's liable to make a run to get here and back on board it.'

Between them the spider and the fish had done me no harm; although it surprised me neither of the two men had thought of looking under the landing-stage, until I realised that it was such an obvious refuge, so open, that they would have dismissed any possibility of my choosing it before even considering it. Thus I remained in this place of concealment, eyeing the river for fear that a man-eater might rise up out of it, and seeing the beginnings of such a monster in the changes of light in the water and in the eddies made by the tide around the piles.

Intermittently, I could hear movement deep in the island as the search for me continued. Time was now working for me as I realised the sailing barge must be due. But if the master and the Trafalgar veteran were in league with my pursuers – even though it seemed that the reason for the three from the cutter wanting to capture me had not been disclosed to the former two – what chance would I have of doing anything else but fall into their hands if I made any move whatsoever from my present position? If I could make my way across the island, perhaps I could take the aborigine Henry by surprise and still slip away in the cutter.

Before I had an opportunity to try to carry out this move, from upstream I saw the sailing barge approaching after coming around a bend in the river.

The Trafalgar veteran had stationed himself forward of the mast, shading his eyes as he peered ahead towards the landing-stage. As if because I was not there, he cupped his hands around his mouth and began to shout.

'Ahoy! Ahoy, there!'

As his calls echoed up and down the river, and the barge bore on closer to the landing-stage, several men and women passengers came to where he stood on the deck, sharing the anxiety which he was showing for me. All a pretence on his part, of course. It had obviously been prearranged that when the sailing barge returned here, I would be found to be missing.

The barge struck the landing-stage hard, causing it to sway and shudder, so that I was very nearly dislodged from my precarious perch. But I clung on yet.

The Trafalgar veteran gave voice to another 'Ahoy! Ahoy, there!'; and after I again failed to respond, he called upon the passengers to volunteer to help him search the island for me.

It seemed all agreed. The planks above me bent and boomed as they hastened ashore, led by the Trafalgar veteran.

They were my saviours those passengers returning to Port Jackson from upstream settlements – I clambered out and hauled myself up over the edge of the landing-stage and stood upright on the planks.

From the barge deck, the master gave an astonished cry: 'How the devil did you get there!'; while the Trafalgar veteran, stopped in his tracks, swung around and stared – and from the stare he gave me, he could not have been more surprised had the naval hero (whose good name he had allegedly defended to the extent of being transported) appeared before him.

Stepping over the low deck railing of the barge, I replied to the master, 'Oh, it was getting rather too hot to be out in the open.'

He scowled as he caught on to my meaning, while the other passengers, realising no search was necessary, returned to the landing-stage, then to the barge, followed by the Trafalgar veteran who kept looking back to the island as if wondering to what point in the bush and vegetation he should direct a helpless – and apologetic – shrug.

My hat had been on an elliptical course from the landing-stage and back near it due to the swirl of the currents and the tide. Using a boat hook I recovered it without difficulty; it had suffered no damage that a drying out would not soon cure.

The three would-be abductors had wasted no time in departing from the island after giving up hope of capturing me, for once the barge had sailed downstream clear of the next bend in the river, the cutter was well ahead and making fast time now that the wind blew off the land and towards the sea.

It was slowed down by the shoal of jelly-fish, and the barge gained some distance upon it, but we did not draw close enough to be able to see the three men aboard it as more than male shapes. By the time we reached the mouth of the Hawkesbury and turned south for the run in the open ocean to Port Jackson, the cutter was a small sail far ahead.

No comments or questions were forthcoming from either the barge master or the Trafalgar veteran about how I spent my interlude on Pirrip Island, although from their cheated and peeved expressions there was much they would liked to have been told. No doubt there would be some reckoning to be faced by them when they met up with the three occupants of the cutter, at least one of whom must have been following me when I called at the quay in Sydney Cove the previous afternoon.

That evening, to avoid any further attempts at abduction, I dined in my room at the hotel and remained there completing letters I had started the night before – to the Pockets and several other friends in Cairo – and preparing for an early start the next morning to be at the coach station for the journey over the Blue Mountains.

The landlord had knocked on my door soon after my return to tell me that he had made it his business to speak to the Constable who had investigated the theft of my two keepsakes; and that he had been informed by the Constable that the whereabouts of Cannibal Jack was unknown. I could have enlightened him on this point but refrained.

Some hours later in the evening, he knocked again, this time to hand me a note that had been delivered for me. It was from Mrs Brewster. She said that since I was travelling on the Friday rather than the Thursday, this had given her an opportunity of getting a letter away to Emma Rushmore to forewarn her of my arrival. She felt sure that her old friend, as she described Mrs Rushmore in the note, would be most eager to meet me and would be making all necessary arrangements to have me taken care of.

The note was, of course, in Charlotte's hand. I had so built up her likeness in my mind to another that now I saw something of Estella in every stroke, curve and dot her pen had made on the paper.

CHAPTER 8

The landlord took my letters for posting and locked away my
luggage, except a hand-portmanteau which I carried as I set
out on foot for the coach station well ahead of the departure
time of seven sharp.

As I did so, I have to confess that I questioned the wisdom of
prying any further into Abel Magwitch's past, and whether this
journey to the earliest scene of his labours – to where he had
conceived the idea of secretly making me a gentleman – might
be best not undertaken; but then, when I remembered that
others seemed bent on either obstructing me in my quest or
beating me to what it might yield, all my doubts were shed and
my determination renewed.

The coaching station proclaimed its whereabouts through
the strong odours of horses and hay emanating from behind the
inn where it was situated. It was a rectangular yard with stables
for horses on one side facing bays for coaches on the other, and
the office and waiting-room mid-way between them. The clerk
interrupted the silent tick-tocking of his quill pen to dip the
point into an ink-well and place a mark against my name on the
list of the six passengers who would be travelling inside the
coach.

With the day growing warmer by the minute, it was evident
that we were to be in for a hot passage, although considering we
were so close to the combination of the Antipodean Midsum-
mer's Eve and Christmas Day, this was only to be expected.

When I remarked that the journey looked like being a warm
one, the clerk replied, 'Never mind, Mr Pirrip – once you start
up into the mountains it will surely become cooler.'

Eager to be obliging, he called a lad to take my portmanteau
and load it on the stage-coach, which had been rolled out into
the yard where another boy was giving its green and black
livery an energetic polish, bringing up a gloss that reflected the

sun with such strength that it dazzled my eyes as I went to the waiting-room, to which the clerk had directed me.

Here I found a number of passengers gathered, dividing themselves in much the same way as they were to travel: those who were to ride on the outside of the coach – so far a family of young parents with two small children, a boy and a girl – on hard wooden benches at one end of the room; and those who were to be inside the vehicle, on upholstered seats at the other end.

Three of my immediate travelling companions were present. A middle-aged couple of substantial means and self-indulgence, if one was to judge from their expensive attire and their ample physical proportions; a couple with a high regard for themselves, too, from the lofty nature of their expressions, through which they seemed to be serving fair warning that they were unlikely to be indulging in much social intercourse with other travellers. They were already giving unmistakable indication of this by the way they maintained dogged indifference to the overtures of the third inside passenger, a man who was endeavouring to engage their interest by deftly keeping three small ivory balls aloft with one hand, a feat which was watched from the other end of the waiting-room with goggle-eyed rapture by the two children.

On my entering the waiting-room, this man transferred his attention to me, and after making three balls and a fourth chase one another through the air with even greater rapidity, he allowed them to click home in his hand, whereupon he swept off his stove-pipe hat, which was of an alarming orange colour, and bowed extravagantly, as if I might be the entire audience of a packed hall.

'Sam Bullwinkle,' he said, introducing himself as he came upright again. 'Juggler and Magician.' He handed me a card on which was repeated what he had said, together with a printed claim that his legerdemain and sorcery had astonished the eyes, confounded the minds, and all but stopped the hearts of countless thousands, including the Crowned Heads of Europe and other Dignitaries. Adding to what was not on the card, he said, 'I am proceeding to distant settlements in the wild interior of New South Wales where no one of my calling has hitherto displayed his wares.'

74

This I could well believe.

It is said that when you are journeying, especially in foreign parts, you fall in with persons you might never encounter in the normal intercourse of life. Sam Bullwinkle was certainly such a one. His flamboyance was not confined to his speech alone. His frock coat was a marvel which it seemed to me must have called for the services of an architect as well as those of a gentleman's tailor to bring about its construction. Such a coat, being a garment in which its owner spends so much of his life, is, in a sense, a sort of alternative abode to the place where he normally resides. Some, it might be said, are tattered hovels, offering little refuge from the elements; others, in the manner of terrace houses, uniformly undistinguished, although warm in winter even if rather too hot in summer; and a few, such as the blue creation occupied by Sam Bullwinkle, Juggler and Magician, imposing edifices, veritable palaçes, to which other frock coats in comparison are so much rubble.

With collar, cuffs and several tiers of pockets adorned with silver braid, it seemed to call for the presence of a sentry on duty outside. And, indeed, as the wearer of this wonder of sartorial architecture slipped the ivory balls into one of its capacious pockets, a candidate for such a post came into the waiting-room, a tall stern man of some sixty years, who paused and looked around about, as if stiffly confined within the narrow space of a sentry-box, before making his way to the upholstered end of the room, thus identifying himself as the fifth of the six passengers to be seated inside the coach. His hat, which had a wide brim, was pulled down close over his eyes.

As Sam Bullwinkle hastened to make himself known to the latest arrival, he moved away from me, leaving behind him – whether from his person, the frock coat or something contained within its ramifications, I had no way of deciding – a faint musty odour which I recognised, although only to the extent of it being one I had experienced at some time in the past; long back in the past.

After pausing to hear what the one-man pantomime had to say, but declining to accept one of his cards, the tall man gave a nod and a grunt before heading to a seat a short distance away from the middle-aged couple. And that was the sum total of

75

what anyone was to extract from him, at least until a certain stage of the journey had been reached, a nod and grunt – most times in that order, except when the grunt received precedence.

His name was Tolchard, something I discovered when the booking clerk came in to announce that the horses were being harnessed between the shafts: he addressed the passengers by name from his list as he told them that it was time to go out to be shown to our allotted places on the coach. Likewise, I learnt that the middle-aged couple, who walked as if taking very great care not to tread where lesser mortals had placed their feet, thereby defiling the surface of God's earth, were the Reverend and Mrs Chilblud. It appeared that the sixth inside passenger had yet to report – and the failure of that passenger to arrive on time began to cause the clerk to use the feathered end of his quill pen as a fan to cool his agitation.

The young couple and their children climbed to the top and took the rear seats near where the guard was securing parcels, packages and an open basket of fresh vegetables. Within the coach, the two Chilbluds faced forward, sitting opposite Tolchard, Bullwinkle and myself, who thus had our backs to the horses. The coachman, another stickler for punctuality, paced up and down, repeatedly taking out and staring at the face of a steel-encased watch. He carried a whip, and in between consulting his time-piece he drew the long leather thongs through a clenched hand, as if to make it more supple, and so enable him to use it with greater precision when called for on the horses' flanks.

Somewhere over the rooftops a town clock started to strike seven. Before it had run its full course, the coachman was suggesting that the clerk had made a mistake about the sixth passenger; but the clerk was adamant, despite his own anxiety to get the coach away on time, so the coachman had no choice but to try to control his exasperation while the horses on their part, having caught on to his ferment, had to be held and stroked by the stablehands. Restless sounds came from the harness and trappings as if they, too, were impatient to be away and jingling.

Without the forward movement of the coach to create a flow

76

of air, it became stifling inside as ten minutes elapsed, and then a two-horse carriage swept into the yard to be brought to a hasty standstill.

It looked like a vehicle I might have seen before, and I realised this was so when I recognised both the driver up top and the postillion who leapt to the ground and ran to the side of the carriage to open the door.

At this point I closed my eyes, having resigned myself to another instance of Mrs Lucy Brewster's interference. To ensure that I did not steal a march on her and somehow manage to get to the hidden Magwitch fortune before her, it seemed that she intended to accompany me on the journey to the west.

As my eyes remained closed, a woman's laughter approached the coach. After having heard Lucy Brewster's laughter, and remembered it to the point that I found the recollection of it offensive, I knew that what I now heard was not hers. And when my eyes snapped open I saw that it was Charlotte.

The postillion carried her cases which he heaved up to the guard to be secured to the roof, while the clerk helped her up into the coach where she took one of the forward-facing seats opposite me, next to Mrs Chilblud who squeezed her husband into the corner – not so much out of concern to make room available as to keep herself as far apart as possible from someone of coloured blood.

Looking across at me, her eyes sparkling with mockery, Charlotte said, 'Surprised?'

'Delighted,' I replied.

'Then Mama was right,' she said, referring to her foster-mother.

'About what?'

'You being delighted – and surprised.' She threw back her head – and it might have been Estella's laugh that filled the interior of the coach. 'She thought you should have some company, considering it's such a long journey and you're a visitor to these parts.'

In other words, Lucy Brewster was sending her along to keep an eye on me on her behalf.

As I came to this conclusion, Tolchard raised the brim of his hat and Charlotte noticed him for the first time. It would be an exaggeration to say she was startled; but unquestionably a momentary look of recognition passed between them.

The rumble of the coach wheels over the ragged road surfaces, the steady pound and occasional broken tangle of hoofbeats, and the innumerable creaking and straining sounds all combined to render verbal exchanges difficult, unless conducted almost at a shout.

Even so, Charlotte managed to keep up a sort of conversation, leaning across to me to point out passing sights – including the turn-off to a property which Abel Magwitch had once numbered among his possessions. It was like being face to face with a living shadow of Estella, the same precocious and provocative manner, the same teasing smile – and, even though Charlotte did not know the root cause of my fascination (which, let it be admitted, was swiftly developing into what should be more correctly described as an infatuation), she was very much aware of the impact her presence and her attentions had on me. All of which was openly eyed by the two Chilbluds; by the man Tolchard, when he chose to lift the brim of his hat marginally above the level of his eyes; and, of course, by the celebrated Sam Bullwinkle, whose eyes had become so bulbous that they might have been two of his ivory juggling balls jammed into his sockets and painted with startled bright-blue irises.

At the first stop to rest and water the horses, and exercise the passengers, which was at a staging-post on the way across the coastal plain to the foothills of the Blue Mountains, Charlotte led me away from the others on the pretext of wanting to show me some small wild orchids in the grasses by the roadway. She plucked one, and as she handed it to me, looking knowingly into my eyes, she asked, 'How did you enjoy your round trip to the Hawkesbury River yesterday?'

Being, as I have already stated, resigned to Lucy Brewster's interference, this to an extent cushioned me against now showing any surprise.

'It was most interesting – especially seeing the island Abel Magwitch once owned.'

'You didn't go ashore there, I hope,' she said, with a shudder.

'As a matter of fact I did.'

'What about all those horrible spiders?'

'They did me no harm.'

'Uncle Abel set them free there. To breed.'

'I thought he used the island to distil illegal spirits,' I said, bewildered to the point I was ready to believe that breeding spiders had been one of his money-making ventures.

'He used the spiders to keep inquisitive people away,' Charlotte said.

As she shuddered again, I felt secretly exulted. I had made a discovery. Although Lucy Brewster might have listening posts everywhere in the colony, providing her with a flow of information about everything and everyone, she apparently had not learnt what had happened on my trip to the Hawkesbury River. All she knew was that I had gone there, not what had transpired. But my exultation was, I fear, dismally short-lived. It followed that she had had no hand in the attempt to abduct me, so therefore Cannibal Jack and his two companions represented a second party not altogether favourably disposed towards me.

If any dismay at this deduction showed on my face, there was fortunately no danger of Charlotte seeing it, because she knelt to pick another orchid, then rose with the two bunched together, holding them up for me to admire while she sprang another surprise on me.

'Your name really should be Magwitch, shouldn't it?' she said.

'Magwitch? *My* name? How can you make such an extraordinary statement?'

'He was your father.'

'He was not!' I replied, raising my voice so much that the Chilbluds, Tolchard and others looked sharply in our direction, thus appearing to add to Charlotte's enjoyment of my discomfort.

'Oh, but he always spoke of you as his boy,' she went on. 'His gentleman – his son.'

This I did not doubt, for on the night he had come to me at my chambers, had not he said, '*Look'ee here, Pip. I'm your second father. You're my son – more to me nor any son.*'? It had been

79

sickening enough to me then; now it was infinitely more so after discovering that he'd had blood on his grimed and veinous hands – blood that could also be on my hands since his crimes had been carried out for my benefit.

I would have gone further to rebut her suggestion, except that Sam Bullwinkle sidled up to us and proceeded to demonstrate his magical skill by producing a tiny orchid from somewhere behind Charlotte's ear and another off my coat lapel, places where no flowers had been until he produced them. And then, when he danced off, there was no further chance to take up the matter with Charlotte as the coachman returned to the driver's seat while the guard cried, 'Take your places, thankee!'

The journey continued through much the same countryside as had extended from the outskirts of Sydney – undulating terrain well grassed and liberally shaded with healthy species of gum trees which frequently thickened to the proportions of forest. Even so, after three hours of it, this Antipodean parkland would have become somewhat monotonous but for glimpses of settlements, mostly small farms with a few cows, sheep, goats and hogs visible; the wide-wheeled wagons we overtook with whole families walking at their sides; a number of native camps; and the inevitable parties of convicts working on widening and repairing the roadway and strengthening bridges.

Occasionally, what might have first been taken for groups of animal statuary came to life, and as if on a signal – which I presently realised was the sound of our coach and horses – what might have been the creations of some sculptor obsessed with making copies of the one model, a species of kangaroo (which Charlotte told me were wallabies) bounded for shelter in all directions with mighty hops of their strong rear legs. I had another glimpse of the exotic fauna of this land when a strung-out flock of small green parakeets wove themselves into the shape of a knot which they as swiftly untied as they flew on out of sight.

At one stage I drew out the sketch maps I carried, and noted other tracts of land Magwitch had owned, in all amounting to many thousands of acres; areas where I might have been lord of all – the trees, the animals, the birds. And perhaps the hidden Magwitch fortune, too.

All through this I was conscious of occupying myself so that I could avoid the amusement waiting in Charlotte's eyes, should I ever glance towards her. Whenever I did so, I was on the alert for anything that might pass between her and Tolchard; but I saw nothing akin to that one initial look in which I had glimpsed recognition of each other. Not that there was much opportunity for any such interchange, as Charlotte presently succumbed to the general drowsiness of all inside the coach, her lids growing heavier until they slipped down over her eyes.

The Chilbluds had already both nodded off and were bobbing side by side with the movement of the coach. Sam Bullwinkle was also asleep. As for Tolchard, he looked so much like a long-serving sentry that I felt he might well be permanently awake, but the wide brim of his hat had dipped down so far over his face that I could not tell. In any event, I myself was soon to be numbered among the slumbering travellers.

The stumbling of the horses and the jarring of the coach, as one wheel or all dipped into holes in the roadway, woke us briefly from time to time. It was just as we were settling down again after a jolting more severe than the others that we were disturbed by another sound, one originating within the coach itself. A gasping, as if someone were struggling for breath. Indeed, as I came awake, I had the odd feeling that one of my travelling companions was being strangled by another of them. Until I saw that the Reverend Chilblud's wife was acting in an alarming way – staring across the coach and extending a shaking hand towards the person of Sam Bullwinkle, while seemingly possessed by a terror of such magnitude that she was unable to release the scream bottled up within her.

When I looked towards the juggler and magician I had an answer for the cause of that musty smell I had detected emanating from him.

I was thrust back in the past, to the unkempt garden at Miss Havisham's house near my old village home in England, to a cage in a corner where in the presence of Estella I was shown a small family of white mice – and now on Sam Bullwinkle's coat, as if it might have been some fairytale castle in which they resided, several white mice with pink noses, ears and eyes were roving about, while others peered from under pocket flaps – and one through the silver braid strands of an epaulette.

The Reverend gentleman's spouse might well have exploded herself apart, had she not been able to loose a scream – one of monumental dimensions, which not only woke all within the coach but reached outside, so that the coachman brought his vehicle to a swift halt as the guard jumped down to investigate what sounded to them like attempted murder.

Mrs Chilblud abandoned the coach with great alacrity for one so ample and was promptly followed by her husband.

Sam Bullwinkle was peremptorily hauled out when the guard was told that he was accompanied by travelling companions not listed among the paying passengers.

'Who give 'ee leave ter carry livestock?' the guard demanded of the juggler and magician.

'These are pets,' Sam Bullwinkle sought to explain. 'Performing pets.'

'They have no authority to perform on my coach!' the coachman proclaimed from his perch overhead.

While his wife was a blubbering mass, the Reverend Chilblud was aboil with outrage. 'Do you mean to say,' he said, addressing Sam Bullwinkle in booming tones of indignation, 'that you carry such vermin around with you on your person?'

'Vermin?' the juggler and magician protested. 'They're tame, clean and never come out – unless I give them the signal.'

'And what, pray, is that signal?' the Reverend Chilblud inquired.

With his lips slightly apart, and the tip of his tongue just visible between his teeth, Sam Bullwinkle gave a low sibilant whistle, a sound so faint that had you not been listening for it you might not have heard it.

To the delight of Charlotte who came out of the coach now, and the family of four leaning over the side of the roof – but to the renewed horror of Mrs Chilblud – several of the white mice popped out their heads from various places on Sam Bullwinkle's coat.

A loud despairing moan from Mrs Chilblud made the mice vanish again.

'I must've done it in my sleep,' Sam Bullwinkle chuckled.

'Done what?' demanded the coachman from aloft.

'Whistled.'

'You've done quite enough,' the coachman went on very sternly, consulting his watch and growing even more vexed. 'We're losing time. Back on board everyone!'

The Reverend Chilblud led the way, supporting his shaken and trembling wife. Sam Bullwinkle also made to go back inside, but the guard raised an arm to bar the other's way.

'Not you.'

Sam Bullwinkle stopped, good-naturedly raising his eyebrows for an explanation.

'If you insist on carrying livestock,' said the guard, pointing to the roof of the coach, 'then you travel up top.'

Sam Bullwinkle did not argue, pausing only to retrieve one of the white mice from Charlotte who had plucked it off his coat inside the coach and had been stroking it, just as I remembered Estella having fondled one of the creatures taken out of the cage in the corner of her foster-mother's garden.

As the coach moved off once more, Charlotte looked across to me, another teasing smile on her lips; and remembering our conversation at the previous staging-post before we had been interrupted, I could not help but feel that she had something more in store for me.

I received confirmation of this when we were being ferried by a large flat punt across the river that flowed below the foothills of the Blue Mountains. Charlotte joined me where I stood at the end of the punt.

'Have you changed your mind?' she asked me.

'About what?' I asked, genuinely puzzled by her question.

'Not being Uncle Abel's son?'

'No,' I said, this time in no danger of unduly raising my voice. 'I told you I was not – and I am not.'

'Dear me,' she sighed. 'I don't know whether to be sad or pleased about that.'

It was on the tip of my tongue to retort that because of the unpleasant discoveries I had been making about my late benefactor, I was extremely pleased that there should be no blood relationship to him; but since I had the feeling that

Charlotte would be elaborating on her statement, I remained silent and allowed her to go on.

'For if you were his son, that could mean that we would be related. You'd be my half-brother, I'd be your half-sister.' And then with her eyes searching deeply into mine for my reactions, she added, 'That's assuming, of course, that he *was* my father.'

Confronted with the same light blue that I had seen in the eyes of Abel Magwitch – and, also, in those of Estella – I asked myself whether Charlotte had come along on this coach journey to keep a watch on me for Lucy Brewster or just to be with me so that she could try to secure confirmation of the identity of her paternal parent.

'When he returned to England,' Charlotte now asked, 'did he ever say he had a daughter in New South Wales?'

'No,' I replied, relieved to be emphatic on this point, because it was the absolute truth. 'Abel Magwitch never discussed any such matter with me – nor in my presence.'

'Aren't you curious to know?'

'I would be *interested* to know,' I parried. 'Perhaps you can tell me? Did he in fact have a daughter here?'

'Me, of course. The trouble is, I have no way of proving it.'

If there had been tears in her eyes, she could not have moved me more. Nothing would have been easier for me than to confess to Charlotte why her many enchantments had touched me so deeply. If I were to reveal that this was because she was so like the person I believed to be her half-sister, it would surely lead to other questions, the answers to which would give her grounds for sharing my convictions; but those answers would at the same time implicate me.

Something whispered to me that this could be dangerous; and as I prepared to try to make some evasive comment, the punt ground on to the river bank.

CHAPTER 9

If that clerk from the coach office had been with us now, he would doubtless have had his quill pen with him, and I would have been tempted to borrow it from him to wag the feather in admonishment at him for making such a wrong prediction. He had said we could expect it to be cooler when climbing higher in the mountains, but as we wound up along the ridges it became even hotter. We could see, and presently smell, the reason for this: the sky ahead was cloudy with smoke from bush fires.

Since these fires had broken out in ravines and gullies to the left of the road, the coachman and guard decided to press on. The wind was blowing steadily from the right, so that it appeared we were in no danger of running into any conflagration; until, after mounting a rise, topping it, then plunging steeply into a gully, we were suddenly in an area which had burning on both sides of the roadway. Having descended into it so unexpectedly and at such a rate, the coachman had no choice but to keep going, and so he raced us through a hot tunnel of choking smoke.

Scorched if not singed, and fortunately unscathed, we came up out of the gully to run along a ridge which brought us to a flat area with massive rocks either side of the road. On our left, the bush still smouldered after having been burnt out, but the vegetation on our right remained untouched.

Directly ahead was another gully seething with fire, so the coachman brought his four horses and his vehicle to an immediate stop.

Unable now to retreat or advance, we waited for the fire to burn itself out; and as we did so, everyone came out of the coach wherein the heat had become intolerable.

While we were out of reach of the flames, our situation was not without certain perils. Snakes of a dark brown and copper slithered across the road from the side that had been burnt out

85

to the side that was untouched, as did many crawling creatures, including what I took to be Antipodean species of centipedes. A haze of light smoke hung about the trees in the bush to our right, in those gaps between the high ancient-looking rocks, and presently we became conscious that many birds had taken refuge among the branches and foliage, mostly a type of mountain parakeet. From the burning side, other birds appeared out of the heavy smoke on our left to alight among the others on our right.

Since the flow of the wind continued to be from the right to the left – that is, towards the burning side – we had reason to feel that the fire would not be able to cross the road in the face of it, and therefore we had justifiable grounds for believing we were safe – until Mrs Chilblud, without warning, added to her reputation for being able to produce screams of operatic proportion by unleasing another, and accompanying it with an operatic gesture, dramatically raising a hand in the direction of what was apparently some flying threat.

It passed through my mind that one of Sam Bullwinkle's white mice might have sprouted a pair of wings and taken to the air to terrorise her until I, too, saw the cause of her dismay and shared her fear of what seemed must inevitably happen.

Out of the smoke on the burning side flew a grey bird of a species I could not identify – but there was no mistaking what was entangled in its claws. A yard-long length of dry twisted vine that flamed furiously at its far end, a burning taper that would surely ignite the untouched bush should it reach that far – and there seemed no way, short of some lightning intervention by the Almighty, of stopping it from doing so.

Yet, as the bird and its taper soared overhead, there was an ear-numbing blast that multiplied itself by bouncing about within the enclosure made by the rocky outcrops; and, as I recalled the sensation of having my young ears roughly boxed by my sister, the bird suddenly – and miraculously – turned into a shattered mass of feathers which, with the burning brand, plummetted to the roadway.

As we stared, not comprehending what had happened, a youthful-looking man, who appeared to have been attired in tattered clothing at the expense of a weather-beaten scarecrow, and who carried a long-barrelled firearm with a wisp of burnt powder curling away from its muzzle, danced out from behind a big rock and proceeded to execute a lively jig in his broken boots over the fallen vine to put out the flames.

Having done this, he treated his dumbfounded audience, both out of the coach and on top of it, to a cheerful grin, even if a partly-blackened one. As three companions stepped out from concealment behind other rocks, all armed, he proceeded to go through the routine of cleaning out the barrel of his weapon in readiness to reload it.

The three were similarly attired to the marksman in filthy rags, their faces smudged with smut and soot from the bush fire – except that this was not so apparent on the features of one of them since his normal colour was black. Two of their pistols, those in the hands of a tallish bushranger and one who was short and thick-set, were pointed at the passengers, leaving the weapon in the hand of the aborigine to divide its aim between the coachman and the guard.

The bushranger cleaning the musket was clearly the leader of the quartet, and he was first to speak, revealing his origin to have been somewhere in one of London's down-river districts.

'Deepest 'pologies,' he began, in tones, though cheerful, far removed from the apologetic. 'We seem to 'ave bailed you up.' He paused to allow the coachman and the guard to glower at him and to grin boldly back. 'Believe me, it was quite un-planned. After bein' driven outa where we was by the fires, we were taking shelter 'ere when along you comes an' stops.'

He sought confirmation of this from his three companions, all of whom readily responded with similar brazen grins, so that despite their assertions of innocence I must record that I immediately asked myself whether, following close on the heels of the previous day's attempt to capture me, this was another – and that my journey to see former Magwitch properties beyond the mountain range was doomed to go no further than this trap along the way.

Apart from ensuring that we all remained totally submissive, which they did quite simply by making us keep our hands raised above our heads, the first concern of the four bush-rangers was to obtain food. Not only for themselves. The nose-bags of feed carried on the coach were fitted to their horses, which were brought out from behind shielding rocks. As for themselves, the four had a choice: the family on the roof of the coach had a basket of provisions with them, but this was passed over once the lid of the Chilbluds' hamper was turned back on its hinges, revealing a mouth-watering feast of delicacies – pastry pies, meat and fruit; legs and wings of chicken and turkey; thick slices of ham, pork, mutton and beef; chunks of cheese; jars of calves' foot jelly; bottles of cider – all of which were ravenously pounced upon, reminding me of when I had handed stolen food to my benefactor on the marshes near my boyhood home and passengers' refreshments to the convict who had tried to escape far out in the Indian Ocean by swimming from the transport to the emigrant ship.

As they saw their precious victuals vanishing before their eyes, the Chilbluds became increasingly incensed; but no one had yet ventured a single word, the temporary deafness which that gun-blast had occasioned possibly somehow also rendering us dumbstruck. The Reverend Chilblud, as might have been expected, was the first to break our silence, giving anyone who might have been concerned for his welfare cause for alarm, since he sounded as if he might be in dire danger of drowning himself in the rising tide of his own outrage.

'If you have any regard for what is good for you,' he said, addressing himself primarily to the leader of the four bush-rangers, 'you'll lay down those firearms and give yourselves up. You'll not escape punishment, but if you hasten to do as I advise, it might possibly alleviate the severity of your sentences. Life, perhaps, in lieu of hanging.'

'Is that so?' said the main recipient of this advice, aiming the muzzle of his musket at the Reverend Chilblud's throat, as if converting it into a pitchfork in readiness to toss a turnip, 'You've a lot to say for yerself. Let's 'ave a better look at yer.'

To do this, the bushranger sought to remove the Reverend Chilblud's hat, an impressive item of clerical attire, broad, high-crowned and made of dove-grey felt which, alas, was doomed to be besmirched by blackened fingers since the clergy-man was unable to retreat swiftly enough to carry it beyond the bushranger's reach.

Spluttered protestations from Chilblud and gasps of indignation from his wife, as the bushranger paraded about in the hat which had taken the place of his cap.

Although the Chilbluds had done nothing to endear themselves to any of those who travelled with them, I assumed that we all shared something of their shock at this show of impudence – until, when looking to one side out of my concern for Charlotte in this crisis, I was dismayed to find that she was shaking with laughter. This I fear only served to encourage the bushranger into greater excesses of impertinence, swaggering about, doffing the parson's hat to the coachman, the guard, one or other of the passengers; and to his companions, who roared their delight. How long he might have gone on doing this I cannot tell, but suddenly he brought himself up into a halt in front of Chilblud, staring the clergyman in the face.

'I do declare! We meet agen.'

'Again?' said the other. 'I have no recollection.'

'Depends what y'are t'day. Reverend or Worship – parson or magistrate? First time you was chaplain aboard that big tub o' rotten timber that brought me out 'ere.'

As I learnt of Chilblud's dual role in the life of the colony, the bushranger introduced himself and revealed something of his own background.

'Spikey Simmins. Transported for gettin' m'hand caught in a stranger's pocket. Later brought up before you fer helpin' m'self to the Governor's goldfish – an' fryin' 'em for supper. Remember now?'

'I fear it still escapes me.'

'Well, I ain't forgot. Y'sent me fer trial, an' I got seven years – of which I'm happy t'say I done only three months before takin' to the freedom of the bush.'

After establishing that Chilblud in his magistrate role was on his way to conduct a court session at Hartley, the inland valley settlement, Spikey Simmins proceeded methodically to relieve us of our possessions, both valuables and further items of clothing, some of which he tossed to one or another of his three companions. Sam Bullwinkle's orange stove-pipe to the aborigine; while Tolchard's hat went appropriately to the tall bushranger.

When Tolchard stood bare-headed without making protest, Spikey became curious.

'You ain't got much to say for y'self,' he said.

Tolchard remained silent, standing stiffly upright, as if the sides of his invisible sentry-box had confined him more tightly by coming even closer together.

'Don't be tongue-tied,' Spikey said, using the muzzle of his musket lightly in the middle of Tolchard's chest to prod something out of him.

Tolchard responded with a grunt.

'I said – don't be tongue-tied.'

Spikey administered a second but sharper prod, and this time Tolchard responded with a blunt, deep-throated answer that had a familiar drone about it.

'I have nothing to say.'

'At least you ain't dumb,' Spikey said, continuing his jabs and thus being told that Tolchard was a commercial traveller bound for Bathhurst.

But Tolchard did not need to say anything more for me to realise that I had heard that voice of his before: when I clung under the landing-stage on Pirrip Island. He was the other masked man whose reflection, along with Cannibal Jack's, I had glimpsed on the water. It appeared, therefore, that the attempt of the previous day to abduct me was unrelated to what was happening now.

As he was forced to speak, Tolchard's eyes met mine. I took no steps to disguise my recognition of his voice, and his realisation of this was apparent from the arrogant way he returned my look. Even though we had not actually met on Pirrip Island, it was an acknowledgement that we had been very close to doing so.

Coming next to Sam Bullwinkle, Spikey decided that there was one prize that must be his personally; and although totally unaware that any other residents of it were involved, he insisted on becoming the principal occupant of the sartorial extravaganza, laying his musket on the ground while he took over tenancy; and then, after buttoning the frock coat all the way up the front, he picked up his weapon again and strutted around with it slung over his shoulder like a long-barrelled cannon leaning across a battlement.

This performance delighted Charlotte who continued to laugh in defiance of the disapproving glares from me and all the others, except the two children who were so intrigued as to be without any fear of Spikey.

Digging into one of the coat's side pockets, he brought out an ivory ball, which he tossed to the children who caught it between them in mid air. He then extracted something else he found, a long string of coloured silken flags, and as he did so there was undoubtedly not one of those who had travelled on the coach who did not wonder when the first of the white mice would appear. A dozen tiny flags, a score, two score, three score appeared before the string came to an end, still without the tip of a pink nose or a white ear. The bushranger then handed the string of flags to Charlotte as a sort of reward to her for the encouragement she had been giving him.

'Any time yer'd care to band up with us,' he said, as he made his presentation, 'yer'd be more'n welcome.'

Instead of taking exception to this scandalous suggestion, Charlotte laughed the more, thereby I fear displaying something of the same streak of mischievous perversity that had so bewildered me in Estella.

It came my turn to empty my pockets. Spikey decided he would have the coins I carried, but not my bunch of keys; my fob watch and diamond tie-pin he also decided to have – and my pocket book, in which he discovered the two rough sketch maps folded among other papers.

He twisted them about, upside down, sideways, and I assumed they would only confuse him as to what they represented; but to my great surprise he made something of them.

'Unless I'm badly mistaken,' said he, 'these maps show the whereabouts of the properties that used to belong to Magwitch.'

The name that kept dogging me wherever I went in the colony struck a response among others present. Mrs Chilblud emitted a startled cry, quickly covering her mouth, but too late to save her from claiming Spikey's immediate attention.

' 'Ullo! What does Magwitch mean t'you?'

With his wife so flustered that she was incapable of answering, the Reverend Magistrate took over.

91

'In the capacity of ship's chaplain, I made several voyages out here from England. My good wife accompanied me on one of them, as matron to the women prisoners. Abel Magwitch employed many men on his properties, and since I had the opportunity to assess the capabilities of the male prisoners, he approached me to select suitable men to be assigned to him on arrival in Sydney.'

'What about the rations?'

The good wife writhed as her husband managed to look blank, although it seemed to me that his composure had been disturbed for a flickering moment.

'Rations?' he repeated.

'The voyage I made out 'ere was a very 'ungry one. We never got our full quotas of rations, because half of 'em was with'eld until we reached Sydney, where they was sold off. One o' Magwitch's men was main purchaser of such – an' the ben-eficiaries was the captain an' his officers, which included the ship's chaplain.'

'How dare you make such a preposterous statement! Slanderous!'

Spikey's reply was to take a luscious slice of ham from the Chilblud's near-empty hamper, flap it disdainfully at the clergyman, then bite into it as he came back to me to take up where he had left off.

He handed my hat to the aboriginal bushranger, so after its experience at Pirrip Island this item of my attire was also having an adventurous time of it. He wanted to know how the two rough sketch maps had come into my possession. He used his musket at my throat to hasten my explanation out of me, and so he heard why I had come to the colony. Not that he accepted what I told him as the truth.

Waving the two rough sketch maps at me, he said, 'Every piece of land listed 'ere has been combed over. First of all by the Agents of the Crown – every square inch of every square yard of every acre Magwitch ever owned. An' what did they find fer all their trouble? Nought.'

Just like Lucy Brewster, he assumed that I had some clue or inkling as to where the hidden Magwitch fortune might be found. I protested that I had none, but he was determined to prise something out of me, and kept the muzzle of the musket pressed hard against my wind-pipe.

Sam Bullwinkle, meanwhile, reduced to a tailor's dummy wearing only a grey flannel vest above his waist, appeared to have decided to lighten the proceedings with a tune which he whistled between his teeth.

'That's what I like t'see, a cheerful captive,' Spikey said. 'Makes a change an' a pleasure t'have one such on our 'ands.'

His three companions agreed that the juggler and magician was indeed such a rare phenomenon. The rest of us might have been fitted with tight transparent masks to hold our expressions very still, for it was clear to us what Sam Bullwinkle was trying to do by whistling that little tune.

Sam Bullwinkle had not furnished us with any specific population figures covering the number of four-footed inhabitants of his coat; but I had clearly seen a dozen of them at the one time, so it was with the expectation that the appearance of at least this number was imminent that I watched as Sam, in his role of Pied Piper, continued with his whistling.

In the event, all of twenty white mice decided to appear at much the same time, something which at first totally escaped Spikey Simmins.

It was left to his three fellow outlaws to register combinations of horror and amazement, for it seemed that their leader had suddenly been infested with a plague of white mice. The effect was so marked on the aboriginal member of the four that the pistol began to shake violently in his hand, its aim swinging high and low, near and wide.

Spikey was thus alerted to the fact that something untoward must be happening to his person – and when he saw that his coat was alive with the little rodents, chest, arms and shoulders crawling with them, he tried to shed the coat by tearing it off. But the brass buttons held fast in their holes, so that to escape he had to undo every button – and once having managed this, he threw the garment aside and stumbled back away from it, as if afraid it might leap up and attack him.

The confusion was such that I am a little uncertain as to the actual sequence of the stages of the surrender, except that it was a complete capitulation. I found myself in possession of the musket while between them the guard and the coachman had retrieved or otherwise taken charge of the three pistols. All thanks to Sam Bullwinkle, Juggler and Magician, who took immediate repossession of his two-sleeved abode. Its smaller residents were by this time out of sight in its various nooks and crannies.

Valuables and items of apparel, none of which had come to much harm, were also retrieved and repossessed – although to hear the Reverend Chilblud's fulminations, Spikey Simmins had so desecrated his precious grey felt hat that to wear it again the clergyman should first have it exorcised.

He then adopted his role of magistrate, which in his view entitled him to usurp the coachman in authority, so that on his instructions the four captive bushrangers were tied back to back with rope two at a time on the one horse, while the remaining two horses of the four that had been fitted with nose-bags were strung behind.

The fire in the gully immediately ahead had burnt itself out, and the road was clear as far as could be seen, so the coach was reboarded and got under way.

Magistrate Chilblud proposed not only to deliver the four outlaws into custody but personally to hear the charges against them. No one seemed to disagree wth this – except Charlotte. Not that she said anything; it was entirely in her eyes. Her sympathy lay all too clearly with the bushrangers, especially Spikey Simmins.

Apart from the perverse trait which I have already mentioned, I could only ascribe this tendency to something originating in her ancestry. And she was, after all, the daughter of a violent criminal and the native woman he had allegedly abandoned.

CHAPTER 10

The clerk at the coach office, from which we were now over fifty miles distant, was to be proved right after all. By the time we reached the next staging-post, which was beside a coaching-inn, rain clouds had gathered in the place of the smoke – and heavy showers, which we were shortly to experience, were to have the effect of putting out the fires and cooling the air.

However, the temperature within the coach, while on the one hand abating the further we climbed on the ascending Western Road, in another sense remained as high as if we were in an oven. The two Chilbluds, from their ruddy colour alone, still boiled with outrage, even though, if they so wished, they had the consolation of being free to visualise the four bushrangers hanging by ropes from the blackened boughs of trees. Charlotte, as it seemed to me, remained seething because of the reverse suffered by Spikey Simmins and his three companions, and from time to time she leant out the open side window to look behind towards the four prisoners on the horses. They were undoubtedly suffering great discomfort, even though the coachman proceeded at a reduced speed, something he had loudly complained about having to do before getting under way.

As for Tolchard, whenever our eyes met (and they did so frequently now we were obliged to keep such a close watch on each other that we might both have been in sentry boxes), he greeted me with a sharp burning stare which somehow conveyed intense dislike and the threat of having something most unpleasant in store for me should he have half a chance.

Charlotte's concern for the captives had been noted by the Chilbluds to the extent that they had openly voiced their shock at her conduct to each other. Since my main concern was for her, when we stopped at the staging-post and were out of the coach, I attempted to lead her to the adjoining coaching-inn where we were to take refreshments. It was my intention once inside to warn her that I considered it most unwise for her to be so open with her feelings in the presence of the Chilbluds; but since she chose not to accompany me, I found myself telling her this there and then.

'Why should I care about them?' she demanded of me.

'As a magistrate, Chilblud could be in a position to do you much harm.'

'In what way, for heaven's sake?'

Lowering my voice, because the clergyman and his wife were not far away from us, I said, 'You might find yourself arraigned on a charge of aiding and abetting the four prisoners. It's just the sort of thing that man might try to do – especially if encouraged by that wife of his.'

'What nonsense you talk!' she answered (almost the very same words Estella had once flung at me), and with a scornful toss of her dark tresses, she left me to find someone from the staging-post who could assure her that the prisoners, who remained mounted back to back under a large tree where their horses were tethered, would be provided with food and something to drink.

Throughout this, the Chilbluds took careful note of what was happening, evidently not trusting the spirited young half-caste woman to be left alone with the four captives. And rightly so.

Only when satisfied by the man in charge of the staging-post that the four would be cared for did Charlotte deign to accompany me into the coaching-inn; and only then did the Chilbluds also do so.

Already within and seated at the main dining-table were the father, mother, boy and girl; Sam Bullwinkle; and the coachman and the guard, the former so concerned with keeping to his timetable that he had detached his steel-encased watch from its chain and set it up on the table-top in front of him so that he could note the flickering passage of every second. He was still hoping to get through to a coaching-inn further on in the one day, despite serious delays so far, and was therefore entitled to register greater dismay than others present at what Chilblud said when he rose to address the company.

'If I may have your attention!' he began, speaking somehow

in the same way as he walked, as if intent upon trying to place his words in the air where those of others had not befouled it. Having secured our all-round attention, he went on, 'When we reach Hartley, where I am due to take up my magisterial duties, I propose to commence them by convening a court immediately upon our arrival, so that the four desperadoes who waylaid us on our journey here will be duly dealt with. Therefore, one and all, you will be required to remain there as witnesses.'

This came as such a blow to the coachman that he almost turned the table over – and his watch – as he rose from the bench.

Anticipating his protest, Chilblud continued, 'A small sacrifice to make, surely, to see that justice is done.'

Muttering that Chilblud had no authority to do this and that he would seek an opinion from the man in charge of the staging-post, who it seemed had some grasp of legal matters, the coachman strode out of the dining-room, after whipping up his timepiece from the table-top, and reattaching it to its chain as he went.

Charlotte viewed the coachman's rebellious attitude with undisguised delight; and when the guard also rose, she looked at him in anticipation of further protest. Although this was not to be. He came around the table to my side and leant down to speak close to my ear in a low voice.

'Could I have private words with you, sir? Outside.' He spoke in a tone which left me in no doubt that he was very serious about something.

Rising from the bench and excusing myself from Charlotte, who made it plain that she would prefer to come too, I left the dining-room in the wake of the guard, going to the back of the staging-post and sheltering under the wide eaves from the rain that was spattering down and becoming heavier.

'Now,' I said, 'what's on your mind?'

'Would you be interested in meeting someone who served as a shepherd with Magwitch – and under the same Master?'

'I would indeed!'

'He works here. Has done so for many a long year. As an ostler.'

The guard pointed in the direction of an open shed where a

97

thin, stooped, white-haired man of advancing years was rubbing down one of the horses that had been unharnessed from our stage-coach for resting here.

'Name of Weedin,' the guard went on to inform me. 'Transported – but now on a conditional pardon. Though I must warn 'ee, he's not given to talking much.'

'I can only try. I'm indebted to you.'

The guard surprised me a little by according me a small bow as he referred to the part I had played in apprehending Spikey Simmins and his companions. 'Me an' the coachman, sir – we're indebted to 'ee.'

I thanked him, although protesting that mine was but a minor role.

' 'Twould be best,' he said, 'were 'ee to speak with him alone.'

Taking his point and thanking him again, I stepped out into what had now become a downpour and headed for the open shed where the ostler moved to another of the horses from the stage-coach. He looked up at me slowly when I approached and I made him out to be about seventy, which would have been the age of Abel Magwitch were he still alive.

'Mr Weedin?' I asked, stopping near him.

'Aye,' he said, 'Jock Weedin. Who might you be?'

So I told him, and when I had finished, he said, 'So this b'ain't the first time ye've been in the colony.'

'Let me assure you, this is my very first visit to this part of the world.' I would have gone on to contradict him at greater length, except that suddenly I realised to what he alluded and recalled what my benefactor had said to me on his return to England:

'When I was a hired-out shepherd in a solitary hut, not seeing no faces but faces of sheep till I had forgot wot men's and women's faces wos like, I see yourn. I drops my knife many a time in that hut when I was eating my dinner or my supper, and I says, "Here's the boy again, a looking at me whiles I eats and drinks!" I see you there a many times as plain as ever I see you on them misty marshes.'

As I told the ostler about this, and repeated what my benefactor had said, the mistrust vanished out of the old man's eyes.

'To know that,' he said, 'you really must be his boy that was.'

Believing that he would now be better disposed to open up to me, I asked, 'How well did you know Abel Magwitch?'

'How well could anyone ever know that man?' he said. 'Some knew him as a brutal and unforgivin' monster, but me – me, I knew him as a friend. For didn't he stand up on my part to the Master, to which we was both assigned, me an' Magwitch. When that Master sold the rations which were provided for us, or made me turn out my pockets so's he could take possession of the few shillin's I had put by from work done arter the hours of our assignment, it was Magwitch who threatened him. And it was Magwitch which got me my rations and my few shillin's. He was never but a friend to me, even if he did make me swear my life away.'

'On a clasped black Testament?' I suggested.

'Aye,' he said, looking at me as if I must possess clairvoyance.

Recalling how my benefactor had extracted an oath from my friend Herbert Pocket, I asked, 'Did he tell you to take the Testament in your right hand?'

'He did that.'

'And did he say,' I asked, repeating as best I could what Abel Magwitch had said, ' *"Lord strike you dead on the spot, if ever you split in any way"*?'

'He did, too.'

'Do you still feel bound by that oath?'

'An oath is an oath – 'specially if made on the Good Book.'

'After all these years, surely you're not still bound by it. Especially as Abel Magwitch is no longer alive.'

'Of that I have no proof.'

Nor did I have proof, except that of my own bodily eyes, when my benefactor had passed away peacefully in the prison hospital, after having been sentenced to death by hanging for breaking the terms of his conditional pardon by returning to the land where his crimes had been committed. I could do no more to convince the ostler than simply and truthfully give an account of Abel Magwitch's last days, his last hours, his last mortal seconds – and when I saw that the old man took my word for it and accepted that his former fellow shepherd was indeed dead, I asked, 'Why was it he made you take the oath?'

' 'Twere the will.'

'What will was that?'

'Our Master's.'

My benefactor had said, '*I got money left me by My master (which died, and had been the same as me) and got my liberty and went for myself.*'; so I said, 'From what I gathered, this Master of yours had also been transported.'

'He had – although he'd successfully forgot it.'

'And I also gathered,' I went on, deeming it unnecessary to mention that my informant had been Charlotte's foster-mother, Lucy Brewster, 'that in his will, he left all he possessed – land, sheep, buildings – to Abel Magwitch?'

' 'Twere what the will said.'

I now realised the ostler had been brought by my questioning to the point at which he must either abide by the undertakings of his oath to Magwitch or decide that he would no longer be bound by them.

At this point, the guard started to go around announcing that the overnight stay would be made at this coaching-inn because of the delays so far. The coachman was evidently in no condition to pass on this information; I saw him pacing about in a state of speechless anger.

' 'Twould be best left till later,' the ostler now said. 'After dark, sir.'

He named the hour and I agreed, but I had to endure the interval wondering whether the old man would continue now that he had been given time to reflect on what he had already revealed.

It was pitch darkness and wet as we met at the back of the stables. I took great care when going outside the coaching-inn, because I kept wondering what had happened to Tolchard who I couldn't remember having seen since the coach arrived here.

Jock Weedin held a small lantern which he had told me he would carry. He turned it down to the smallest possible flame. He had hesitation written all over him, so I offered him a handful of the coins that had been temporarily in the custody of Spikey Simmins. After eyeing them for some moments, he agreed to accept them.

Standing closer to me under the eaves of the stable where we were well-sheltered from the steady rain that had kept falling, he began by referring to the fact that Abel Magwitch could both read and write while so many others, including the ostler himself and their Master, possessed neither of these accomplishments.

'That is so,' I said. 'He was taught to write by a travelling giant, and to read by a deserting soldier.'

I did not yet understand why the old man had wanted to establish this, because when he started to speak, he referred first of all to the way Magwitch had been able to get along well with the natives whom many considered thieving savages.

'Thanks to what Magwitch gleaned from them about the heights and levels to which the flood waters had reached in the past – often in the past of their legends, too – our Master had been fortunate to suffer very few losses when the neighbouring river broke its banks. Magwitch had seen to it that all the sheep were herded on to high ground. But the Master remained ungrateful, and he riled Magwitch by boasting how he had prospered, saying he must make arrangements so that, if anything happened to him, his good fortune would be shared by his wife and his children who were still in England. Although until now he had never spoke of them without a mention of how pleased he were to be shed of them. He provided the sheet of paper, the jar of ink and the pen for Magwitch, who he instructed to write down the contents of his last will and testament. Which Magwitch did, and which I saw him doing, because our Master called me in to be present while it was done. And once it was complete, Magwitch beckoned over a native called Trout; and to our Master and me and the native, Magwitch read the will out aloud, after which our Master put his mark to it – and as a witness, so did I, and as a second witness so did Trout, who used the diamond shape of a fish to sign his name. But what Magwitch wrote and read out was not what our Master told him to write. While our Master thought he was bequeathing his worldly goods to his wife and his children, Magwitch was bequeathing them to hisself. Unseen by our Master, he looked up an' gave me a terrible deadly wink with his eye; and after it was all done Magwitch told me what he had wrote instead, because of our Master's ingratitude and his treatment of us. He said that if ever on our Master's death – which he believed would not be too distant in the future – I was questioned, I was to forget what our Master had said and to say that he had left his all to his loyal, hardworking servant, Abel Magwitch, just as was set down in the will. And to make it certain I would speak thus, Magwitch had me on oath on his little black Testament.'

'So your Master died and you were questioned?'

'Aye, I were. By a Court of Justice.'

'And I take it you adhered to your oath?'

'So help me God.'

Lucy Brewster had told me that my benefactor's Master had been struck by lightning and killed, so I asked the ostler if what I had gathered on this point was correct.

As I expected, because I felt there was bound to be another reason, the ostler shook his head.

'No,' he said. 'Although his death did take place in a thunder-storm, one of the first after the drawing up of the will. Magwitch was with our Master at the time – and he used a stone to smite him a blow on the head, after which he suffocated him until he was dead, and then singed his hair and his clothing to make it look like as if he were struck by a bolt of lightning, which was fierce at the time, killing some sheep and setting them on fire.'

The ostler told this without feeling or emotion, but it chilled me so that I seemed to feel the cold of it in the very marrow of my bones.

'Were you a witness to this, too?' I asked, not believing that so mild a man could have endured seeing such an act and yet still be able to give such an unemotional account of it.

'No,' he said again, with another shake of his head. 'Magwitch boasted to me about it.'

'He *boasted*?'

'Aye. Thought I would be pleased. As he were hisself.'

Now I took a turn at shaking my head, doing so in disbelief and horror – not only at this frightful example of my late benefactor's brutality but more so at the lengths to which he was prepared to go to secure the means to secretly make me a gentleman. If ever I felt that the blood of Abel Magwitch's dark deeds was also on my hands it was now.

The ostler looked down as he opened out his hand to reveal the coins I had given him, and it seemed that he felt my generosity merited something more of him. Raising his eyes to mine again, he said, 'Word gets around swiftly in a small place such as this – 'specially when a coach comes in with the like of Spikey Simmins in tow as a prisoner. And captured, it would seem, by a bunch of mice. Amongst what's been said, I've heard tell as you're searching for Magwitch's hidden fortune.'

'That's not strictly correct,' I said, still so sickened that I felt it was time I gave up my pilgrimage and sought a return passage by ship to Egypt, lest I be confronted with even more ghastly revelations about my late benefactor's activities in the colony. I told the ostler why I had come to New South Wales; then granted that, since having heard of the hidden Magwitch fortune, I was on the alert for anything that might lead me to it, even if only motivated to reach it before others who I felt should not gain possession of it.

'I've been told,' said the ostler, 'as you're on the coach as far as the staging-post after Hartley?'

'Yes. And I expect to proceed from there to a property which Abel Magwitch once owned. The Rushmore Estate.'

'You're heading in the right direction,' said he, with a meaningful nod, the significance of which I did not yet fully grasp.

'Are you trying to tell me that the fortune is hidden on the Rushmore Estate?' I inquired.

'Where it is hidden I have no idea, none at all. All I know is that you're heading in the right direction to meet up with someone who knows the details of what that fortune is an' where precisely it lies concealed. That someone is Edward Rushmore, the husband of the woman who was transported on the same ship as Magwitch. 'Twere Magwitch hisself who told me, the very last time we spoke together, which was when he last passed through here – as it was to turn out, a matter of just a few days afore he secretly took a passage back to the Old Country. Not that you'll find it all that easy to get as much as a single word out of Rushmore.' And before I could question him about this, he added, ' 'Tweren't the only clue he gave me either.'

'About the hidden fortune?'

'Aye. He showed me two things I had already seen a many times before. The little black Testament and the pack of cards he used for his game of Patience. Holding them up, one in each hand, he patted them against each other, saying to me, "*Put these two together, Jock, an' somewhere in between them both is also the secret wot only me an' Eddie Rushmore as knows*".'

Because I felt such an elation at the discovery of why the Testament and the pack of playing cards had been stolen from my hotel room, I very nearly succumbed to the temptation to tell the old ostler about it. I had been mistaken about Cannibal Jack's reactions outside the Sydney grog-shop. What I had interpreted as fear had been fascination – amazement that such key items should have found their way back to New South Wales.

Spikey and the other three prisoners had been removed from their horses and taken to a shed where they were roped back to back again for the night.

Early in the morning we were woken by a loud commotion in the yard outside, and as we hastened out in various states of dress and night attire, those of us who had busied ourselves were just in time to glimpse Spikey and his companions whooping and hollering as they prodded their horses into galloping escapes, leaving the ropes that had bound them lying on the straw and sacking in the shed. In escaping thus, they had been forced to abandon a musket and three pistols, but no doubt they considered the loss of these weapons a fair price to pay in exchange for their freedom.

In a voluminous ecclesiastical gown, the Reverend Magistrate Chilblud presided over an immediate inquiry, the early sun reflecting on his vast bald pate as it gathered height and strength in a rain-washed but clear sky.

Holding up the ropes, he pointed out that the one binding Spikey Simmins back to back with the aborigine member of the bushranger band had been sliced through with a sharp instrument, probably a knife, while the other rope had been unknotted and loosened.

'Therefore,' he said, 'it is my opinion that someone first severed this rope, thus enabling Simmins and the native ruffian to untie the rope binding the others. Whoever wielded the knife must have made a swift visit to the shed.'

He looked around under a frowning brow, until his eyes came to the coachman at whom he stared for some moments, only to switch his attention very sharply to Charlotte when the comical side of the situation so overcame her that without any prompting she started to laugh.

This may well have been taken as evidence that Charlotte had some direct hand in the escape of the prisoners; until when the coachman was preparing to depart with fresh horses harnessed between the shafts of the coach, the guard noted that one of the passengers was missing.

'Where's Mr Tolchard?' he asked.

Only now was it realised that the tall surly man had to all intents and purposes vanished soon after the coach had arrived here the previous late afternoon. No one had glimpsed him since; nor was there any sign of him.

CHAPTER 11

After reaching a high point on the mountain range, the Western Road descended steeply into a valley. The rain stopped but water streamed off the slopes, turning the roadway into a torrent in which the coach slewed about, so a fallen tree trunk was attached by a length of rope to the back axle to be dragged along and steady the vehicle.

At the bottom of the valley, which appeared to be extensive and fertile, lay the village of Hartley where the courthouse was being repaired.

After having had only Charlotte and myself for company, the Reverend Magistrate Chilblud and his wife could not part with us quickly enough and wasted not one of their precious highly-honed words in farewell, confining their feelings to sullen glowers which somehow included both of us in the responsibility for the escape of Spikey Simmins and his three companions.

Since the family of four and Sam Bullwinkle remained up top, that left only Charlotte and me inside the coach as it started out for the next staging-post where we were to disembark. I was acutely aware now that I was alone with her for the first time. Something of my feelings must have conveyed themselves to her, since she began to act as if I was not there, confining all her attention to the passing scene which she viewed from the opening at her side. In doing this, little did she realise that she was acting exactly in the way I had experienced with the one person to whom I had given my heart completely and without reservation whatsoever: Estella, who had been part of my very existence, part of myself. I had lost her, and my heart had been cruelly wounded, yet the rough common romantic boy still apparently dwelt in me and I began to wonder whether, by coming to New South Wales, I was to find someone who would fill that gap so long vacant in my life.

The snob also still dwelt in me, I fear, because I had no sooner imagined the prospect of life with Charlotte at my side than I found myself confronted with the problems that would arise because of her mixed blood. Yet these problems were mainly confined to a society such as that I had left in England, and had been transplanted here in New South Wales. Were I to return to Cairo and spend the remainder of my life in Egypt, Charlotte would in no wise be out of place: there were many instances of marriages between white and coloured in the community in which I had moved there with Herbert and Clara Pocket – and they, God bless them, would have no prejudices. Indeed, I could imagine their delight were I to return from my pilgrimage with the half-sister of Estella as my bride.

My eyes were on Charlotte as these thoughts passed through my mind; and it was as if she had sensed something of their import, because she glanced at me, giving me an aloof, mocking smile, and then stabbed me to the very pit of my heart by saying to me loudly enough to be heard above the noises of the coach and the horses, 'I wonder which way Spikey headed when he got away.'

It was as if all along in avoiding my eyes by looking out that open side she had been but watching for Spikey and his three companions.

The next staging-post was situated where the great sweep of the interior plains began, and waiting here was a carriage to take Charlotte and me to the Rushmore Estate, as Lucy Brewster had pre-arranged. Once again I had the feeling of being manipulated, again of being the hunter who was also the hunted.

The shadows were lengthening, the land bathed in a glow as the dropping sun shone from the west where the sky was almost clear of clouds. We had been travelling for twelve hours, and within another darkness would fall.

The Estate, by European dimensions, was a kingdom. And the entrance to it proclaimed it as such, having a cast-iron gate with coats of arms on both its halves and a solid gate-house made of stone blocks to one side of it.

The gate-keeper appeared at our approach, a burly man who

must have stood at least six feet in his prime, now bent over, with white whiskers and beard, and an unusually large head of white hair bald on top. His eyebrows, however, were black and bushy. As he opened both halves of the gate to let the carriage enter, I glimpsed his large powerful hands and I had the odd feeling that I had seen them somewhere before. It was no more than an evanescent shadow, and possibly brought about because at the same time there hung on the air a faint scent that also had some connection with the past.

For the present I thought no more about it, for there was much to see, despite the failing light, as we were driven on a narrow road through pastures where sheep grazed in small scattered groups, their fleece pink as the sky turned roseate with sunset. While a single view might give the impression that the animal population was small, when it became apparent that these pastures were square miles in extent, then I realized that many thousands of sheep must graze here. The land was undulatory, hillocks dominated by clumps of gum trees, and presently on such a hillock and among such trees we saw the Rushmore homestead; a squat structure under wide eaves with verandahs all around, the total length of which I judged would provide a tolerable walk for anyone seeking exercise in the shade.

With two servants to take our luggage, Emma Rushmore came down the verandah steps to meet us. After the vulgarity of Lucy Brewster it did not necessarily follow that I expected to be confronted by someone like that woman; but they had both come to the colony as convicts, so I had been prepared to find some trace or taint of this. However, I can say no more than that, in this remote place, I was greeted most graciously by an elegant well-bred Englishwoman. It was impossible to associate her with someone who had been transported for robbing poor boxes at churches and wantonly setting light to barns and hayricks in order to join a lover.

'Welcome to Rushmore,' she said, taking my hands in hers, her warmth extending to my companion. 'And, Charlotte, my dear, how nice of you to accompany Mr Pirrip. You look more lovely every time I see you.'

Lamps were lit inside as she led us to a large room furnished and decorated with taste and artistry. I was to learn later that the water-colour paintings on the walls, scenes of the interior this side of the mountain range, were her own works. Also, that a tapestry which caught my eye, especially as a lamp shone immediately below it, had been woven by Charlotte.

A meal had been prepared for us, so after being shown to our rooms, where we refreshed ourselves, Charlotte and I joined Emma Rushmore for dinner. There was no sign of her husband, Edward, nor was any mention made of him. Mrs Rushmore, thanks to Lucy Brewster's letter (penned for her, of course, by Charlotte) knew the reasons for my visit to New South Wales, both commercial and sentimental. No mention was made that evening of Abel Magwitch either, that subject, by undiscussed yet mutual agreement, also being left till the morrow.

At breakfast, after a sleep so sound that it might have continued indefinitely but for the immense chorus of birds that woke me, there were only two of us at the table.

'Charlotte has gone horse-riding,' Mrs Rushmore explained. 'She felt you would like to speak to me alone.'

That was true; although I had reservations about Charlotte's stated motive being the real reason for her absence. I had as yet no call to alter my belief that she had been sent along by Lucy Brewster to keep a close watch on me.

Not wanting to appear ungracious I said, 'That was very thoughtful of her.'

'Before receiving Mrs Brewster's letter,' Emma Rushmore went on to tell me, 'I had, of course, heard of you.'

'From Abel Magwitch, no doubt,' I said.

'Many, many times. He lived for his "young gentleman".'

I must have cringed visibly, because my hostess looked at me in alarm.

'You must forgive me,' I hastened to explain. 'I have cause to be grateful to him. Without his patronage, I would be a blacksmith hammering my life away at a fiery forge. But now I find I have occasion to abhor him, the more I learn of the lengths he went to try to make a gentleman.'

Once again, I heard his voice, booming as it had been doing more and more within my head; while his coarse face again rose before my eyes, as my young face had apparently risen before his at a solitary hut not far distant from where I was now. On what had been his first Master's land:

'*Yes, Pip, dear boy, I've made a gentleman on you! It's me wot has done it! I swore that time, sure as ever I earned a guinea, that guinea should go to you. I swore arterwards sure as ever I spec'lated and got rich, you should get rich.*'

'In that case,' said Mrs Rushmore, bringing me back to myself before I wandered off any further, 'I think we understand each other. I, too, have cause to be grateful to him – and to abhor him. How much did Lucy Brewster tell you?'

There was no need for reticence on my part since Mrs Rushmore was insistent that she wanted me to be frank, so I told her how I knew of the circumstances which had brought about her passage to Australia, and how Magwitch had favoured her and treated her as a lady, protecting her from the attentions of the seamen and marines, and arranging for her to take a seat at the Captain's table, while he had left Lucy to fend for herself.

At this point, Emma Rushmore corrected me.

'That is Lucy Brewster's version. She could have been with me had she so chosen, but she was out to get Magwitch for herself – and she threw herself at the seamen and marines just to try to make him rescue her from them. She only ever wanted one man . . . Magwitch.'

'How is it,' I inquired, 'she is called Mrs Brewster?'

'To gain some respectability. It was Magwitch or no one . . . and it nearly killed her when he had a child by a black woman and not herself.'

'Was that child Charlotte?'

'I believe so, despite Magwitch's repeated denials.'

For the same reason of caution, I refrained from mentioning the evidence I possessed of Charlotte's resemblance to Estella. I was still wary of putting myself in a position where I might have to adjudicate on Charlotte's paternal parentage. However, I did venture an observation.

'If Charlotte were Magwitch's daughter, then she would be the legal heir to his hidden fortune. That is, assuming there were no other claimants. If so, to part of it.'

Though as fine as a gossamer veil, a little of Emma Rushmore's ladylike manner dropped when she said, 'If that were so, I wouldn't put it past Lucy to try to step in and gain control of it. She has an insatiable craving for money.' Then, regaining all her composure, she went on, 'Perhaps Lucy and I know each other too well. Because Magwitch kept in touch with both of us while he was here, we never lost contact – and after he left, we continued to keep in touch.'

Were I to have passed an observation now, I would have found myself obliged to say that it seemed to me that it was my benefactor's wealth as much, or even more, than his person that had caused the two women to remain in contact with each other; but I kept this to myself and allowed Emma Rushmore to speak without interruption.

'It was on that voyage out here that I heard of you for the very first time. Magwitch spoke of your kindness to him on the marshes, and how grateful he was – and how he would like to repay you some day. It was because of my gratitude to Magwitch for his kindness to me on the voyage that I persauded my husband Edward to give him what help he could. You see, Edward had been granted a conditional pardon while Magwitch was still assigned. Soon after Magwitch gained his liberty, and even though he inherited land, stock and money from his Master, his plans were such that he needed more. More land, more sheep, more money. Edward was still struggling and owed much himself, but he found a way to provide Magwitch with a loan. I admit that Edward's terms were stringent, but only because he himself was in the situation where he had to make repayments. Magwitch prospered, and paid back everything. He continued to prosper, while we, alas, had reverses. Bad seasons when disease struck our flocks, when floods drowned hundreds of sheep and carried away buildings. Edward now turned to Magwitch for help – and it was forthcoming – except that Magwitch's terms were fearsome – and when Edward had difficulty in meeting the times of his repayments, he was harried and threatened. Not by Magwitch himself, but by those heartless creatures who worked for him. The very dregs of the colony. With unyielding harassment they persecuted my husband, poor man. If you feel you can start the day off with a shock, Mr Pirrip, then let me show you the effect it all had on him.'

Since I offered no protest, from the breakfast room Emma Rushmore led me down a long corridor which divided the homestead into two parts. At the end of this corridor, she paused before opening a side door, and said in a low voice, 'If you'd sooner not . . .'

I shook my head; I had agreed to what she wished to show me and had already braced myself. Besides, wasn't this the man who, according to the ostler Jock Weedin, had been told the secret of the nature and the whereabouts of the hidden Magwitch fortune?

The picture I had built up of Edward Rushmore was based on the understanding that he'd had the strength of character to stand up against the injustices he saw in the society in which he lived. Even though he had done this some thirty years earlier, I still expected something of that courageous nature to show in him. And to have won the heart of Emma Rushmore, who must have been a beauty of note at that time, I assumed that he would have been a handsome man and that something of this would also still show despite the intervening years.

It was therefore a greater shock than I had prepared myself for when Emma Rushmore guided me into the study where he lived out his days. Books and a collection of firearms covered all four walls, while someone incapable of opening the pages of the volumes, or of using any of the weapons, sat swaddled in a rug in a chair, the husk of a man of letters and action, skin and bone somehow holding together the living remnants of a noble human being.

She took me to the front of him, in line with the fixed glazed stare of his eyes, and she spoke loudly, slowly and very distinctly to introduce me.

'Edward, this is Mr Pirrip . . . Mr Philip Pirrip . . . Pip . . . Magwitch used to talk about him.'

The utter absence of any sign that Edward Rushmore had either heard or comprehended was most unnerving to me, and I felt foolish and helpless as I said, 'How do you do, Mr Rushmore.'

Still not the merest indication that anything had got through to him.

Emma Rushmore tucked his rug in either side of him, then planted a soft kiss on his brow, before leading me out of the room and back into the corridor where I stood shaken at what I had seen.

'He suffered a series of paralytic seizures,' Mrs Rushmore told me. 'At first he lost only some of his movements, then all. At first only part of his power to speak, then all. But we believe he can still see, even if only in a blur – and that he can hear, even if only faintly. He has no way of communicating with us, none whatsoever – and without the soft foods and liquids we give him, what little there is now left of him would soon wither away to nothing. It was a terrible thing for one man to have done to another.'

Again I felt I shared some of the blame for the tragic predicament of that man in the study, and the sensation of empty sickness, which I had started to experience whenever thus reminded, came over me once more.

Something that had long perplexed Emma Rushmore now confronted her, and she said to me, 'I could never understand why Magwitch should have gone out of his way to be so harsh to Edward.'

Even though I had given no consideration to this question until this very moment, I had little trouble in finding a reason – or so I thought. Abel Magwitch had stood in awe of Emma Rushmore, a lady; a woman by birth, upbringing and education far beyond his reach. Edward Rushmore suffered no such shortcomings, and so my benefactor had been jealous of him.

'The last time we saw Magwitch,' Emma Rushmore resumed, 'was within a week of his leaving the colony for England. We were on our first, smaller property then. He boasted to me how he had amassed more than enough for you to live as a gentleman for the rest of your life. Furthermore, he had another fortune secreted away, should the first ever run out. He asked me if he could bid goodbye to Edward – alone, if he might, since he had something special he wanted to say to my husband. I suspected nothing. On the contrary, I had visions of Magwitch saying something, as a farewell gesture, that might heal the wounds of their dealings with each other. Yet when Magwitch came back to me, he stunned me by telling me that he had not only boasted to Edward about his "hidden" fortune, but had actually told him what it was and where it could be found – knowing that my poor darling had no way of ever passing on such information to any other living person. It was a horrendous thing to have done – and I told Magwitch so. Rarely have I ever completely lost my temper, but this was such an occasion. I ordered him from my house and wished him the very worst that Fate might ordain for him.'

Out of breath, Emma Rushmore stopped for some moments, then spoke in a quieter voice. 'Forgive me, Mr Pirrip, but whenever I recall it I become worked up about it all over again.'

'You have every reason,' I said in an equally quiet voice, because I was appalled – and I abhorred my benefactor more than I had ever done, this time being unable to find any saving grace for his actions, as in the case of the Master he had murdered, since it seemed that man might have earned something of what had been meted out to him.

It was at this point that I realised I need go no further than this Estate to solve the mystery of who had sent word ahead to England to inform Magwitch's sworn enemy Compeyson that *his* sworn enemy was on the way back from New South Wales. Emma Rushmore would have had every justification.

At the same time, I began to wonder, as others before me had obviously already done, how the secrets Abel Magwitch had revealed to Edward Rushmore could be obtained from a man incapable of communicating with any other mortal being.

CHAPTER 12

Two hours passed without any sign of Charlotte and I began to worry. The weather was fine, the air untainted with any of the smoke or tang of the fires from the mountains, although the land was heavy after the rain and the creeks swollen with water.

Emma Rushmore appeared unworried. As she pointed out, on her visits here Charlotte frequently took long horse-rides and could in fact go for half a day at a time and still remain within the boundaries of the Estate; also, that there were places where she could shelter if she wished to rest – out-houses and huts, including the very hut where Abel Magwitch as a solitary shepherd had been struck with the idea of secretly making me a gentleman and where many times he had 'seen' me and 'talked' to me.

'He used to spend a lot of his time alone with you,' Mrs Rushmore told me. 'He used to go off in his "caravan" – a covered wagon hauled by a pair of oxen as formidable-looking and nearly as wily as himself. He used to say to me that he had spent a week or two *"alonger his boy"*.'

After all I had been discovering about my late benefactor, I was greatly surprised to learn that he had risked going any-where on his own. In fact, I had been told by the landlord in Sydney that towards the end of his time in the colony it was something he never dared do. So I questioned this.

'Not completely alone,' Mrs Rushmore informed me. 'He took along a man almost as big as himself, a Welshman, a man of many trades including water-divining. Thanks to him, Magwitch made sure there was a good supply of water on any land he purchased or took over. Although he could really have risked going alone. He had so many men sworn to him that if any harm had come to him those responsible would have been hunted down and dealt with.'

There was still no sign of Charlotte. After trying to be

patient, my anxiety got the better of me. In Cairo I had been horse-riding regularly (we went out on horses in preference to camels on our archaeological expeditions), so was experienced in the saddle, and chose a big bay on which to ride out. There were tracks in all directions which I might follow, but having no idea which one Charlotte had taken, I kept as far as possible to high ground, bringing my horse to a halt every so often and looking around for her.

For miles whichever way I faced, the landscape was a parkland, the only living things being sheep, many species of birds, and swarms of flies and biting midges. Between hillocks I occasionally found ponds and small lakes, some of these thick with game – duck, geese, pelicans and other water birds. When I came upon them suddenly, it only needed one bird to show alarm and all the others took to the wing, soaring high into the air and milling about for some time after I had moved on.

It was when in the distance that I saw birds similarly disturbed that I concluded they had been sent aloft by someone passing by, so I headed in that direction and presently saw Charlotte riding casually side-saddle. She halted when she saw me approaching at a gallop; and when I had stopped beside her, she said, 'I was on my way back to the homestead to pick you up.'

As I told her how anxious I had become, there must have been an overtone of my growing feelings for her, and she eyed me watchfully. Her skin had a deep copper glow which I took to have been brought about by the combination of the open air, the exercise of riding and the natural colour of her skin; but then I detected a simmering excitement within her.

She did not delay in telling me the reason for this.

'You've been followed,' she said.

I quickly looked around about, but there was no person in sight.

'Not now,' she said, laughing. 'Yesterday. From that last staging-post.'

'Followed by whom?' I asked.

'Three men. That's all I was told.'

'You were told?'

'By a friend.'

'What friend?'

Delighting in leading me along, she said, 'I'll give you three guesses – and some help. His name begins with the letter after "R".'

'Not Spikey Simmins!'

'And what, may I ask, is wrong with Spikey Simmins?'

'My dear Charlotte,' I said, 'Spikey Simmins is a thief and an outlaw, certainly not the sort of person a young woman of your repute should have dealings with.'

'What a silly pompous man you are!' she cried, and once more in the very same tone and manner used by Estella when she had admonished me.

Stung by her taunt, and feeling foolish for having in fact been so pompous, out of a sort of desperation I seemed to embroil myself even more.

'What were you doing meeting up with him?'

'Merely keeping an appointment,' she coolly replied.

'An appointment?'

'Made at the coaching-inn – if he should somehow manage to escape.'

'Charlotte,' I said, 'I would hate to have to tell you what I am thinking.'

'Don't bother – I know. That I had a hand in that escape?'

'I fear so.'

'What about Mr Tolchard?'

'He was blamed for the simple reason that he branded himself as the obvious culprit by disappearing at the time.'

'Keep blaming him then!'

Putting an end to my cross-questioning, Charlotte went on, 'I was returning to the homestead because I'd seen the hut where Uncle Magwitch used to "talk" to you. I thought you might like me to take you there.'

Although reluctant to give up before establishing who in fact had assisted Spikey Simmins and his three fellow bushrangers to abscond, I dropped the subject at the prospect of being able to see this hut. A visit to it was something I had hoped I might make, and immediately I told Charlotte this she wheeled her dappled grey horse back in the direction from which she had come, then started off into a gallop, forcing me to do the same, never allowing me to come abreast of her on my mount, increasing speed whenever I tried to do so. Not only did we scare birds up off their calm-water resting places but also sheep from their grazing – sheep, that I realised were of the merino variety bearing the vaunted Magwitch strain of wool.

For twenty minutes we proceeded at a reckless pace, until among trees on the side of what was a fully-fledged hill rather than a hillock, a small stone hut rose into view, revealing itself as what might have been an isolated prison cell as we came to a stop alongside it. Four very solid walls constructed of rocks bonded together, an entrance with a sound if weathered wooden door, and on one side a small narrow window with a number of rusting iron bars set horizontally into the stones.

From the outside, especially at a distance, it looked much smaller than it revealed itself to be once I had stepped inside. At its rear there was a cramped stone grate and a short flue leading to a fist-sized hole up near the roof for smoke to escape. No doubt in the bitter winter, which I had been told was experienced here, a fire was necessary. In fact, there had recently been one in the hut, as I noticed from the fresh ashes in the grate.

This then was the tiny grate at which Abel Magwitch had stood to warm his hands. I imagined him having to stand stooped, because had he been upright, his bald head, tattooed as it was with wrinkles, would have been against the rough wood beams of the roof. Just by imagining his presence in the hut it began to feel overcrowded, so I left it to his ghost and stepped back outside. Here I stood where he must have taken his stance after seeing what he had imagined. My head reverberated with his voice once more:

'I see you there a many a times as plain as I ever see you on them misty marshes. "Lord strike me dead!" I says each time – and I goes out in the open air to say it under the open heavens – "but wot, if I gets liberty and money, I'll make that boy a gentleman!"'

Here had begun the crazed romantic dream that had led him callously to cheat and murder his Master: all in the cause of making me a gentleman. Here had begun the long calendar of threat and crime: all to make me a gentleman. Here had begun what had led Abel Magwitch to turn poor Edward Rushmore into a living human husk: just to make me a gentleman. And all in a place as far removed as any other place could be, within the bounds of Earth, from those misty marshes where we had first met: the wild-eyed convict on the run and me, a village lad petrified with terror.

What Charlotte now divined, and what she now chose to say, but acerbated my sense of shared guilt.

'It was here he used to "see" you.'

'Do you think I don't know that?' I cried, a plea to her not to make the pain of it all the more excruciating.

'And "talk" to you,' she went on, prepared to spare me nothing, so that I could but groan.

And then, taunting me in another way, she added, 'Just as I used to "talk" to you.'

Some of the mist from those far-off marshes might have gathered in my eyes, such was my bewilderment as I stared at her.

'At least, to your portrait,' she explained. 'And you used to "talk" to me,' she said. 'At first when it was in Magwitch's house, you on the wall and me standing below, you used to tell me that one day you would come sailing up the harbour in a ship and carry me off to some kindly place where people didn't turn up their noses and look down on me because of my coloured ancestry. Even though my skin was dark, you used to tell me that I was beautiful . . .'

This sudden revelation released such a flood of emotion within me, being such a parallel to what I had been thinking about her, that I was poised on the very verge of telling her that even though there was much in that portrait I considered false, what had been spoken was the truth, and that she was indeed beautiful and that I had in fact contemplated being able to take her to a place where the colour of her skin would not matter, and that she was the embodiment of someone I had loved and lost. My hands reached out to take her in my arms, but she made a game of this too, as she had done when riding our horses here, and she turned away and slipped back inside the stone hut, leaving me all atremble and unable for the moment to move lest I take a tumble to the ground.

'Have you seen what are on these walls?' she asked, calling to me from within.

When I joined her inside, I found her dusting off the stone surfaces to reveal more of the names, initials, dates and other markings scratched, cut and scrawled there.

Perhaps Abel Magwitch had contributed something; and as I peered, thinking of him using his great horn-handled jack-knife to engrave his two initials with its tip, I got the impression that he was in fact at work, because I started to hear a sound such as his jack-knife might have made – and looked to where Charlotte stood and saw that she was using a knife to pick out a letter.

'It's "P", if you're wondering,' she said. ' "P" for "Pip".'

But it was not the letter that riveted my attention.

Realising this, and starting to laugh, Charlotte showed me the knife, a folding one that could be disguised as a lady's hand comb and slipped into the side pocket of her riding habit – or into the basket she had been carrying when we crossed the mountain range by stage-coach.

As we both accepted that this knife was evidence of what had happened to a certain rope at the staging-post beside the coaching-inn, there was no need for any question to be put into words.

For an answer she gave me a laugh that filled the hut; a laugh that suddenly could get out of the hut only by way of the barred window or the chimney flue, because the door which swung outward slammed shut and stayed rigidly closed.

With my flattened palm, I thrust my hand at the door, but it did not budge. I put my shoulder and all my weight to it, but it gave no more than a fraction of an inch, there being something jammed against it from the outside to keep it firmly shut – as I was to learn, a stout stake that had been prepared as part of the trap that was about to be sprung once we were inside.

There was the rap of metal on metal at the narrow side window, and I turned to see that the sound was made by the barrel of a pistol striking one of the horizontal iron bars, while outside behind the weapon, bending down so as to be able to see inside, was the face of the stage-coach passenger who had vanished at the coaching-inn.

Aiming the pistol at my heart, Tolchard said, 'Well, now, "young gentleman" ' – and if I had any lingering doubt as to whether this man and the masked pursuer whose reflection I had glimpsed when I hid under the landing-stage at Pirrip Island were not one and the same, it was dispelled as I heard his voice now – 'there's many a man still alive in the colony who'd give an eye or an arm to be where I am today. To be face to face with the young gentleman who drove Abel Magwitch to do what he did. I swore that if ever I had the chance to get even with that person, I would kill him – and take great pleasure in so doing.'

The deadly danger that now faced me also faced Charlotte, and I cast a sideways glance towards her, expecting her to at least show some concern, if not fear, but was amazed that she was able to appear so calm, merely bemused. With the feeling that I was caught not only in a trap but in a web, I recalled the brief look of recognition that had passed between Charlotte and this man on the stage-coach.

'But for you,' Tolchard went on, giving the bar a rap with his pistol barrel to demand my full attention, 'Magwitch would not have undertaken that voyage back to England, in which case my good friend Compeyson would not have come to his death by drowning.'

'You say Compeyson was your friend,' I said, realising that I had at last an inkling of how the intelligence of my late benefactor's return to the land from which he had been exiled had preceded him.

'As far back as our days at a public boarding-school. We grew up together, we worked together. He was still serving out a sentence when I found myself expatriated here for life, but we managed to keep in touch after he was released.'

'You spied on Magwitch for him all those years.'

'Put it how you like, "young gentleman".'

'And you sent word ahead of him that he was returning.'

'That I did. To Compeyson, my friend.'

'May I ask how you discovered he was returning?'

'You may. But you'll get no answer to that.'

He levelled the pistol at me with the barrel still aiming at my heart, and with his other hand he placed on the ledge of the narrow window, under the lowest of the iron bars, first the black clasped Testament and then the second of the two keepsakes that had been stolen from my hotel room in Sydney, the pack of playing cards.

'You know, and I know, what Magwitch left hidden away,' Tolchard said to me. 'And you know, and I know, that the clue to its whereabouts is hidden somewhere in this book and these playing cards. Magwitch boasted it was so. And unless you had some clue, why would you be here in New South Wales?'

I wanted to protest the true reasons for my visit, but Tolchard gave me no chance to speak.

'Much as I would like here and now, without ado or delay, to carry out my long-cherished threat to kill you, I'd be prepared to come to some other arrangement if you are prepared to share all clues with me. So there they are.' He tapped the book and then the pack of cards with a finger. 'Busy yourself and come up with some answers.'

With that, he stepped back from the narrow window, letting more daylight return into the hut and allowing me to see who was outside with him. I had expected it. Cannibal Jack and the aborigine Henry.

With my face close to the iron bars, I called out to the wizened little man with the Maori tattoos in blue lines on his face. 'Now I know who climbed the drainpipe to my hotel room.'

It could not have been the aborigine, because, if you recall, there were bootmarks on that drain-pipe, and the native wore nothing on his feet.

Cannibal Jack glanced sourly towards the hut, making no comment to me but he muttered to the aborigine who smirked; and then they both started to gather dead sticks to make a fire.

Charlotte took the Testament and the cards from the ledge, and, after examining them, handed them to me.

'They are desperate men,' she said.

'You don't seem much afraid of them,' said I.

'I've a brave "young gentleman" to protect me. Besides, I'm sure you're going to find something in this book and the cards that will appease Mr Tolchard.'

'You're much mistaken,' I retorted. 'Just as your foster-mother was several evenings ago when she decided I'd come to New South Wales to try to find that secret fortune. Believe me, until she mentioned it, I knew nothing of its existence. Nothing whatsoever. Although now, after what I've learnt, it's my intention to do my best to be the first to find it.'

'So your trip to the colony could well turn out to be a very profitable one.'

'I'm not interested in the hidden fortune for myself – but I'm determined to do all I can to make sure it doesn't fall into the wrong hands.'

'And whose might be the right hands?' she inquired.

'Abel Magwitch's legal heirs.'

'Including yourself, surely.'

'*Not* including me. I was not related to him – and he never put any settlement in my favour in writing before he was captured. But certain people would have a claim.'

'Such as an illegitimate daughter?'

Again, I was very much on my guard not to be drawn in on this issue and finding myself having to give my opinion; so I chose not to reply, confining myself to making an examination of the Testament and the playing cards. I did so with a closeness I had never subjected them to before, starting with the Testament.

For years at a time I had not opened the Testament, but left it in a box with the playing cards and a few other treasured possessions in my rooms in the Cairo villa where I lived with the Pocket family. On the rare occasions when I had taken it out, I had always looked first at the owner's name at the front, in his crude but bold hand. With affection, too. Until now, I had never observed that there were other places in the Testament where a hand holding a quill dipped in ink had been at work. Most pages had been left untouched, but here and there a ring had been drawn around a single letter in the text.

I must have reacted with visible sharpness to my discovery, because Charlotte moved even closer to my side, bossy in manner and in tone.

'What have you found?' she demanded.

'Nothing of any significance, I'm sure,' I said dismissively, closing the Testament.

She snatched it away from me, opening it at where she judged I had been looking. Whether it was the same page or not, I do not know – but she found a similar marking around one of the letters in the text. Holding the page nearer the incoming light, she wanted to know what this signified.

'I have no idea,' I said. 'And that's the truth.'

From the outside, where I realised he had been listening, Tolchard appeared at the barred window again and interjected. 'Busy yourself and find out. By the time I get back, I'll expect an answer.'

He didn't say where he was going; but after he took lines and hooks from the saddle-bag of his horse and headed down to the bottom of the hill with the aborigine, I guessed it was to the river to fish, and that the fire Cannibal Jack was building up was being prepared to cook their catch.

Leaving Charlotte to try to make what she could of the encircled letters – and she kept holding up the Testament again and again as she found more such markings that she wanted me to explain – I occupied myself with the playing cards. Perhaps there were some markings on them, too, so I went through the entire pack, searching the front and the back of each card, but finding no more than the one marking they had in common, the grime of old age – until, as I turned one of them over, I noticed that it seemed to give off several twinkles of light.

Taking great care to make my closer scutiny very casual so as not to have Charlotte at me with fresh demands, I turned over the same card. It gave off the same twinkles – and then I saw that this was because there were minute holes in it, about half to a full dozen of them, the size of pins. Indeed, they may well have been made by pricking through it with a pin or a needle.

Thereafter, other cards revealed similar tiny holes, but never in the same pattern. I wondered if they might have been 'marked' cards, for instance the Seven of Hearts having seven such holes in it, and perhaps one to four more holes added to denote what suit it was – Spades, Hearts, Diamonds or Clubs; but the face value of no card matched up with the holes in this way.

Meanwhile, Charlotte had gone back to the start of the Testament, and was reading each encircled letter aloud, obviously hoping that strung together they might start to make sense. There was, I fear, a conspicuous lack of coherence in what this process yielded; but I did not interrupt her as it now became imperative, in view of what I saw through the narrow side window, that Charlotte should remain fully occupied with the Testament.

Across from the clump of trees, where we had left our horses tethered in shade within reach of grass at which to nibble, there crept a man armed with a piece of broken tree branch the size of a male arm and shoulder. He was attired in a shirt and trousers of coarse material marked with red arrows, and wore shoes and hat of the type issued to convicts. As Cannibal Jack continued to tend his fire and bring a sooty iron pot of water to the boil, he was in total ignorance of the threat approaching him in swift silent strides.

As Cannibal Jack crouched on his haunches and used a stick to prod the fire, the interloper raised the broken piece of branch high above him, paused for a moment to steady his aim, then brought the bludgeon down with a mighty smite, clubbing Cannibal Jack at the back of the head and sending him sprawling with little more than a light grunt.

That grunt, however, was picked up by Charlotte's ears. I tried to stand against the narrow window so that she might not see out, because the interloper was heading at a run towards the hut. As he did so, I recognised the convict who had swum from that floating prison to the emigrant ship far out in the Indian Ocean. There he had failed in his bid for freedom; but here, soon after his arrival in the penal colony, he had apparently succeeded, if only to the extent of temporarily being at large.

Charlotte pushed me to one side and looked out, just in time to see the convict reaching the hut.

With a great outraged gasp, which seemed to me grossly misplaced coming from someone who, like myself, had little hope of escape from this lonely cell without some outside help, Charlotte turned on me, as if I was guilty of some atrocity for trying to organise our deliverance.

Before she could say anything, the wooden door was open, and the convict was standing outside, holding the strong stake that had kept it securely shut.

'I'm right 'onoured to be able to return a kindness, sir,' he said to me, using the stake to beckon us out while with his other hand holding onto the broken tree bough just in case he needed it again as a weapon.

Charlotte shrank back inside the cell, and I had to take hold of her arm and bring her out into the open with me.

'This man's set us free, don't you understand,' I said, trying not to raise my voice.

I thought it must have been fear of the convict that had caused her to hold back, for he looked almost as forbidding as when he had swum between those two ships and stood in the moonlight on the emigrant ship's deck. Although she no longer held back, she seemed in two minds about availing herself of this chance to escape Tolchard and the other two. Her indecision allowed me to retrieve the Testament from her and shove it into my pocket where I had already thrust the pack of playing cards.

'You've rendered me a greater favour that I was able to do you,' I said to the convict.

'You but tried, sir,' he said, and waving us towards where our horses were tethered, he added, 'Make haste.'

As I thanked him, he set off in another direction and was soon out of sight, offering no explanation of how he had come to be here at such a convenient time, although I suspected he had been sheltering in the hut. That would account for the recent ashes in the grate. I wished him well.

The heat from the fire performed for Cannibal Jack what a bucket of cold water is more often called upon to do, and he stirred as Charlotte and I hastened from the hut across the sloping hillside to our horses. I urged Charlotte to hurry so that we could make good our escape while we had a chance. She was keeping up with me, until she stumbled and let out a cry; then bent down, rubbing her ankle, complaining that she had caught it in a grassy hole and twisted it. She kept on, limping, but the damage had already been done.

Her cry hastened Cannibal Jack's recovery – and as soon as he made out what was happening, seeing me helping Charlotte up on to the saddle of her horse, he let out a shout remarkable in its strength for one who had so recently been rendered so apparently lifeless that I would not have been at all surprised had he been dead.

'Hold hard!' This I ignored, and with Charlotte on her horse, I hastened to mount mine as he cried, 'Wait there, you!'

Declining to oblige, I swung my horse around towards the way we had come, as Charlotte did her dappled grey, and we set out to return to the Rushmore homestead. As we departed from the vicinity of the lonely hut, we glimpsed Tolchard and the aborigine, in response to Cannibal Jack's shouts (which continued with growing lustiness), pounding up from the river, then halting askance as they saw us going, before racing to the copse where they had left their own horses.

While we had a handy start, they would soon overtake us if Charlotte were allowed to set the rate at which we rode. In marked contrast to the headlong fashion in which she had arrived at the hut, she seemed now content with a little more than a canter, and I found myself slowed down to her pace; until, as we reached the top of a hillock, I looked back and saw Tolchard and the aborigine had drawn so close that if we did not speed ourselves we would be recaptured well before reaching the sanctuary of the homestead.

It occurred to me that this was perhaps what Charlotte was trying to bring about; for as much as I hated to have to entertain the possiblity of it, I was forced to admit to myself that there must be some link between her and the man who had played such a fatal part in relaying the intelligence which had been passed back to England ahead of Abel Magwitch's ill-advised return there.

Conscious that I had two vital items back in my possession again, the Testament and the pack of playing cards, I decided that it was up to me to set the pace, and I used the heels of my boots to spur the bay horse into a fast gallop.

Charlotte proved more than equal to the challenge, bestirring her mount and keeping close up with me.

Even so, Tolchard and the aborigine still gained ground on us. I knew so little of this terrain that there was no turning I could take to attempt to throw them off. It was a matter of trying to out-ride them.

And then, while being pursued from the rear, I saw that we were being intercepted from another direction – by four horsemen – and, as I involuntarily pulled on the rein to slow down my bay until I could decide what to make of this new situation, Charlotte came right alongside me, amused at my concern.

'It's only Spikey and his friends,' she said.

Spikey Simmins and his three bushranger companions also knew about the hidden Magwitch fortune and no doubt also believed that I had some knowledge no one else possessed – so they, too, would be eager to waylay me.

If we out-distanced Tolchard and the aborigine, we still had to somehow avoid the four bushrangers.

Until less than seventy years earlier, New South Wales had been unnamed – indeed, an empty space of uncompleted coast-line on the known map of New Holland. The interior until little more than two decades years ago, as far as Europeans were concerned, had been unexplored, inhabited only by small bands of blacks. Now it seemed it was becoming crowded with whites, for Charlotte and I not only had Tolchard and his aborigine at our heels, and Spikey and his companions coming at us from one side, but immediately ahead of us, preceded by loud barking, there appeared a detachment of a dozen soldiers with two large dogs on the leash.

The sight of them had the effect of bringing Charlotte and me, and both our pursuers and interceptors, to a quick stop. Looking around to these two parties, I saw the members of each backing their horses into the shelter of trees, so as to keep out of sight, yet still be able to watch what happened between us and the detachment.

A Sergeant brought the soldiers to a halt, but the two men with the dogs on the leash had to pull back hard to prevent the animals rushing at us.

Charlotte was dismayed. 'What are soldiers doing here?' she asked, no doubt fearful for Spikey.

'Isn't it obvious? They're on the hunt for that escaped convict,' I told her. 'For heaven's sake, don't mention we've seen him.'

The Sergeant came right up in front of my horse and saluted, before asking exactly what I had expected. I felt that I was repaying the escapee for his kindness by assuring the Sergeant that we had seen no one of the convict's description, an assertion which Charlotte backed up with her eyes so large and innocent that I could not help but realise, much as I had come to adore their loveliness, how easy it would be for them to betray and lead astray.

The Sergeant told us that the convict had been assigned to a timber-cutter in the valley on arrival in the colony only a few weeks ago, and that he was a notorious escaper and that on the voyage to New South Wales he had swum through shark-infested waters from a prison transport to an emigrant ship, where he had terrorised passengers and crew before being hunted down from the rigging. I could have given the Sergeant an eye-witness account and a correct version of what had happened, except that I didn't want to miss the opportunity that his arrival had given me to turn the tables on both pursuers and interceptors.

Pointing to where Spikey and his companions were concealed, and then to where I had seen Tolchard and his aborigine taking shelter, I said that since both parties appeared to be acting in a suspicious manner they might have something to hide, which could well be information as to the whereabouts of the escapee.

Thanking me profusely, the Sergeant about-turned to his men, divided them into two parties, each with a dog, then sent them off at the double in the two directions.

Charlotte was furious at me; but after all the laughing she had done at my expense, for once I enjoyed being able to see the humorous side of a situation.

Neither party waited for the soldiers or dogs to corner them; we glimpsed Tolchard and his aborigine, and Spikey and his companions, heading for the forests which lay at the foot of the steep valley slopes, where hide-outs abounded. Thus it seemed we were to be able to complete our return to Rushmore homestead without fear of further interference; but as we passed near the gate-house, we saw two tall men in dark clothing on large horses questioning the gate-keeper.

Charlotte aimed some of her smouldering fury at them.

'You know who they are, don't you,' she said.

'No,' said I. 'But they look important.'

'They *think* they are.'

'Who are they then?' I asked.

'Agents of the Crown,' she told me. 'But they won't get anything out of that old gate-keeper.'

Instead of answering the two Agents, the gate-keeper seemed to be biting the side of a forefinger, a mannerism that had something familiar about it, one which I would have thought about more at the time, except that I found myself becoming overwhelmed at the number of different parties who had converged here – all, without question, interested not so much in me as in what they believed I could lead them to: the hidden Magwitch fortune.

CHAPTER 13

Emma Rushmore assumed that I had managed to meet up with Charlotte out on the Estate and that we had continued horse-riding together, so neither of us informed her otherwise. And since she made no mention of anything connected with them, we assumed that she had heard nothing of any bushrangers, escaped convicts, soldiers or other intruders abroad among the sheep and wild life on her property.

Dinner that night was an elegant meal. Mrs Rushmore insisted that I should take the seat at the head of the table, so there I sat with her on one side and on the other Charlotte. In the candlelight, she looked even more exquisitely lovely than on that first night at 'The Mansion' by the harbour. In Egypt, I had seen many striking women of mixed white and coloured blood: tonight it was as if we were in the presence of an Eastern Princess.

She had many a soft and beguiling smile for me, yet each one became another stab into the wound made in my heart. That she could be attracted to anyone so vulgar and worthless as Spikey Simmins somehow subjected me all over again to the distress caused me when Estella had chosen to pass me over, to spurn my love, and marry that brute, Bentley Drummle. Besides which, I had to face the fact I could not trust her. She had almost deliberately led me into being trapped with her in that lonely shepherd's hut; and when the convict had set us free, she had been slow in seizing the opportunity to escape.

Throughout the meal, I was acutely conscious of what I carried on my person, the Testament and the pack of playing cards; and while I had already been able to investigate them at length in the privacy of my room, I had been unable to discover anything of significance from encircled letters in the one or from the series of tiny holes in the other, so that I was anxious to be alone with them again.

My room had a tall glass door opening on to the wide verandah that bordered the homestead on all four sides. Somewhere out on the darkened acres, two parties might well be stealthily moving towards the hillock on which the homestead stood: Tolchard, Cannibal Jack and their aborigine; and Spikey Simmins and his three fellow bushrangers. Also, the Agents of the Crown could well have designs on the two Magwitch relics. Or even someone from the homestead itself. Against any such internal intrusion, I turned the key in the lock of the door to the corridor. Likewise, after shutting the glass door to the verandah, even though it meant excluding the cool night air, I turned the key in it too. Then I drew the curtains across the glass doors, but not completely. I wanted as much seclusion as possible while I sat at the corner table where there was an oil lamp for light, but at the same time I felt I must be able to look out. With the curtain fully drawn, prowlers could be at the other side of the verandah door before I knew it. This way I might obtain some warning of such an approach.

And so it was with one eye on that gap in the curtains that I took out the Testament and the list I had made of all the letters marked in it, having set them down in the order of the pages starting from the beginning on a sheet of my personal notepaper.

T R S W T H T E
T H E E G E A B
E H O H C O E C
T O N V E E E L
E R F N A H L G
E T N M D S E W
C M E D

After reading these letters from start to finish, then in reverse, it all remained gibberish. I wondered if this might be another language, but it seemed unlikely as Magwitch knew only English, even though having a certain fascination for other tongues, something which had driven me to distraction when he was first in hiding with me, since when he had enough sleep and had won another game of Patience (and marked his win by jamming his ugly horn-handled jack-knife into the table-top), I had been obliged to read aloud to him from my books. Not in English.

'*Foreign language, dear boy!*' And as I read in French or German, althought not understanding one word I said, he would take pride in the cleverness of the young gentleman he had created.

Putting the Testament and the list of letters to one side, I brought out the pack of playing cards again. Taking one card which seemed to bear an average number of the tiny holes, I placed it on another sheet of my notepaper and used the point of my diamond tie-pin (retrieved, of course, from Spikey Simmins) to prick through each hole on to the paper, thus transferring the pattern. I then lightly linked the tiny holes with a pencil mark.

My archaeological interests in Egypt helped me now, since I had been involved with Herbert Pocket and other enthusiasts in spending some of our leisure time in excavating ruins (which that country certainly did not lack). We would uncover widely separated traces of a building, a palace or a temple – a corner, an entrance, another corner, the positions of which we transferred to paper – and then link them up, thus obtaining a glimpse of the whole as it once was, even though much remained to be actually excavated.

The result in this instance was a sort of crescent curve which made no sense to me either.

Oh, that I had paid more attention when Abel Magwitch had been playing this game and so acquainted myself with its basic rules! Or allowed Cannibal Jack to play another such game outside the grog-shop in Sydney town before interrupting him.

The only thing I could recall of my late benefactor's playing of the game was that he laid the cards out in a certain way and that after much turning over of one card and another, and moving them about, when the game was finished – assuming it was one that he completed and therefore won – the cards ended up in exactly the same pattern, except they were upside down. The four Aces in the pack, after starting in a line at the bottom, ended up in a line at the top. Having remembered this much, I was fortunate enough to be able to call up a mental picture of how Cannibal Jack had ended his game, and it was with the four Aces in a line with the cards of each suit strung down below them vertically in the order of King, Queen, Knave, ten, nine, eight, seven, six, five, four, three and two.

(Even this brought a memory of Estella rushing back. The very first time I met her on my visit to Miss Havisham's dismal old-brick house, when she watched as Estella and I played cards together – beggar-my-neighbour – and to belittle me, Estella derided me by saying, 'He calls the Knaves, Jacks, this boy!')

Naturally, I wasted no time in setting out the pack in that remembered pattern. I was not sure of the order of the four Aces from left to right, and although not a regular card-player I believed that one suit had preference over another, so I placed them on that basis: Spades, Hearts, Diamonds, Clubs. Then, after moving the lamp so that the light shone over the pattern of the cards, I examined the tracery that the pin-holes now made. It seemed to be a long wavering line with smaller patterns clustered about half-way down and on the right of this line.

To be able to see this more clearly, I placed sheets of my notepaper on the table, then laid out the cards over them so that I could prick through each hole with my tie-pin. With most of the cards it was necessary first of all to locate where the holes had originally been made and then insert the point of my tie-pin to open them out again before laying them on the notepaper. No doubt I missed some, but not enough to matter, because, after gathering up the cards into a pack again, a visible outline of indentations on the sheets of notepaper indicated a rough map.

As I lightly linked one indentation to another with a pencil, there emerged what appeared to be a boundary, or perhaps even a shoreline, wavering from side to side down the sheets of paper, with squares, triangles, circles and oblongs all to one side. I knew of no place or location this might represent – and was aware that any linking together of the pin-pricks would result in what looked like a map. Even so, that long wavering line seemed pretty definite.

Here before me was undoubtedly the key to the location of the hidden Magwitch fortune, although it was ironical that I should be going to such lengths to try to establish its whereabouts when under the same roof that very information was in the possession of Edward Rushmore.

It was now that I heard a light footfall on the boards of the verandah outside and realised that a little earlier I had paid no attention to the same sound, because it came at a time when the discovery of the map absorbed all my attention to the extent of making me almost oblivious to anything else.

I turned down the wick of the lamp, slipped the Testament and playing cards into my pocket and collected all the sheets of notepaper. Rather than present myself as a target by going to the gap between the curtains, I went to the side of one of them and drew it aside a little.

As I peered out into the darkness, I heard the baying of dogs in the distance, a sound which was replied to by the barking of the dogs chained at the back of the homestead. If there had been a prowler on the verandah, it might have been the runaway convict. As I waited and watched, the baying of the approaching dogs grew louder and the response by the homestead animals so spirited that the household was woken and lamps started to throw light out on to the grounds surrounding the verandah.

Near several trees growing almost trunk to trunk, there was a sudden movement as a beam of light struck; someone slipped away, and all I caught was the glimpse of the back of a man; a very brief glimpse, but enough to recognise the gate-keeper.

His presence did not necessarily prove that he had been responsible for the footfall on the verandah, but he had certainly been some distance from the gate-house.

With the entire household now awake, the detachment of soldiers arrived, and I heard the Sergeant telling Mrs Rushmore that they were on the trail of the escaped felon and had been led in the direction of the homestead by their dogs. (So perhaps the convict had been on the verandah after all.)

Emma Rushmore had no hesitation in avowing that no escapee was here under her roof. She invited the Sergeant to have his soldiers inspect the premises if they wished to satisfy themselves; but the Sergeant did not press, and when she suggested the detachment might shelter here for the rest of the night, the Sergeant readily accepted the offer.

The soldiers were housed in a shed near the main homestead building, close enough for me to retire to bed with the feeling that I need fear no trouble from any intruders. Again, I had reason to thank the runaway convict.

After such a long, energetic and eventful day, from the instant I put my head on the pillow I fell into a long sound sleep. I woke refreshed, aware from the light coming in between the curtains of the start of a golden day outside. As I lay in a lazy mood, the events of the previous few days passed through my mind. And then, as I have said, shortly after wakening from a satisfying sleep, the mind puts together little bits of this and that, and without any apparent mental effort on your part, you find yourself in possession of the answer to something that has been puzzling you.

The gate-keeper. The shape of his head. His cavernous eyes. The smell of scented soap. The biting of the side of a forefinger. It seemed beyond the realms of credibility that this man, now aged, should be in New South Wales – and perhaps it could be a whole collection of coincidences – but otherwise unquestionably the gate-keeper who had slipped off into the darkness when lamps were lit up in the homestead during the night was the man who had defended Abel Magwitch at the Old Bailey; my one-time guardian, the man responsible for Miss Havisham adopting Estella – the London lawyer, Mr Jaggers.

CHAPTER 14

Despite the strength of the light outside, it was still an early hour. After the disturbance of the night, the other occupants of the homestead were all still asleep.

This was my opportunity to slip off alone to try to satisfy myself on a matter I knew would pester me until I had an answer one way or the other: the identity of the gate-keeper. Since the Testament and the pack of playing cards had already been stolen once, I took the precaution of putting them in my pocket – together with the sheets of notepaper on which there remained two unsolved conundrums.

Once outside, however, I had second thoughts about going as far as the entrance to the Estate on my own, no matter how fresh, calm and innocent this fair morning seemed. Tolchard, Cannibal Jack and their aborigine had still to be accounted for, and what guarantee did I have that Spikey Simmins and his three ragged disciples were not somewhere in the vicinity? There were also those Agents of the Crown. To set out alone might be to turn myself into an easy picking. I could, of course, go to the stables, saddle up a horse, and trust that by covering the distance between the homestead and the gate-house at a sudden fast gallop I would arrive there before any lurking party or parties could make any move to try to waylay me.

The soldiers who had given me the feeling of protection during the night now solved this problem for me. Two of them had been posted to stand by on watch at the entrance, and two more were about to set out to relieve them. As they marched side by side, I followed close behind them, after informing them that I was taking an early morning walk as far as the gate-house. They made no objection, although for a walk, since they marched at a lively pace, it turned out to be a brisk one.

Had they any idea as yet where their quarry, the escaped convict, might be in hiding?

'No, sir,' one of them replied. 'Not as yet. But we'll run him to ground soon enough.'

They might have been speaking about a wild animal, and the sympathy I felt for the runaway extended to others also fugitive, now or in the past, so that in spite of the abhorrence I had built up to so much of what Abel Magwitch had done, I again found myself feeling he'd had justification for some of it.

A side door was open in the stone gate-house building, and as I peered inside, I was greeted by a voice from the shadows.

'Hah, Pip! I've been half expecting you.'

This was unquestionably the voice of Mr Jaggers, as clear and peremptory as ever. The man who came towards me as I stepped into the room was nearly ten years older than when I had seen him last. While his beard, whiskers and hair had gone white, his complexion remained dark, and his eyebrows, now that I saw them at closer quarters, were if anything blacker and more bristling. His beard, of course, was new to me.

His large hand extended towards me and I grasped it and joined him in a brief shake. He had never been a man to show warmth and did not do so now.

'I read of your arrival in the *Clarion* – and from a certain source I gathered that you might pay a visit to the interior.'

Leaving me to wonder whether he had received this information from Emma Rushmore or another source, he gestured me to a chair and then stood opposite me, as if in front of the fire in his office in Little Britain, leaning over to look at his boots, then straightening up to show me a frown above eyes that seemed to have withdrawn further into his head with the passing of the years. The smell of the scented soap he used when washing his hands was most pronounced (so I assumed he must still wash them as frequently as ever), and he bit his great forefinger hard as if through it he was giving his memory a sharp jog.

'Let me think. It would be four years ago that Wemmick – my clerk if you recall –'

'As if I could forget.'

'It would be four years ago that Wemmick told me he had written to you in Cairo. I believe I am right in saying it concerned a stranger who had been making an inquiry as to your current whereabouts. The inquirer could have been an

Agent of the Crown – but he could, just as easily, have been the emissary of another party interested to acquire certain information which they had cause to suspect might be in your possession. I believe Wemmick dealt with the matter adequately.'

'Most adequately, Mr Jaggers,' I said. 'And how is Wemmick?'

'Retired to the property bequeathed to him by his aged father. Had he not retired, there would unfortunately have no longer been a position for him at my offices in Little Britain. I had been obliged to vacate them in order to comply with a change of domicile forced upon me almost exactly a year ago. But I see you know nothing of the circumstances.'

I confessed that I had indeed no knowledge whatsoever of the misfortune that had apparently brought Mr Jaggers, the famous criminal lawyer, to this outpost in a distant penal colony.

'Put it to you this way, Pip. Did you not once dine with a certain attorney at law at his house and meet his housekeeper, a woman of wild Gipsy blood, whom he had sheltered, and whose violent nature he had the power to keep under his control?'

'I did, Mr Jaggers,' I said solemnly, knowing him to be referring to his own house and to Molly, the mother of Estella, who had been tried for the murder of her rival and had been acquitted at the Old Bailey after Jaggers had stood for her. The rivalry had been over Magwitch, father of Molly's child; and the child had been delivered to Jaggers, and through him adopted by Miss Havisham and brought up in total ignorance of who her parents had been.

'Put it to you that after many years of abiding by the terms under which the lawyer had stood for her – that she would abandon all claim upon her child – she suddenly decided that she must find the daughter from whom she had so long been parted. Put it to you that the lawyer refused. Put it to you that the woman became so violent that she attacked the lawyer with a hatchet. Put it to you that to protect himself the lawyer had snatched up the nearest article that came to hand, in this instance a crutch-headed stick which had been bequeathed to him on the gallows by an unsuccessful client. Put it to you that in his protection of himself the lawyer had delivered a blow which not only subdued his attacker but broke a blood vessel in her head. Put it to you that the woman died, that the lawyer was arrested, charged and sent for trial. Put it to you, Pip, that one who has dedicated his life as a lawyer to the defence of the criminal classes, and on their behalf endeavoured to defeat the purposes of justice, can expect little mercy from those who devote themselves to upholding it. Prosecutors, judges and the like. Put it to you that the lawyer found himself subjected to their long-felt desires to revenge themselves for the defeats he had caused them; and that what might have been a case of manslaughter, for which there were clear grounds, remained that of murder, for which the sentence of life was imposed. Need I put more to you, Pip?'

No, there was no need for Mr Jaggers to do so. I shook my head. He had explained all. That is, all concerning how he came to be in New South Wales. Not how he came to be employed on the Rushmore Estate, although I was not kept long wondering about this.

I gathered that while it was the practice to limit the age of convicts for transportation to about fifty years, in the case of Mr Jaggers there were officials who not only wanted him well out of the way but also to be made to endure the greatest possible hardship and humiliation.

That despite this, on the transport he was treated as a celebrity, not only by fellow felons, to whom he was something of a legendary hero, but also by the crew, and given a place at the Captain's table.

That on arrival in Sydney he had found himself assigned to Mrs Lucy Brewster, who believed that a former lawyer of his accomplishment might well prove useful in her service.

That because of the heat of the Sydney summer, which at his age he found difficult to endure, Mrs Brewster had arranged for him to spend the hottest months in the cooler airs of the interior and had temporarily passed him over to her old friend and adversary, Mrs Rushmore.

That he was gate-keeper only when the regular man at this post was assigned to other tasks, at the present time repairing boundary fences. And that his main task was a simple one in that he was called upon every other day to read aloud to

Edward Rushmore, from the Sydney newspapers and, when they came, periodicals from the other side, 'Even though,' as he went on to tell me, 'it is like speaking to a locked safe.'

He gave me a sharp, penetrating look, and I knew and he knew what was locked inside Edward Rushmore, the secret of the nature and whereabouts of the hidden Magwitch fortune. Even a lawyer as skilled in the art of cross-examination as the great Jaggers would not expect to extract anything from a locked safe, the keys to which in this case had been destroyed by paralytic strokes.

Since the subject of the hidden fortune had now been brought up, even if without any direct reference to it, I told Mr Jaggers why I had come to New South Wales and that until my arrival I had known nothing whatsoever of the fortune's existence.

'You are sure of that, Pip,' he said, giving me another hard look, one which seemed to go right through to the back of my head.

'I am absolutely positive.'

'You had Magwitch's pocket-book of papers in your possession.'

'I did – but only for a short time. Are you suggesting there was something about the hidden fortune among them?'

He gave me a slow nod.

'It was bursting with papers, but I fear I didn't go through them,' I said.

'Didn't your late benefactor make any reference at all to another fortune?'

'Once, perhaps. The first time he produced his pocket-book.'

Abel Magwitch's voice sounded in my head again:

'*There's something worth spending in that there book, dear boy. It's yourn. All I've got ain't mine; it's yourn. Don't you be afeered on it. There's more where that come from*'

In my own words, I related this to Mr Jaggers who then recalled that while in prison, after his fight to the death with Compeyson and his capture, Abel Magwitch had provided information which had enabled the lawyer to draw up a list of possessions which he believed I would inherit. That was the list I had brought with me to Australia.

'I thought it would never end,' said Mr Jaggers. 'And the

more he added to it, the more infuriated I became that you should have allowed it to slip through your fingers.'

'You made that point,' I said, remembering again his having said this to me at the time.

'He kept wanting to know whether I thought it would be adequate for your future needs as a gentleman. Enough? I assured him that it would allow you to live like a Prince to the end of your days. Just as he told you, he told me that there was more. Knowing that nothing of it would ever be yours, I was impatient to get the list complete. He was about to add even more to it, but then mumbled something to the effect that it might be best left undisturbed. Perhaps you can shed some light on this, Pip?'

Eyeing me, he adopted an old ruse of bringing out his handkerchief and holding it to his nose, as if my reply would not be of much interest to him. I simply shook my head.

Mr Jaggers now revealed something that I did not know.

'From the Agents of the Crown who confiscated the pocket-book, I learnt that there was a note referring to certain concealed wealth, and that the key to it had been secreted in two of his prized possessions, neither of which he had described in this note.'

Both Mr Jaggers and I – and others, unfortunately – knew those two prized possessions to be his Testament and his pack of playing cards, items which I now carried on my person, although I deemed it highly judicious to make no mention of this. For had he been the prowler during the night, his purpose could well have been to try to lay hands on these very items.

Biting his forefinger again, Mr Jaggers took a few paces to either side of his imaginary fireplace, then came back to where he would have stood with the tails of his coat up to gain warmth from the flames, and he looked at me most watchfully as he said, 'You accepted that you had no claim to Magwitch's wealth, and you told me that you intended to abide by that resolution – and that you would never allow yourself to be troubled by the hopeless task of trying to establish such a claim. Do I remember rightly, Pip?'

'You do, Mr Jaggers. And I have abided by that very resolution.'

'So you have no interest in the hidden wealth we have been speaking of?'

'On the contrary. That is another matter. My interest is not in it for myself, but to try to ensure that no one without any claim to it lays hands on any particle of it. My aim is to see that it should go to those legally entitled to inherit it.'

'Such as, Pip?'

'Such as, for one, Estella, Abel Magwitch's daughter. And any other child he might have fathered.'

'Such as?' he repeated in his bullying manner.

'Mrs Brewster's foster-daughter.'

'Charlotte?'

'Yes.'

'You have, of course, evidence that Charlotte is such a child?'

'Of course.'

'Tell me.'

'Don't you recall how I came to discover Estella's true parentage?'

'Refresh my memory, Pip.'

'I saw her in her mother – and also in her father. The likeness in each was unmistakable. And now I have seen a likeness between Estella and Charlotte – so Charlotte, too, must be Magwitch's daughter.'

'Take nothing on its look, Pip. Take everything in evidence.'

I persisted. 'I have no doubt. The likeness between Charlotte and Estella is remarkable – in many ways.'

'Let me put something else to you, Pip. A child can bear little or no resemblance whatsoever to a parent. I give you an instance. You have met Mrs Lucy Brewster?'

'I have,' I said, quite utterly mystified at the sudden introduction of her name.

'Tell me, then – where have you seen her parent?'

'Lucy Brewster's?'

Mr Jaggers gave a heavy nod of his massive head, his eyes now boring into mine from their sockets.

'But I have never seen her parents, father or mother.'

'You have, Pip. Her mother. You knew her well.'

'Lucy Brewster's mother?'

'Indeed. Her father was Abel Magwitch's one-time partner,

Compeyson. Lucy Brewster is the illegitimate daughter of –'

'Not Miss Havisham!' I cried.

'Miss Havisham,' said Mr Jaggers, going on to say what in my incredulity I had interrupted. 'I was not at this time in Miss Havisham's councils. It was early days for me in my legal career. An acquaintance of mine was articled to the lawyer who handled the matter of the disposing of the child. For a sum of money a chimney-sweep was persuaded to take her into his family – and promised a number of annual increments to ensure she remained there. Giving no reasons, of course.'

At this revelation, I could only shake my head; and when Mr Jaggers said, 'What evidence is "look" now, Pip? Where in Lucy Brewster can you detect the faintest shadow of Miss Havisham?', I could but keep shaking it.

Until, that is, I remembered having seen a fleeting similarity when at dinner at her house. I told Mr Jaggers of this.

'Have you given any thought to it since?' he asked.

'None at all,' I admitted, although now I realised from whom Lucy Brewster had inherited her longish nose.

'When I raised the matter with her,' Mr Jaggers resumed, 'Mrs Brewster freely admitted to me that she had no notion as to the identity of her parents. When I said that through my legal connections I had reason to believe that she may well have been the daughter of a genteel lady, she immediately wanted to know whether any money might be gained from this source. When I said no, that it had all gone to an adopted daughter whose husband had managed to dispose of most of it, she immediately lost all interest.'

What interested me was Mr Jaggers' mention of Miss Havisham's adopted daughter – interest being an infinitely mild way to describe the intense curiosity that seized hold of me. What did he know of Estella? I begged him to tell me.

'I regret to have to inform you that her life has been most unhappy. She became separated from her husband, who had treated her abominably. Only a matter of weeks before my departure from London, I heard that Drummle met his death from an accident following his ill-treatment of a horse. For all I know, the lady could be married again.'

Jaggers knew, of course, that an observation such as this

144

would cut me to the heart, which it did. From behind the protections of his handkerchief, he took his satisfaction from my misery, and then returned to one of his favourite subjects.

'So, Pip, what further evidence have you of the blood relationship of Estella and Charlotte?'

I tried to argue that what had come out in Lucy Brewster, her avarice and scheming, could well have been in her blood; for Miss Havisham's brother, Arthur, who had introduced the unfortunate woman to the scoundrel Compeyson, was a waster and a gambler.'

'Still not evidence, Pip!' Mr Jaggers retorted.

I checked off the remarkable similarities of appearance, nature and manner in Charlotte to Estella, claiming these to be grounds for my conclusion which could not possibly be ignored. After all, Magwitch was strongly suspected of being Charlotte's father; her doubts seemed to be based entirely on his denials – and Lucy Brewster had told me that such disavowals arose from his refusal to admit that he had been consorting with a native woman.

Mr Jaggers heard me out with ponderous nods of his head, and a bite or two of his forefinger. Then he said, 'If I may sound a warning to you, Pip – I know Miss Charlotte, and I have had a number of conversations with her. It would seem that she is most anxious to establish the truth or otherwise of the alleged identity of her paternal parent. Take great care. Be prepared for such consequences as there may be should you tell her why, in your opinion, she is Magwitch's blood daughter.'

'What specifically do you mean by that?' I asked.

Only because of my insistence did Mr Jaggers elaborate.

'It has been my observation – indeed, my experience – that such knowledge, which can be likened to a verdict from a jury or a sentence from a judge, can sometimes produce the most unexpected reactions. On the one hand, it can bring calm, on the other distress; there is no hard and fast rule. Furthermore, sometimes such clarification is sought for reasons altogether different from those you might have been led to assume. In short, you can never be sure what you might precipitate.' And holding up his hand in a gesture of finality, he added, 'Enough, Pip – the subject is closed – I will say no more.'

That Mr Jaggers should put into words something of the nature of the caution I had felt each time the opportunity had arisen to tell Charlotte what I believed was both strange and disturbing.

'In coming to New South Wales,' Mr Jaggers went on, 'it would seem that you are discovering much more than you bargained for.'

What alternative had I but to agree, albeit ruefully. As an instance of unexpected discoveries, I cited in particular the lengths to which my late benefactor had gone in order to ensure that I should be brought up to live the life of a gentleman, and what a dreadful shock it had been for me to discover that Abel Magwitch had even resorted to murder to help to make his wildly romantic dream a reality. Mr Jaggers raised his hand at me again.

'If that is what you believe, Pip, I fear you are wrong. Magwitch may have appeared to do much for you, but nothing – I repeat, nothing – was done for you alone.'

This I just could not believe and my stare of astonishment was met by an expression of contempt at me for my naivety.

'Behind all was his desire for revenge. Revenge for the way he was given a larger sentence than Compeyson for the same crimes, including that of putting stolen notes in circulation, because he lacked Compeyson's education, social graces and circle of friends. Revenge for the way the colonial gentry still treated him as their inferior, even when he had accumulated great wealth. In short, revenge against the society which had discriminated against him.'

Mr Jaggers saw the impact of his suggestion on me and nodded, then looked out the door.

'Hah!' he said, sighting someone approaching. 'Here's a man from the homestead to take over the gate from me. A moment, Pip, and I'll walk back up there with you.'

He went to an adjoining room and I heard the sound of water splashing, and the smell of scented soap drifted to where I sat dumbfounded, listening once again to that voice from the past and seeing its owner, the slouching fugitive of the marshes, with that savage air no dress could tame:

'. . . *dear boy, it was recompense to me, look'ee here, to know in secret I was making a gentleman. The blood horses of them colonists might fling up dust over me as I was walking; what do I say? I says to myself, "I'm making a better gentleman nor ever you'll be." When one of 'em says to another, "He was a convict a few years ago, and is an ignorant common fellow now, for all he's lucky," what do I say? I says to myself, "If I ain't a gentleman, nor yet ain't got no learning, I'm the owner of such. All on you owns stock and land; which on you owns a brought-up London gentleman?"'*

Again I heard him, seeing him looking around and snapping his fingers:

'Blast you every one, from the judge in his wig, to the colonist stirring up the dust, I'll show you a better gentleman than the whole kit of you put together!'

'So!' said Mr Jaggers, noting the look on my face as he came back to me. 'I perceive I have given you food for thought. Come!'

Outside the door he handed over the post of gate-keeper to another servant. The light was brighter, the air warmer, and Mr Jaggers was about to start off through it along the roadway to the homestead. I hesitated to accompany him, for had he not been close outside my bedroom during the night? To return alone in his company to the homestead could be to hazard myself and those items I carried.

There were no soldiers in sight, either – and ahead lay clumps of trees where other parties could be lying in wait, should my misgivings about Mr Jaggers be unfounded.

Sensing my unease and putting his perceptive finger on the cause of it, he said, 'Should you be concerned that certain marauders might be abroad and waiting, let me assure you, Pip, you're more than adequately protected.'

At first I thought he was referring to himself, and that he was armed. He lifted a hand slowly, as if its weight were now telling on him with age, and I saw that he was pointing to two tall men in dark clothing on dark horses on a hillock to one side of the roadway leading to the homestead.

'Agents of the Crown,' said Mr Jaggers. 'It might well be that you will come to find their presence an encumbrance, but I very much doubt that you'll be left out of their sight until that hidden fortune comes to light and they have duly confiscated it.'

Mr Jaggers carried along with him the smell of scented soap, strong even in the open air. I was surprised to find him still using it, because many years before I had come to the conclusion that he did so to wash off the contamination of what he was doing in employing his talents to get the better of justice on behalf of his criminal clients. I was aware, of course, that he might still resort to this type of soap out of habit; but I remained surprised nevertheless because it did not seem to me that he had the same call to use it any longer.

CHAPTER 15

By the time I reached the homestead with Mr Jaggers, I was quite light-headed; but then my head had been reeling before leaving the gate-house after all the revelations there. I had so much to digest, and so much to decide, that I felt I must be on my own again.

My room had been entered and searched, so I was thankful that I had taken those two precious items with me. Anticipating that something of this nature might happen in my absence, I had left a cupboard door ajar very slightly and several drawers pulled out marginally, and then marked their positions with a pencil very faintly. The door and the drawers were nearly as I had left them, but not quite; so I had no doubt that at least one intruder had gained entry to the room.

Mrs Rushmore and Charlotte had both presumably been still abed when I left earlier and so had been in the homestead; it could have been one of them. For that matter, it could have been anyone in the homestead, for I was not to know how many people were also on the hunt for the hidden fortune. However, I was inclined to nominate Charlotte as the prime suspect, for the reason that I was convinced that she had some liaison with Tolchard and his two companions and that therefore she could have been attempting, on their behalf, to again steal the Testament and the playing cards.

Now that I had settled the identity of the man I had glimpsed the previous night, my next objective was to try to match up the map I had shaped from the pin-holes in the playing cards with some existing map or place. While the long winding line that dominated the map I had formed had at first appeared to me as possibly a shoreline or a boundary fence, it could just as easily be a, a river, a track, a stream – or even a lengthy marking on the surface of the ground itself. The squares, circles, oblongs, triangles and other shapes I had made by linking one dot to another could be houses, gardens, ponds, halls, wells, even crazy mazes – the possibilities seemed endless.

Where was I to start my search? Here on the Rushmore Estate seemed as good a place as any. Since Emma Rushmore had purchased this property when the confiscated Magwitch land holdings were put up for sale, some sort of map or plan or survey must exist. And since I had made no secret of the reason for my visit here – to satisfy a certain curiosity by looking over what might have been mine – why should I not be equally interested in sighting any such document, one which would give me, so to speak, a compact bird's eye view of the entire Estate?

While conducting these solitary deliberations, I had remained cloistered in my room where I'd had breakfast brought to me by a servant. As I left the room and stepped out into the corridor which divided the homestead, from its far end, where a door stood half open, I could hear the voice of Mr Jaggers as he read aloud to Edward Rushmore from an English newspaper with tidings now many months old after its long journey by sea. It was a report about the proliferation of new railway companies throughout the Kingdom – and the lawyer read as if addressing a judge and jury rather than a man who had been turned into a human counterpart of a locked safe.

From a housemaid busy dusting, I learnt that Mrs Rushmore was in a day room near the front of the building. Here I found her painting in oils, with a half-completed scene of neighbouring pastureland on her easel.

After complimenting her on her artistic skill, I told her that I had been wondering whether there might be a map or survey plan of the Estate.

She was able to oblige and eager to do so.

'There are numerous maps and plans,' she said. 'I'll take you to Lamont, they're in his safe-keeping.'

On the way back down the corridor to the rear of the homestead, she explained that Lamont was her clerk. Nearing the door to Edward Rushmore's room, from which the voice of Jaggers continued to come, she stopped and looked at me with concern.

'I know who that is,' I said. 'I met him earlier – after taking a walk down to the gate-house.'

'I hadn't mentioned he was here. I was afraid it might upset you to learn of his fall from grace.'

'He explained how it happened,' I said.

And so we passed on, Emma Rushmore leading the way to a small room which had been converted into an office, and where her clerk, Lamont, was seated at a desk and perusing one of the English newspapers which he had spread out over several open ledgers.

He rose as we entered and, after closing over the newspaper, stood attentively.

'Catching up with news of home, I see,' said Mrs Rushmore.

'Such as it is after all this time,' the clerk replied, his accent marking him as coming from the north of England. 'Jaggers kindly left it with me until he needs it.'

Now that more of the pages of the open ledgers lay revealed, I saw that the columns of entries and figures had been executed in a most ornate copperplate hand, rich with scrolls and other embellishments. Emma Rushmore saw what had caught my attention, and said, 'Lamont not only keeps my books in good order but, as you can see, he turns them into works of art.'

As Lamont bent forward in a bow to my hostess with whom I hastened to agree, I realised that this short and mild man of some forty years must be the notorious Felix Lamont whose forgeries of bank notes were said at his trial at the Old Bailey to have been even more perfect than the originals. He had been arrested in the year I left London for Cairo and, if my memory served me correctly, sentenced to transportation for seven years. At the time my personal fortunes had been at such a low ebb that I had been acutely aware of the efforts by others to fend off financial disaster, even if by legally unacceptable means.

After telling Lamont what she wished him to show me, Mrs Rushmore left us together, saying as she went, 'If you need me, Mr Pirrip, I'll be in the day room with my painting.'

From a shelf in the office, Lamont took down several folders containing survey plans and maps, all in all some fifty documents covering not only the main Rushmore Estate and other

151

local properties formerly held by Abel Magwitch but also almost the entire area mapped or surveyed from where the coastal range finished and the inland plain began.

The former forger was so anxious to learn why I should want to inspect all these documents that I did not dare take out those sheets of notepaper with the long curving line and the other shapes formed from the identations. I would have liked to have been able to refresh my memory, but instead I had to rely on the mental image I had recorded. As I examined document after document, Lamont's curiosity remained such that I added him to the list of those I could have grounds to suspect of having entered my room when I was absent at the gate-house.

Several times during this examination I had occasion to be inwardly excited. It seemed I had discovered something to match up with that long winding curve, until closer inspection convinced me that the two were not identical. Thus, a river that could have been that curve I was seeking, was not; nor were a boundary and a road. In the end, I thanked Lamont for his help and suggested that he return the folders to their shelf, certain that they did not contain what I was searching for.

Lamont came part of the way with me to return the borrowed newspaper to Mr Jaggers. As I continued along the corridor towards the front of the homestead on my own, I was aware that the inspection of all those maps and survey plans had not been a waste of time. Many were marked as having originated at the lands office in Sydney, while others were the work of surveyors and surveying companies, the names of which I had committed to memory. I was able now to come to a quick decision as to what to do next. Return forthwith to Sydney and pursue my inquiries there, after seeking out the ostler Jock Weedin on the way. Without my revealing too much about what I had discovered, perhaps he could recall something else that my late benefactor had said to him concerning the Testament and the playing cards.

In the day room, Emma Rushmore had been joined by Charlotte who had a flushed look about her that reminded me of the previous morning when I had met up with her and learnt she had been at a rendezvous with Spikey Simmins.

'Must you really leave us so soon?' Mrs Rushmore exclaimed, surprised and much dismayed that I planned to depart after such a short stay.

'I'm most grateful to you for all your hospitality,' I said. 'But I've been neglecting my duties. After all, the main reason for my being in New South Wales is to promote the business interests of my firm and partners in Cairo.'

Even though I had been according neither attention nor thought to this aspect of my visit to the colony, it did have a basis of truth.

As I should have expected, my decision brought a sharp and immediate reaction from Charlotte. 'What about the other old Magwitch properties out here,' she said. 'Surely, now that you've come all this way, you're going to look them over, too?'

I was tempted to retort that with strangers at large and intent upon trying to interfere in my affairs, I was disinclined to as much as take one step outside the homestead; but my visit to Lamont had furnished me with a better answer.

'In a sense,' I said, 'I've already looked them over.' And Emma Rushmore backed me up when I described the sort of bird's eye view I'd obtained in the clerk's office.

That Charlotte was very much put out was apparent to Mrs Rushmore, and it seemed to me that it was as much embarrassment as anything that prompted her to excuse herself, saying, 'If you must go, Mr Pirrip, you must. I'll have arrangements made for tomorrow morning – you'll need to leave very early to pick up the Sydney-bound stage-coach.'

Alone with Charlotte, I found her more like Estella in manner than she had ever been, showing the same anger and petulance at not being able to get her own way.

Making it an accusation at me for my lack of consideration for her, she said, 'I suppose you realise that this means I'll have to leave, too.'

'I don't see why you should,' I said, even though I understood all too well that Charlotte was under instructions from her foster-mother to accompany me on the full round trip to the inland and back, in other words to keep a constant check on me. I also understood why she wanted to remain here, so I added, 'If you've some reason to stay, then stay.'

Well aware of what I was hinting at, Charlotte confirmed what I had suspected: that she had indeed met up with the bushranger earlier while out horse-riding. Although she did so in a way I hardly expected. As she subjected me to a hot haughty glare, I prepared to repeat in no uncertain terms what I thought about Spikey Simmins and his outlaws; but her anger melted away, and with a sweet smile and a few nimble words she cut me short.

'Isn't it wonderful!' she said. 'There are five of them now. Spikey met up with your escaped convict – and he's banded with them.'

Thus I was forced to abandon my intended tirade and to accept that since Spikey had assisted someone who I had been at pains to help – and to whom I was indebted – I ought to consider myself obliged to the bushranger. Nevertheless, I was greatly exasperated at finding myself put in this position. So much so that it got the better of me, and I found myself saying, 'Did you by any chance also meet up with Tolchard?'

Charlotte looked at me coolly and boldly. My jibe was a telling thrust back at her, and she hesitated, although only momentarily, before turning it away.

'Why should I want to meet up with him and risk getting myself locked away in some empty hut?' And then, with a degree of feeling for which I could not account – and at which I thought I may have been unduly severe with her by what I had inferred – she added, 'Please understand – it is no wish or design of mine that that man is here.'

With a fresh pout of her lips and a flounce of her skirts, she left me on my own to sit in a chair and try to still my confusion by staring into the distant hills in the scene on Mrs Rushmore's easel.

Who had informed Tolchard of Abel Magwitch's return to England remained as much a mystery to me as ever; although I still considered that Emma Rushmore had grounds for doing this after what my benefactor had done to her husband to bring about his present tragic condition. She had known some days in advance of Magwitch's departure that he was secretly quitting the country. On the other hand, Lucy Brewster also knew that he was due to leave, so the informer could just as easily have been the person who Jaggers had told me was Miss Havisham's illegitimate daughter.

Not that Magwitch had ever been unmindful of the perils involved in the action he was taking. Had he not said to me, '*If the danger had been fifty times as great, I should ha' come to see you, mind you, just the same.*'?

Now, after the argument Mr Jaggers had put to me, how did I feel towards my late benefactor and his motives regarding myself? If I were to accept his argument, there was no longer occasion for me to feel that I shared the guilt of his crimes and machinations. It made me a victim of his endeavours rather than a beneficiary. I need no longer feel that I must leave the colony as soon as possible for fear of delving deeper and discovering even worse things done by him in my name.

To match my thoughts, in my mind I conjured up a picture of him again, and it was as if the mental image had been given substance, because before my very eyes there appeared a tangible likeness of him. It was no illusion. Emma Rushmore had returned to the day room so silently that I had not heard her (stepping lightly, no doubt, because she had perceived me deep in thought). In her hands was a pencil sketch of Abel Magwitch as he took a nap in a chair similar to the one in which I now sat.

'It's not to be compared with that portrait of you by the Royal Academician in Lucy's house,' she said. 'But it was the best I could do at the time. I had to work rapidly to catch him before he woke.'

He had been depicted lying in the large easy chair, and he might well have had his great horn-handled jack-knife down by his side and his pistol concealed under the cushion, for here was the lawless felon whose criminality no soft pencil line could disguise. It was not difficult to recall him in that ditch on the marshes when he caught up with his hated adversary Compeyson, before they were both recaptured, tearing and fighting like a wild beast.

After having held the sketch in my own hands, I started to return it to Mrs Rushmore.

'Would you like to have it?' she asked; and when I hesitated, she said, 'I thought you might. Do please keep it.'

As I thanked her – even if, in view of my changed attitude to Abel Magwitch, doubting whether I should want it near me – Mrs Rushmore glanced around, expecting to have found Charlotte still with me.

'She left,' I said, refraining from explaining that relations had become strained between us. Not that our hostess needed to be told this, since she had seen the beginning of that situation before leaving us together.

'A dear girl; but, oh, so strange,' Emma Rushmore said, appraising me gravely to ascertain whether I might be prepared to discuss Charlotte with her. Finding me apparently ready to do so, she went on, 'Lucy Brewster treats her like everything else – another possession. That young woman is crying out to be set free.'

Since I had been nursing the romantic notion of returning to Egypt in the company of a bride, I was tempted to tell Emma Rushmore that if Charlotte needed rescuing, then I had a certain course of action under consideration. Something of what I had in mind could have communicated itself to her, because what she proceeded to tell me contained a warning of what I could be letting myself in for by becoming intimately involved with the half-caste beauty.

'Charlotte has stayed with me off and on since she was a girl. She loves horse-riding, and she's most proficient at it; but I confess that every time she rides out, I'm fearful that she may not return. You see, Mr Pirrip, on several occasions she has disappeared – and I've had to send out search parties to find her. On one occasion she was found in a native encampment, happily joining in the gathering and cooking of food. On another, with some escaped convicts from the road gangs. She'd been stealing food and taking it to them. With all her civilised accomplishments, it seems incredible that she should have sought out such low company. I'm sure, Mr Pirrip, that you're as confounded by such conduct as I am.'

I said nothing, but thought of Estella.

CHAPTER 16

As we took our leave of Emma Rushmore in the early dawn light, Charlotte was in a sullen sulky mood, as Estella would have been at having to depart against her wishes.

How curious it was that I should have had to travel to such a distant place to learn what had become of the one to whom I had been in thrall since my boyhood. I had occasion to reflect thus as the big iron gates were opened for our carriage by the person who had imparted this information to me, Mr Jaggers. He saw me seated beside Charlotte, but gave me little more than the perfunctory nod he would accord a stranger – the 'little more' being a sharp stare which served to remind me of the caution he had given me against disclosing anything to my companion about the suspected identity of her father.

I had been hoping that we might have a protective escort on the drive to the staging-post, and was not to be disappointed. Under a tree, in which the remnants of the dispersing darkness still clung, two Agents of the Crown waited on their horses. They allowed us to pass, then trotted in our wake a respectful distance.

After delivering us to the staging-post – the one west of Hartley village where we had disembarked, the carriage returned to the Rushmore Estate. A wait ensued, which Charlotte, whose mood remained unchanged, sought to blame me for – even though the coach was dead on time, which was to be expected since it was the same coach that had brought us here with the same stickler for time in charge – and the same guard. If they were concerned that my presence on their galleon of the road might attract the unwelcome attention of pirates of the landlubber variety, no doubt their minds were put at ease by the appearance of the Agents of the Crown who stood by, still at a respectful distance, which they maintained as we moved off.

Three passengers were already on board: a man and wife in their forties, returning to Sydney town after being in service together on a country property; and an old lady whose white cockatoo was in a cage up on the roof, from where it kept squawking its name. As a pendant she wore something which Charlotte much admired, a star sapphire apparently picked up in her fowl yard.

At Hartley village, where the horses were changed, we were entertained (if that is the right word for it) by a furore emanating from a cottage where the Reverend Magistrate Chilblud and his esteemed wife had been installed. During the early hours, uninvited visitors had left them in much the same sort of physical relationship to each other as had been imposed on the four bushrangers captured on our way into the interior. Rope had been used to tie them back to back. Artisans and convicts working on the courthouse building heard muffled cries coming from within the cottage and broke down the door to gain entry, after which they released the Chilbluds who appeared in night attire to proclaim the outrage perpetrated on them by the very same bushrangers whose escape had been criminally assisted a few days earlier.

After the Chilbluds had checked their possessions, they found valuables, money and food to have been stolen – also the clergyman's handsome grey felt hat which, no doubt, now sat firmly on the tousled head of Spikey Simmins. Indeed, Charlotte, who was openly delighted, confirmed this to be so.

'It becomes him,' she murmured to me, and it was a whispered wound; it meant she had seen him in the pre-dawn darkness.

As the horses toiled up the incline where, during the descent, a tree trunk had been attached to the back axle of the coach as a drag, my vulnerable state must have been all too evident to Charlotte who proceeded to tease and taunt me. She insisted that I should admire the elderly lady's star sapphire, which I did, since it was a fine gemstone.

'Did Magwitch have any stones like this locked away?' she asked me.

'He certainly did!' I affirmed, rising to her provocation. The list of his confiscated possessions testified to this.

'So there could still be bags of them hidden away?'

There seemed no point in disagreeing. I still had no clue as to the nature of the second Magwitch fortune – and what Charlotte suggested, even though in devilment, was as good an explanation as any.

A late luncheon was due to be taken in the coaching-inn at the staging-post where I had met Jock Weedin, so I assumed that I would have ample time to have another talk with him.

As the coach came to a stop in the yard, stable boys and grooms proliferated to assist the passengers out and to take over the horses. These practised menials went about their tasks without any particular concern for the identities of the travellers – until I made my appearance, whereupon shouts of alarm and warning issued forth from each man and boy. There was a scramble to be armed, and presently I found myself hemmed in by pitch forks, garden stakes and finally, in the hands of the man in charge of the staging-post, a big musket which he hastened to warn me was loaded and ready to discharge.

'What in the name of goodness is this all about?' I demanded of him.

'As if you didn't know!' he rejoined. 'You left him for dead – and if he hadn't been found in his last gasps, dead he would have been – and his life on your head!'

'For mercy's sake!' I cried. 'Who and what are you talking about?'

'Jock Weedin!'

I was so utterly astonished that it was beyond me to protest, and at the behest of the muzzle of the big musket, the prongs of the pitchforks and the sharp ends of the garden stakes, I was marched off towards the hut where I was to be brought before the man I was alleged to have attacked. Charlotte would have accompanied the party, except that the man with the gun ordered her to remain. As was to be expected, she was incensed at this, and I caught a glimpse of it as I looked back. But then, as our eyes met briefly, she began to smile, as if she might have been taking some dark delight in my predicament. Further shades of Estella!

On the way to the hut, I gathered that Jock Weedin had been found crawling and bloody in the bush some hours after I had left on my westward stage-coach journey to the inland. He had steadfastly refused to name his assailant; but in the minds of my present captors there was little doubt that I was the guilty party, since a stable boy and a groom, both of whom were members of the armed party now escorting me, had seen me meeting the ostler in the stables and engaging with him in close conversation.

This was not proof, I protested – but to no avail. I was bundled into a dim wattle and daub hut, one of a small cluster of such habitations in thick forest, and led to a corner where Jock Weedin lay on a low bed under ragged blankets. His head was heavily bandaged, his face and hands cut and abraded, his eyes blackened and glazed. I was most shocked at what had been inflicted on him.

The man in charge of the staging-post had me positioned close by the bed before raising one of the flaps over an open window; then he roused the injured ostler by gently shaking his shoulder and pointed at me as I stood in the light.

'It was him, wasn't it?'

Any sign of recognition of anyone was very slow to appear in Jock Weedin's eyes; but when it came, it did so with a rush. I could see that he knew who I was – and at that instant I believed that he would identify me as his attacker.

Apparently the man in charge of the staging-post thought so, too.

'So it was, eh! It was this man?'

From the ostler there came no response.

This the man in charge of the staging-post took to be an affirmative answer, and he turned on me.

'Yer'll pay for this!' he averred, and the grooms and stable boys tightened their grips on their makeshift weapons as if in readiness to deal out mass physical punishment to me.

But then it was realised that Jock Weedin was slowly rolling his bandaged head from one side to another.

'What's that meant to be?' my main accuser demanded of the ostler.

'I'm not the man?' I suggested quickly – and as the men

160

around me became more threatening, Jock gave a slow painful nod.

'I'll ask the questions!' the man in charge of the staging-post warned me.

There was no need. Jock Weedin managed to moisten his broken lips with a swollen tongue, after which he spoke in a weak, hoarse voice.

'It was not Mr Pirrip . . .'

'*Not* him?'

'No.'

My accusers had so built up their expectations of having me confirmed as the assailant that they were unable to suppress their disappointment.

'And now,' I said to them, much emboldened since the tables had been turned, 'I'll thank you to withdraw, all of you. If I'm left alone here, perhaps I'll be able to solve the mystery of who attacked Jock.'

The man in charge of the staging-post looked to the ostler for his reaction to this; and on seeing him give another slow nod, he told the grooms and stable boys to leave, and so they filed out of the hut with him and gathered in a bunch outside.

From the open doorway, I said to them, 'If you don't mind, it would be better if you waited well out of hearing distance.'

They acquiesced, retreating further away to the front of another hut, even though with the same show of reluctance to admit defeat.

At Jock Weedin's bedside I told him how distressed I was to find him in such a sorry condition. Who, I asked, had been responsible?

His head rolled from one side to the other, and in a whisper he said, 'I be sworn to remain silent.'

'Sworn?'

'Aye.'

At a point during our first meeting the ostler had stared at me as if I had possessed clairvoyance, and now he did so again when I asked him, 'Was it on a clasped black Testament?' I dug into an inside pocket of my jacket and brought out one of the items I carried, and added, 'This, for instance?'

'How'd 'ee come by that?' he gasped.

'I retrieved it from someone who had stolen it from me. Also these.' I brought out the pack of playing cards for the ostler to see, before returning both items back into the safe-keeping of my inside pocket. 'I imagine him to be the person who battered you – either alone, or in association with his two partners, one a native, the other identifiable by the tattoo marks on his face?'

True to the oath that had been forced out of him, Jock Weedin neither agreed nor denied what I suggested. In any event, I had my answer. It was a combination of his refusal to commit himself either way and a certain look in his eyes that convinced me he had been savaged by three assailants – Tolchard, Cannibal Jack and their aborigine. Likewise, I was equally confident that I knew their motive – to try to extract from Jock Weedin anything that he might have gleaned from Abel Magwitch as to the information secreted within the Testament and the playing cards; or from me.

Despite the precautions I had taken when first meeting the ostler, I had been observed not only by a stable boy and a groom but also Tolchard. Approaching Jock Weedin as I had done, I felt that I had been responsible for the physical harm that had come to him, and now I told him so. He bore no ill feeling against me. Indeed, he seemed more concerned that the same treatment should not be meted out to me.

'Be on your guard,' he whispered. 'Ye'll be shown no mercy.'

After thanking him, I wondered whether – quite apart from the risk it entailed – I should confront him with that long winding line I had formed and ask if he could identify it in any way. I felt I had imposed on him enough already and did not wish to bring him further misfortune. As I hesitated, he began to repeat in a low voice what my benefactor had said to him concerning the Testament and the cards when they had seen each other for the last time:

' *"Put these two together, Jock, an' somewhere in between them both is also the secret wot only me an' Eddie Rushmore as knows".*'

'You've already told me that,' I said, but I barely interrupted him. Fortunately so.

' *"Patience",*' he went on, adding to what he had told me Abel Magwitch had imparted to him. ' *"All it needs is patience".*'

Obviously this was something he had remembered since

talking to me; something that had come to mind when he had been forced to recall the past. As for the map I had formed, had I now chosen to show it to the ostler the information it contained could easily have passed into wrong hands.

Just outside the side wall of the hut there was a light crushing sound of fallen foliage, a foot sinking into debris of leaves and twigs. My assumption was that one of my erstwhile captors had crept to the side of the hut; but when I looked through the open doorway to where they remained assembled, they all seemed accounted for.

My next candidate for the role of prowler was Charlotte, and I went to the open window where the flap had been raised and looked out, expecting to discover her there – but instead I found myself face to face with one of the Agents of the Crown who had been following the stage-coach.

He stood up, completely without apology, simply saying to me, 'Are you having any difficulty, Mr Pirrip?'

'Yes,' I replied. 'Great difficulty in going about my business without outside interference. I'd be obliged to be completely left alone.'

I waited at the open window until the Agent of the Crown, slightly the taller of the two who had attached themselves to us, and apparently the senior officer, had moved off back in the direction of the staging-post. I returned my attention again to Jock Weedin, thanking him for his help and again regretting the trouble I had brought upon him. I felt it was too hazardous to attempt to seek out any further information from him, and presently, after making my final commiserations, I took my leave.

The man in charge of the staging-post stepped forward as I walked away from the hut. Had I managed to establish the identity of the old ostler's assailant? No, I said, I had not – and since Jock Weedin himself had refrained from naming any one person, this in a sense was a truthful reply.

At the coaching-inn, where I had a hurried luncheon so as to be able to rejoin the vehicle by departure time, Charlotte put the same question to me. I gave the same evasive answer.

If I needed further proof that Charlotte had met Spikey Simmins at some hour during the preceding night between the bushrangers' raid on the Chilbluds' cottage and our departure from the Rushmore Estate, she soon provided it by falling into a deep sleep that continued, despite the rough passage of the coach and the intermittent squawking of the pet cockatoo from its cage on the roof.

The fires were all quelled now and the first hints of new growth appeared in the form of patches of soft green mist on the scorched ground and fresh shoots on the blackened skeletons of the trees. The coach thundered through the rocky area where that musket shot had blasted the bird with the flaming torch out of the air – and where Spikey Simmins had come dancing forth. For an entire stage between posts on the downward return journey, Charlotte slept on.

By giving me news of Estella, Mr Jaggers had sharpened my sense of loss. Finding myself with Charlotte's head resting on my shoulder, that feeling was greatly intensified, leaving me all the more susceptible to the allure of the one who had so much in common with my ideal. And so, as Charlotte slept, I fell into a daydream. I imagined myself in place of that portrait of me, listening to Charlotte's words of adoration, then speaking what she had told me she had imagined the portrait to have said to her about her beauty despite the dusky colour of her skin. It was not long before I was in Cairo again with her at my side. And it did not seem such an impossible dream – until I remembered something else that the lawyer Jaggers had said: the warning he had sounded about the consequences of informing Charlotte that I believed I could prove that Abel Magwitch was her father. In the wake of this I recalled the cautions voiced by Emma Rushmore. There was much about Charlotte that I did not know nor understand. But then how much had I not known nor understood about Estella?

Our overnight stop was made at a coaching-inn on the lower slopes of the coastal range. Here Charlotte again questioned me about the identity of Jock Weedin's assailant.

Any revelation of that identity at the place where the attack had been made could possibly have been traced back to Jock Weedin with adverse consequences, should the assailant or his accomplices have come to hear of it. We now seemed far enough away from the scene for there to be no such danger any longer. Besides, I was irritated by her persistence, so I said, 'I wonder what you would say were I to tell you that it was someone you knew – someone with whom you've had clandestine dealings?'

With much consternation, she said, 'Not Spikey? It couldn't be!'

'No,' I said. 'It was not your bushranger friend.'

'Then who?'

'Need I name him?'

Since there was only one other who it could be, this time she did not persist in trying to obtain an answer. Leaving Tolchard unnamed, she said, 'I've already told you – I am not responsible for that man or anything he might do.'

I was prepared to accept this as being the truth; nevertheless, it still did not explain the basis of the association between the two.

CHAPTER 17

It was shortly before dark on a hot mid-summer evening when we reached the Sydney coach station. The air was loud with the shrill of cicadas, as if to remind me that even though I may have survived certain perils on my journey to the inland, much menace still faced me back here.

A rider was dispatched by the coach-station clerk to 'The Mansion', and by the time Charlotte and I had taken some light refreshments in the waiting-room, Lucy Brewster's carriage had arrived.

On her way home, Charlotte set me down at my hotel; and as we parted, she said, 'I'll be able to tell Mama that we've had a very exciting time, won't I?'

'Please give Mrs Brewster my kind regards,' said I.

'Oh, I'll let you save them up till you see her. She's not going to let you alone, I'm sure.'

Of that I felt equally sure.

Charlotte blew me a laughing kiss as the carriage moved off from the front of the hotel – and as it swung around the street corner, I made out two men standing there. Agents of the Crown, no doubt – and I also felt sure that they were not going to let me alone either.

The landlord accorded me a courteous but restrained welcome back.

'Is all well?' I inquired, for I sensed that he wanted to say something to me but was uneasy about broaching it.

'Not entirely, sir,' he replied, relieved to be invited to be open with me. 'It may well be as a consequence of the burglary you suffered – but I've had the feeling that since you left here, there's been an official watch on the hotel.'

I knew, of course, the answer to this: those Agents of the Crown. Out of bravado, I very nearly told him that I had recovered the two stolen articles; but thought better of it and confined myself to saying, 'In that case we should be safe from any further burglary.'

'All went well with you on the trip, I trust,' he said.

'I saw what I went out to see,' I said – and without any elaboration I made my way to my room, where I locked all doors, thus making the conditions even hotter for myself.

The discoveries about my late benefactor which the inland trip had yielded had left me deeply shocked. The outright murder of one man and the brutal treatment of another, acts perpetrated in the cause of making me a gentleman, also made me an accessory. No doubt it was in an attempt to divest myself of this sense of shared guilt that I took refuge in the feeling that I had been a victim of Abel Magwitch's machinations rather than a beneficiary.

With the outside night leaning heavily upon the door and windows, I lay on my bed, wondering how I would pursue my search for the hidden fortune by examining further maps and survey plans without arousing unwelcome attention from others with the same goal in mind. I woke with the answer waiting in my head. Whereas until now I had been at pains not to have my name connected with that of the notorious Magwitch, if I were to gain access to those documents, should I not adopt a bold approach and make use of that link? My story, therefore, would be that I had been the intended beneficiary of many properties which had been forfeited to the Crown following the recapture, conviction and demise of Magwitch – and that I wished to satisfy myself that all such had been duly confiscated and sold off. However, should any of them have been overlooked, then, the law and its loopholes being such as they are, I might have grounds for establishing a claim upon them. The height of optimism perhaps, but I felt it would suffice as an excuse.

And so, on the basis of this pretext, I approached the lands office, and the offices of surveyors and surveying companies (remembering names and addresses from those maps and survey plans shown to me at the Rushmore homestead by the bank-note forger, Felix Lamont).

This ploy of mine was accepted without question at one office, with amusement at another; elsewhere I met with disbelief and suspicion; but I persisted, and by and large I must have examined close on a thousand documents of a like nature.

Each day before going out, I refreshed my mental image of the map I had formed from the line and other shapes I had made on sheets of my notepaper. The first thing I now discovered was that the wavering line I had traced from the pin-points could represent more than a shoreline, a boundary fence, a road, a river, a track, a stream or a lengthy marking on the ground; it could also indicate the edge of a lake or a cliff, trails made by sheep or goats – or even, if it designated something which was in the sea rather than on land, a reef or a submerged shelf.

In the course of this search, as at the Rushmore homestead, I discerned certain similarities and parallels that buoyed up my hopes of having made a discovery; until, on my return to the hotel, where in my room I checked with the original map, I realised that success still eluded me. But, bearing in mind that Magwitch had also said to Jock Weedin – '*All it needs is patience*' – I kept on and did not go entirely unrewarded.

Having declared my link with Magwitch, I came by information I might not otherwise have obtained: in a drawing office, from a draughtsman who had been in the field as a surveyor and had encountered my benefactor many times in the company of the hulking Welshman who I had heard about from Emma Rushmore.

'Something came between them on the last trip they made together,' this man told me. 'Magwitch returned in a fearful state – cut an' bruised very bad, with ribs broke. He explained nothing, except he'd had to fight for his life. I can't be sure, but I don't think the Welshman was ever seen again – nor did Magwitch ever make another such trip.'

While continuing to track down more maps and survey plans, for appearance's sake as much as anything I called on the merchants I had first visited soon after my arrival in Sydney town and took up discussions with them again about importing and exporting. One of these men dealt in hides, and I was confident that there was a market for his wares in Egypt, in particular leather. He was most eager to come to a firm arrangement immediately and told me that there was a ship in the harbour due to sail fairly soon on a route that was to take in Suez at the top of the Red Sea.

Several days passed but nowhere did I sight any map, chart, plan or survey that matched up with the outline I had traced on sheets of my notepaper. Meanwhile, Charlotte had been proved right when she had warned me that her foster-mother would not leave me in peace. Each day on my return to the hotel there was a message from Lucy Brewster inviting me to call at her home; or to lunch or dine at her establishment, the place she had mentioned to me as being where Abel Magwitch had sometimes stayed. I took the precaution of seeking some information about it from the landlord and gathered that it was reputed to be an illicit gambling house, and a place where males of the species desirous of the company of members of the fairer sex could expect to be agreeably accommodated. I thought it much the wiser to decline such hospitality.

The next invitation from Mrs Brewster was a printed one, requesting my company at her annual mid-summer's night fête to be held on the lawns of 'The Mansion'. It was also a Christmas party. Among the entertainments there would be a military band, a fireworks display and exhibitions of juggling and magic by the celebrated Mr Samuel Bullwinkle. Guests would be picked up at a quay in Sydney Cove and ferried by barge to the landing-stage below the house.

When I sought the landlord's reaction to this invitation, he urged me to go. It was one of the events of the year in the colony – all-night dusk-to-dawn festivities.

'Take care, though, sir,' he jokingly warned me. 'It's said that Mrs Brewster runs the party at a profit, like all else she handles. She's said to engage pickpockets to mix with her guests – none of whom would dare, for fear of insulting her, to suggest that they had been fleeced when enjoying her hospitality.'

On the appointed evening, and well ahead of the time nominated to be at the quay, I set out from the hotel after having ensured that all the items I carried on my person were safely secreted well out of the reach of any pickpockets.

In accepting the invitation, I was largely motivated by the desire to see Charlotte again – for, despite the veiled warnings issued to me by Mr Jaggers and by Emma Rushmore, I still clung to the romantic fancy that I could have found someone who might fill that void of emptiness that I had carried with me ever since Estella had rejected me. After all, *half of her was Estella.*

I had fallen into the habit of assuming that even though I walked alone, others would not be far behind. As expected, two men moved out of the shadows opposite the hotel and followed me down towards Sydney Cove. On this occasion, however, one of these two Agents of the Crown stepped out briskly, overtook me and walked along at my side.

'We are aware, Mr Pirrip,' he said, 'of the reason for your continuing search. You do realise, I trust, that anything you might find is by law the property of the Crown.'

'Surely,' said, I, 'the Crown must have been satisfied after having confiscated Abel Magwitch's first fortune?'

'We are but doing what the law ordains, Mr Pirrip. We have reason to believe that the key to what still lies hidden is contained in two articles which were stolen from your hotel room. It would appear that you have since regained possession of them.'

This I neither confirmed nor denied, and allowed the Agent to proceed.

'We have no claim upon them, but should you make those articles available to us for perusal – and should they lead to the hidden resources – then you would be entitled to a bounty. It could well be a handsome one.'

'Are you trying to bribe me?'

'This is not in any way in the nature of a bribe. We are empowered to make such an offer.'

By now I was beginning to wonder whether even Agents of the Crown were to be trusted, so I decided to go about the search on my own and in my own way, and politely declined the proposition. At the same time, I was concerned as to how, or from whom, they had obtained their intelligence; I doubted that the ostler Jock Weedin would have told them, so therefore it must have been either Tolchard and his accomplices or Charlotte.

A vague oppressiveness seized hold of me as I took my place in the barge at the quay among other guests. As I dipped my hand over the boat's gunwale into the water, I realised I was repeating something of what Abel Magwitch had done on the night he was rowed down the River Thames in our vain attempt to save him from arrest by smuggling him out of England – and I recalled what he had said:

'*We can no more see to the bottom of the next few hours, than we can see to the bottom of this river what I catches hold of.*'

CHAPTER 18

For newcomers to the colony, it was a great novelty to have heat instead of cold and biting winds at Christmas, although not for me after living many years in Cairo. Nor was it an experience new to me to be rowed in a private barge; however, the one which delivered me and others to the landing-stage below 'The Mansion' was as handsomely equipped and as smartly manned as any of those on which I had been a guest on the waters of the River Nile.

Although keeping fairly close to the shore, where the incoming tide lapped the rocks, the barge passed near a number of ships at anchor, most of them decorated with coloured lamps and lanterns, some having these far up in their rigging. Greetings were shouted at us, but few of my fellow passengers either acknowledged them or replied. They were a restrained lot, mostly middle-aged couples or older, all presumably of some importance in the community (certainly of much self-importance!); and if not actually prosperous, undoubtedly giving that impression.

Before reaching the point dominated by 'The Mansion', the military band drowned out all other sounds. We approached the landing-stage through waters ablaze with the reflections of gushing flares along the sea wall and others up through the grounds. The big house itself was aglow with lights from within.

No sooner had the barge master seen us safely ashore on to the landing-stage than he directed his team of uniformed oarsmen back to Sydney Cove to take another load of party guests on board, while those he had just left formed a line to be announced by a footman and welcomed by Lucy Brewster, who had Charlotte at her side.

As I shuffled along in the line, noting that among those ahead of me and behind me, were gaitered members of the clergy and military officers in full uniform, I overheard a number of remarks about our hostess. These, I fear, were mainly disparaging. Even though prepared to accept Mrs Brewster's hospitality, some of her guests apparently still felt free to comment on the ostentation of the event. Far from being here to enjoy the festivities, it seemed that they considered themselves under an obligation to be present because of past or expected favours from their hostess. While my sympathy for my late benefactor was at a low ebb, all around me I saw the sort of attitude he had faced even after he had established himself as a man of wealth. He had been extremely sensitive to this, while Lucy Brewster was evidently just the opposite.

When it came my turn at the head of the line, the footman, a tall man, inclined an ear to me to get my name, and then in a loud voice announced me to my hostess, who was richly robed in silks and much jewellery, wearing a tiara on her head again, although a larger one.

'Pip!' she exclaimed, again little endearing herself to me by using my nickname. 'I wos beginnin' ter fink you wos avoidin' me.' Then, belatedly lowering her voice, and at the same time nodding towards Charlotte, 'From all accounts, you two 'ad an excitin' time tergether. See yer enjoy yerself – we'll 'ave a talk later on, eh.'

If there was anything of her mother in Lucy Brewster – apart from the longish nose they shared – it was not her appearance (except insofar as there might have been a parallel between the withered bridal flowers Miss Havisham had constantly worn and Lucy Brewster's tiaras); but there was a certain detectable familiarity of which I was aware, if only because I had been so often in Miss Havisham's company – a witch-like eagerness to conspire, the lowering of her voice and the narrowing of her eyes when she spoke intimately. Even so, without Mr Jaggers' categorical assurance, I would not have been prepared, on the basis of this one similarity, to aver that my hostess was Miss Havisham's child.

It was nothing like the situation involving Charlotte and Estella, in which the similarities were many – and never more apparent than tonight as Charlotte greeted me after I moved forward, allowing Mrs Brewster to welcome the next guests in the line. In a white satin gown, she looked more breathtakingly lovely than on all our previous meetings.

I found myself unable to express this in words, so I seized on something else to say to her.

'I'm looking forward to seeing Sam Bullwinkle again – although I'm surprised he's back from his history-making inland tour so soon.'

With amused langour, Charlotte said, 'He was chased off the stage, I fear.'

This amazed me. I felt sure that his audiences would have been most appreciative.

'By a ferocious rat-catcher,' Charlotte went on. 'Someone let the dog loose on the stage when Sam was doing his act with the performing white mice.'

She giggled, and as I passed on, leaving her to add her welcome to those of her foster-mother's to the guests immediately behind me, I was in no two minds as to the identity of the person who had released the dog. Spikey Simmins had also had his revenge on Sam Bullwinkle for the part the juggler and magician had played in his capture during the hold-up of the stage-coach.

The band played from an elevated wooden platform just below the front of the house where tents had been erected for refreshments. Guests mingled inside the tents, while among those outside waiters moved about with silver jugs of punch. Near the driveway, an ox was being roasted on a spit; and from the waiter who filled me a glass of the punch (which seemed most potent) I learnt that plum pudding was available in one of the tents.

At functions such as this, one tends to make conversation about the weather, the climate and other such subjects to complete strangers, some of whom introduce themselves while others continue to remain anonymous. Much the same happened on this occasion as I carried my punch among the guests. All were new faces to me – except one man I felt I might have seen before. Perhaps in passing in the street.

Out on the water of the bay, a bevy of small craft had assembled so that those on board them could be spectators to the fête. I assumed that in some vessel or other, Agents of the Crown would be in attendance.

Adjacent to where the band played was a lower wooden platform with a polished surface; no one danced here yet, although a few guests had seated themselves on the chairs and the sofas drawn up on all four sides.

I passed by this dancing floor and made my way up the sloping lawn and under the portico of the house which had been thrown open to guests. Servants were in attendance, no doubt as a precaution against anyone who might be tempted to pocket any of the ornaments on ledges, stands and tables. I was drawn, inevitably perhaps, to the reception room where I had first met Charlotte and her foster-mother. As expected, the portrait of me was in the same place on the wall, and I was as displeased as ever with what I saw. Oh, what a false world I had been living in when I sat for that Royal Academician – dinners, plays, operas, concerts, parties – all sorts of pleasures, thanks to someone who was prepared to resort to extortion, murder and other infamy that I should be free to indulge myself. In my own eyes now I was certainly no Prince Handsome – although I tried to picture Charlotte in the place where I stood, imagining that I spoke to her. The fact that the band outside was playing the tune of a romantic air from one of the operas I had seen in London no doubt was in part responsible for the great fondness for Charlotte which welled up inside me. Nevertheless, it was disconcerting to find her suddenly in the room beside me; more so because she held on to the arm of a young military officer.

'I saw you entering the house,' she said. 'I thought this is where I might find you. Admiring yourself again?'

'Certainly not!' I retaliated. And with an angry gesture at my portrait, I said, 'If that were mine, I'd have no hesitation in doing what I did to its twin.'

The young officer stiffened at my vehemence, as if I might have been guilty of using strong language in the presence of a lady.

'Mr Pirrip burnt an identical portrait of himself,' Charlotte explained to her escort, whose only comment was a sniff and a flare of a nostril.

After coolly appraising the portrait and me, and then the

portrait again, the oddest look came into Charlotte's eyes and the oddest tone into her voice as she said, 'Yes. Perhaps I understand how you feel.'

I had no opportunity to pursue the import of this, as the band outside stopped and the footman who had announced the guests called for attention as he introduced Mr Samuel Bullwinkle.

Charlotte excitedly grabbed the young officer's hand and hurried away with him. I followed, after according my portrait a parting glower.

The military bandsmen vacated the raised platform, and through curtains at its rear Sam Bullwinkle made his appearance. Or, should I say, a coat appeared, a most extraordinary coat, with a beaming man apparently in sole residence within its fortifications, a cloth castle with woof and weft in place of brick and mortar. It was the coat, rather than the occupant, which drew a great gasp from the assembly.

After making his initial bow within this stronghold, Sam Bullwinkle proceeded to intrigue the gathered guests with his artistry with the ivory balls, the strings of coloured silken flags and other articles. If he had done no more than his juggling and his sleight-of-hand, he would have satisfied his audience; but, as I knew, the highlight of his performance was yet to come – and when he began his soft, cajoling whistling, I prepared myself as much for the reactions of the onlookers as for the appearance of other residents installed within his coat.

As I expected, there was all-round incredulity as Sam Bullwinkle's whistling lured out the first white mice; and then uproar as he extended both arms, clasped his hands together, making a mid-air rampart around which the mice scurried in a line, crossing his shoulders at the back of his neck, and going around and around.

At the conclusion of all this, Lucy Brewster came stumbling to my side, unsure of her footing on the sloping grass because her eyes were bleared with the tears of laughter. What delighted her most with the impact of Sam Bullwinkle's mastery of the mice was the effect it had had on a number of her female guests who had apparently fallen into swoons and faints. In particular, a certain hard-headed woman, hitherto noted for her imperturbability, who had staged the most impressive swoon of all. This, in my hostess's opinion, proved that the woman in question had social aspirations.

'All she wos doin' wos tryin' ter make out she wos a lady.'

She wiped her eyes to clear them, and her look at me sharpened as she repeated her earlier greeting. 'I really wos beginnin' ter fink you wos avoidin' me.'

'I greatly appreciated your kind invitations,' I said. 'But my time's been full. I've had business matters to attend to.'

' 'Mongst other things,' she said with a fixed, meaningful smile that left no doubt she was well acquainted with the wider scope of my activities.

'True,' said I, declining to be drawn on the subject.

She laughed and led me by the sleeve to a point behind a bushy tree clipped in the shape of a crowing cock. As the firework display began with rockets being launched from down near the sea wall, we were partly shielded from the noise and bursts of light as I found myself having to contend with more specific questions.

'Well, Pip,' she said, 'by now I expect yer've seen all of wot might 'ave been yours, but for Magwitch takin' it into his 'ead to go back to the ole country to set his eyes on the young gentleman wot 'e had created.'

'I expect I have,' said I.

'And yer still ain't resentful about losin' it?'

'I'm not losing any sleep over it.'

'It's a lot to 'ave slipped yer by.'

'It is, indeed – but now that I've discovered how it was accumulated in the first place, I'm happier having no part of it.'

With a contemptuous laugh, she said, 'Yer don't gain nothin' in a place the like of this wifout 'avin' ter soil yer 'ands one way or anuvver.' She swept a hand loaded with rings in the general direction of her guests. 'There's scarce anyone 'ere wot's got 'ands all that clean – judiciary, church, commerce, police, military – you name it, Pip. Clean 'ands an' Noo Souf Wales don't go togevver. That's if yer wants ter get on.'

Her truculence I attributed to her having partaken of her own hospitality; and when she made another all-embracing sweep of her hand, and seemed in danger of losing her balance, I grasped her elbow to support her. This she resented, roughly brushing my hand away. At the same time, on the wall near the honeysuckle, a row of Roman Candles were touched off and they started to flame and spin.

'An' just in case yer got any 'llusions, Pip – Magwitch wosn't much different from anyone else when it come ter gettin' on.'

I could not have agreed with her more. 'He went too far at times, I fear – much too far.'

'Too far?' she said, aggressively defensive to a most unexpected degree. 'When fer instance?'

'When he taunted a stricken man, a man locked within himself so to speak, by telling him where his secret second fortune was hidden.'

'Yer mean Eddie Rushmore, of course?'

'Of course.'

'Magwitch wos fully entitled.'

'To do a cold-blooded thing like that?'

'After wot Eddie Rushmore done ter 'im, definitely 'e wos.'

Apparently there was some facet of the relationship between the two men that I knew nothing about, so I sought enlightenment – and promptly received it.

'Magwitch at one time stood in so good wif someone 'oo 'ad the ear of the Guv'nor that 'e wos hopeful of gettin' a full an' absolute pardon. Which, if yer knows wot that means, would 'ave left him free ter return ter see yer, all legal. But someone 'ad that stopped – an' Magwitch 'ad good reason ter believe it was Eddie Rushmore gettin' some of 'is own back.'

Hearing this, I could not help but begin to see what had been done to Edward Rushmore in an entirely new light; although other instances of my late benefactor's excesses still seemed to stand as crimes beyond forgiveness. I referred to one of them: the murder by Magwitch of his Master.

' 'Ow much does yer know about that scum of the earth?'

So I repeated what Jock Weedin had related to me.

'In that case, yer knows nothin'. 'Wot do yer think that snake in the grass used ter do fer pleasure? An' why wos it 'e built a stone hut wif bars all away on its own?'

'I'll have to leave you to answer that for me.'

'Wif pleasure! 'E used to go shootin' with a gun at people –
livin' people – natives – like Charlotte's mother – fer sport.
And where did 'e keep his live game fer when he went out
huntin'? In that 'ut. Magwitch done a lotta folks a good turn
when he turned hisself into a bolt of lightnin'.' She gave a coarse
laugh at her comparison, then eyed me keenly, knowing something of the change that my attitude to Abel Magwitch would
be undergoing because of this information.

'Makes a diff'rint story, eh, don't it?' she said.

'Considerably different,' I agreed.

At this moment, the one person among the guests whose face
I felt I had seen before came into view – over near the entrance
to one of the tents – and I found myself asking my hostess who
he might be.

'I'm not surprised yer rec'nise 'im – 'e's one of the Agents of
the Crown.'

This seemed the probable explanation – yet what was the
man doing here accepting hospitality which could have certain
strings attached to it, in that favours might be expected in
return?

I put this to Lucy Brewster who chuckled and raised herself
up so that she could speak closer into my ear.

'Some of the present Agents of the Crown wos around when
Magwitch wos 'ere – and he 'ad more'n one of 'em on 'is little
black book – if yer unnerstan'.'

Yes, I understood all too well. Magwitch had had them
swear away their lives on the very little black Testament I now
carried concealed on my person.

With a nudge of her elbow and a wink to go with it, Lucy
Brewster elaborated. ' 'Ow do yer think it wos that Emma
Rushmore an' me was able ter get our 'ands on so many of the
ole Magwitch properties like we done, eh?'

The revelations were making me dizzy. No wonder Lucy
Brewster and Emma Rushmore had been forced to remain on
reasonably friendly terms! It was as if I were being given a
glimpse into a whirling cesspool of bribery and betrayal; and
just to give another stir, Mrs Brewster said, 'Yer'd be surprised
'oo Magwitch 'ad on that little black book before 'e made 'em
kiss it.' And she mimicked the oath he had extracted. ' *"Lord*

179

strike yer dead on the spot, if ever yer split in any way sumever!" ' She gave a hoarse laugh and revealed even more. 'The likes, fer instance, of that parson wot Charlotte says wos on the coach wif yer goin' west.'

'Not the Reverend Chilblud?'

' 'Im, awlright. Took the book in his right 'and, swore wot 'e wos tole – an' kissed it.'

Leaving me to ponder this, Mrs Brewster called across to several guests to ask how they were enjoying the fireworks, and after being assured the display was the best ever, she said, 'Mustn't n'glect my special guest all the way from Ee-jip.' And turning back to me, she asked, 'Any plans for goin' back?'

'Not as yet,' I said.

'Not till yer've picked up all that 'idden wealf, eh?'

Now, because of what I had just learnt about Edward Rushmore and Abel Magwitch's early Master, I had been having profound second thoughts about considering myself a victim rather than a beneficiary of all that had been carried out in my name; I was conscious of one of the first things I had privately undertaken to try to solve, so I said, 'There's something else I'd sooner discover first.'

'Oh?' she said, her eyes becoming slits, as Miss Havisham's eyes might have done. 'Are yer goin' ter let me know wot it is?'

'Certainly,' I said. 'I take it you know a man called Tolchard?'

Her eyes widened momentarily, as if the question had taken her by surprise, but then they swiftly became even narrower slits.

'Wot of it?' she asked.

'On his own admission, he was a friend of Compeyson, Abel Magwitch's enemy. And it was Tolchard who managed to send word ahead to England informing Compeyson that Magwitch was returning there. What I still don't know is this: who informed Tolchard?'

'And yer ain't got no ideas?'

'Oh, yes, I have. It could, for instance, have been someone like Mrs Rushmore. After what Magwitch did to help bring about her husband's tragic condition, I believe her to have had certain justifiable grounds for seeking retribution by informing on Magwitch.'

'Anyone else?'

It was put quietly in the form of a challenge, and I decided to accept it.

'Yes,' I said, 'it could also have been you yourself.'

I must own myself unprepared for what followed. I might well have touched off a human form of firework, for it was as if something akin to the star-bursts breaking in the night sky overhead had exploded within her.

'Me?' she cried. 'Suspect me of that! 'Ow can yer even fink such a thing! I begged 'im not ter go back ter the ole country. I warned 'im wot could 'appen. I told yer that when first yer wos 'ere. I tried an' pleaded all I could. Betray that man? Me? Never!'

The guests to whom she had spoken now stared in our direction; others, too, despite the partial shelter afforded by the sculpted tree. I tried to calm her, but without success.

'I knoo 'e 'ad put the story 'round as 'e was goin' far into the interior ter survey new lands which 'e wos thinkin' of pur-chasin'. An' I knoo that all the time 'e'd had it planned ter smuggle on board a ship sailin' for Plymouth, England. I 'ad all sorts of people comin' ter me ter try ter find out where 'e might 'ave gone, but they got nuffin out of me. Tolchard included. None of 'em. Nuffink!'

It would have been fair to claim that I had never met anyone who I instinctively distrusted more than Lucy Brewster – and I had seen many prime examples of the criminal class lounging about or gathered in whispering knots outside the offices of the lawyer, Jaggers; also in Newgate prison, where Jaggers' clerk Wemmick had once taken me, and where he had walked about among the prisoners the lawyer was defending as if he might have been a gardener among plants. In such company, Lucy Brewster, in my estimation, would have been of that species known as Deadly Nightshade. Even so, I now believed that what she had told me in connection with her relationship with Tolchard was the absolute truth. Emma Rushmore had told me something of the depth of her attachment to Magwitch so it could well have been the one enduring loyalty of her life. I therefore hastened to withdraw my suggestion.

'Of course it couldn't have been you,' I said. 'I'm sorry to have upset you.'

'Sorry won't be the word for it if ever I finds out 'oo it wos wot told Tolchard.'

She left me in no doubt that something very unpleasant indeed would be arranged for the informer, should that person ever be identified.

The fireworks display terminated with blazing stars lighting up the bays and arms of the harbour with lights of different colours. When Mrs Brewster moved to the front of the bushy tree shaped like a crowing cock, I went with her, and side by side we shared the view of the spectacle. As the last of the stars burnt themselves out, leaving the night sky hung with smudges and tendrils of smoke, the military band struck up on the elevated platorm, while the first dancers stepped on to the polished surface of the lower platform.

Because of her white gown, Charlotte stood out as she began to gyrate with her young officer escort.

The sight of her seemed to diminish some of the fury that had built up in Lucy Brewster, and she stood watching and smiling as the flowing beauty her foster-daughter created reached across to us like some intoxicating night sccnt – until, with her forehead furrowing, she turned and, with her eyes reduced to slits again, looked at me and into me.

'Yer know sumpin', Pip – ever since that young lady got back from the journey wif you, she's been actin' very odd. Restless, moody and 'igh-'anded. I wos wonderin' wevver yer might be able ter account for it?'

Even though I was instantly aware of one very good reason to explain such conduct, I hastened to say, 'I'm afraid not, Mrs Brewster.'

'She seemed ter be showin' all the signs of 'avin' fallen in love.'

'Not with me, I'm sure.'

'You ain't plannin' on a return visit ter the Rushmores, by any chance?'

'Not that I know of.'

'Then it can't be you, 'cause Charlotte's talkin' about going back to spend some more time wif Emma.'

Lucy Brewster did not press me any further because two of her guests approached her to thank her before going down to the landing-stage to be ferried back by barge to Sydney Cove where their carriage awaited them. I was left to have to admit to myself that the relationship between Charlotte and Spikey Simmins, despite its being of such short duration, must have progressed much further than I had suspected.

Even though the barge was never empty on its return trips, a large body of guests remained. I had come here with the prospect of seeing Charlotte – and our brief confrontation in the reception room had not been enough to satisfy that – so I stayed on, taking some food in one of the tents and drink in another. Without putting a direct question or proposal to Charlotte, I wanted an answer from her; I wanted to know in my own mind whether through her it might be possible for me to fulfil that foolish boyhood dream of having Estella for my own, even if that Estella should turn out to be her half-sister, Charlotte; in short, I wanted to know whether there was any point in pursuing such a crazy fancy.

In the event, it was Charlotte who made an approach to me, sweeping across the lawn with the hems of her gown skimming the grass. So that I would be unencumbered and free to dance with her, she took the glass of punch from me and handed it to a waiter, then led me over to the lower of the two platforms where we joined other dancers in a minuet.

'And what,' she asked me, as we completed a full circuit of the polished surface, 'was Mama trying to find out from you?'

'Oh, we talked about many things,' I parried.

'I'll say it again,' she said as we danced in time with each other. 'What was it she was trying to find out?'

'Well,' said I, deciding to come to at least one point without further ado, 'she seemed concerned to know if I might be able to explain why you seemed to be eager to return to stay with the Rushmores.'

Our hands were lightly linked; even so, within its glove, I felt hers suddenly tense, and I knew she was disturbed at what I might have said to her foster-mother; but I set her mind at ease.

'Have no fear,' I said. 'I made no mention of the possibility that it might be so that you could meet up with a certain disreputable desperado.'

'My!' said Charlotte, with a flash of Estella's mockery, 'You did well to get your tongue around that.'

'He's not the sort of person you should be consorting with.'

'May I be the judge of that?'

'Only if you insist.'

'People like him are forced to be what they are. Just as your precious patron, A.M., was.'

We danced in silence for some time, one sullen, the other stern. The latter was conscious of what had drawn the sullen to the escapes Emma Rushmore had told him about; her half-caste blood to the natives, and another part of her to the company of runaway convicts. I was tempted there and then to disclose to my dancing partner why I believed the blood of that precious patron, A.M., to be in her veins. Instead I said, 'Have you seen or heard anything further of that man Tolchard?'

Even if she had not answered me, I would have known that my shot in the dark was an accurate one, because her hand in mine gave a tiny twitch.

'Why should you mention him?' she asked.

'Because,' said I, sure of my grounds now, 'I have the feeling that you're afraid of him.'

'Afraid!' she repeated, trying to make it derisive.

'That's the impression I get.'

'But why should I be afraid of him?'

'You're in a better position than me to explain that.'

The band stopped for an interval, and we seated ourselves on one of the sofas at the side of the platform on which we had danced. The silence between us continued, and presently Charlotte stood up as if to leave me; but a naval officer appeared before her, bowed and requested the privilege of the next dance with her, only to be told that she would be partnering me again, after which she resumed her seat on the sofa. Meanwhile, I had been mindful of those words of Abel Magwitch which I had recalled when coming here on the barge: '*We can no more see to the bottom of the next few hours, than we can see to the bottom of this river which I catches hold of.*' He had been referring

184

to hours in the future; what of hours in the past? And so I looked into that part of the river of time, and deep in its waters of the past I saw what could be answers for Charlotte's strange behaviour.

As the band started up again, playing another minuet, we took to the floor once more, and I began to put forward those answers I had discovered.

'You were just a girl when Abel Magwitch left the colony. Did you, perchance, like Mrs Brewster, know that he was smuggling himself on board a ship bound for Plymouth, England?'

We danced some moments, some pretty steps, before she deigned to reply.

'I overheard him telling Mama.'

'Did you, perchance, inform Tolchard of this?'

Her answer to this was to abandon the minuet – and me as well. She swept off the polished platform and across the grass towards a tree trimmed to the shape of a kangaroo; and before I could overtake and stop her, she had reached another shaped like an elephant with its trunk held aloft. As we spoke, we might have been continuing the minuet, with words in place of steps of our feet.

'And why should I have informed Tolchard?' Charlotte wanted to know.

'For that,' I said, 'I have no answer.' For it was not among those that the waters of the past had as yet disclosed to me.

'Perhaps I could suggest one to you?'

'Please do.'

'It was before "The Mansion" was built, when we lived at Mama's establishment. She beseeched Uncle Abel not to go; she said that if he left he would be deserting his own child for another. Me for you. He was violently angry at this – and denied that I was his daughter. He chose to risk all for a glimpse of his make-believe son. So when Tolchard called on Mama to try to find out where Uncle Abel had gone, and received nothing from her – I slipped outside into the street. And when he came out, I told him that Uncle Magwitch had not gone into the interior, but on to a ship for England. Tolchard said that he'd have the information on a fast wool ship leaving for

England that very night – and with luck it would arrive before the ship on which Uncle Abel had sailed.'

Because I was so sentimentally prejudiced in Charlotte's favour, preferring to think well of her rather than ill, I was all too ready to ascribe her betrayal of Abel Magwitch to her having succumbed to an emotional impulse at a time when she was over-wrought with a sense of having been abandoned. Other questions presented themselves, and from those waters of the past I came up with the shadows of other answers.

'Has Tolchard been threatening to expose you to Mrs Brewster?'

'He has,' said Charlotte, in the first of a series of terse confirmations.

'And so you found yourself forced to accede to his demands?'

'I did.'

'And that was why, for instance, you led me to that lonely hut to be captured by him – and Cannibal Jack and their aborigine?'

'It was.'

'Charlotte, my dear – you've been placed in a desperately difficult position, all due to an understandable impulse away back when you were little more than a child. You have my deepest sympathy.'

After hearing me out with her expression concealed under the dark veneer of her skin, what my revelations brought forth from her could not have astounded me more, even had the tree, in whose proximity we stood, turned itself from furze trimmed to the shape of a trumpeting elephant to a live beast of the species on the rampage.

Scorning me, Charlotte said, 'Please don't waste your sympathy on me – after all, I enjoyed it!'

The stunned echo, which was the most I could manage, was little above a whisper.

'Enjoyed it?'

'Forget all I ever told you about standing in front of that portrait of you, and adoring you, and hearing you say adoring things to me! That was when I was an ignorant child. After I heard Mama telling Uncle Abel that she believed I was his daughter, I believed it too. Yet he was too ashamed to admit it.

He put his "young gentleman"' first. After that, I still used to stand in front of your portrait – but only to tell you how much I hated you.'

'*Hated* me?'

'For stealing what should have been mine.'

Since arriving in the colony, all I seemed to have uncovered was treachery and intrigue. I should have been well hardened against further shock. But all of it combined was not enough to soften the impact of this latest discovery. That I should have been so grossly deceived and misused aroused uncontrollable resentment in me, and goaded me into saying what I had been determined not to disclose.

'Lest there be any further doubt,' I said, 'let me tell you something.'

And so, yielding to impulse myself, I went on to reveal to Charlotte that I had known one of Magwitch's daughters, and that I had observed uncanny likenesses in many ways between Charlotte and her; so much so that I was positive that they were half-sisters by the same father, and therefore that Charlotte must unquestionably also be Abel Magwitch's true blood daughter.

The effect of this on Charlotte was shattering. Nevertheless, in my current frame of mind I had scant consideration for her feelings, and took unrestrained advantage of her vulnerability by going on to say, 'Whether you like it or not, you sent your own father to his death.'

Oh, that I had managed in my surrender to bitterness to heed the caution of Mr Jaggers! He had given me adequate warning of the unpredictable effects that might follow the final resolution of long undetermined issues. To some it could bring calm, to others distress – and to Charlotte it brought the latter in high degree, causing her to tremble violently and breathe in terrified gasps. It took some moments for her so to reassert control over herself that she could speak – and then, her blue eyes burning in that burnished face which shone in the light of the flares, she cried at me, 'You're to blame! It's all your fault!' And lifting her long skirts, she turned away, and started to run up past a tree shaped like a spouting whale and through small groups of startled guests, until she reached the front of the big house

187

where, briefly immersed in the play of light made by the flares fixed on iron holders, she disappeared from my view.

After admitting to myself that much of the blame for her distress was mine, as I sat on a garden seat under the trumpeting elephant, I began to shift that blame further into the past, to when I had acceded to Abel Magwitch's threat and brought him food and an iron file; and then, even further back, to when I had strayed into the churchyard where my parents and brothers lay in their plots of earth. Had I not gone there on that bleak, wind-swept afternoon, it would never have come to pass that I should be here now.

In relation to this I recollected a passage from my earlier narrative: '*That was a memorable day for me, for it made great changes in me. But it is the same with any life. Imagine one selected day struck out of it, and think how different its course would have been. Pause you who read this, and think for a moment of the long chain of iron or gold, of thorns or flowers, that would never have bound you, but for the formation of the first link on one memorable day.*'

CHAPTER 19

My concern now was to remove myself from the vicinity of 'The Mansion' and everyone there without further ado. As I looked about me, seeking the easiest and swiftest way to effect this – and deciding that it would have to be by the barge from the landing-stage – I perceived my hostess bearing down on me; and so, after having risen from the garden seat under the bush shaped like a trumpeting elephant, I remained standing beside it.

The haste with which Mrs Brewster approached left her so breathless on arrival that she dispensed with preliminaries and at once broached the matter foremost in her mind.

'That wos a lively tête-à-tête you just 'ad wif Charlotte,' she gasped. 'Wot wos it all abart?'

It was a brazen demand and it rankled me. What if I did tell her what had passed between Charlotte and me? That it had come out that Charlotte had betrayed Magwitch? Lucy Brewster had threatened such dire reprisals that it was inconceivable that I should be the one to reveal the identity of the informer.

With her abrupt departure, Charlotte had virtually swept herself out of my life, leaving me more aware than ever that through her I had been pursuing an impossible fancy – and I was content to let it rest at that. So I simply said, 'We had a difference on a private matter. I doubt either of us has the desire to see the other again.'

Not surprisingly, Lucy Brewster made it very plain that she was unprepared to leave it at that. She was about to press me for something more specific when there was a commotion centred around Sam Bullwinkle and a small circle of his admirers at the point where they had foregathered near a bank of dense bush.

Mrs Brewster took my hand firmly in hers and dragged me across to the scene of the disturbance. Here we found an irate

Sam Bullwinkle, shaking a fist up at the dark heart of a tree. It appeared that a shadowy owl had swept down and plucked one of the white mice off Sam's shoulder and flown off with it.

While Sam's admirers regarded this as an outrage, Mrs Brewster began to laugh – and I started to feel that I had been released from having to parry further questions from her about what had happened between Charlotte and me.

But even while still shaking with laughter, she turned back to me to take up what I had hoped she might have forgotten. As she did so, her face was caught in a certain configuration of light that reminded me of that thrown from the grate on Miss Havisham's features when I had sat at her fireside. Her eyes again narrowed in much the same way as Miss Havisham's had done. Under questioning by Miss Havisham – and in a sense mesmerised by her – I had been powerless to be anything other than all-revealing in my answers. Now I had the feeling that I would find myself compelled to answer her illegitimate daughter's questions in the same frank way. Until, like Sam Bullwinkle and his admirers, Lucy Brewster's attention was diverted to the source of the flickering light. As was my attention. Up towards the big house.

From the drawing room, where mellow light had hitherto prevailed, there was a surge of blazing light – and then a burst of smoke and flame.

Silhouetted against this, a servant in livery plunged down the grassy incline, waving his arms in alarm and crying out to his mistress.

'Mrs Brewster, M'am! Come quickly! Come quickly!'

But before Mrs Brewster could start up the slope, the servant had halted before her, still waving his arms back towards the house.

'It's Miss Charlotte!' he tried to explain. 'She brought in a burning flare and used it to set alight to a picture on the wall!' And, pointing at me as if I might have been in some way an accomplice, he added, 'The picture of this gentleman!'

Leaving the servant to help Mrs Brewster struggle up the slope, I raced ahead. As I did so, the fire within the big house swiftly gathered strength as if the building contained gaseous airs, like the bush on my journey across the mountain range.

Already there was widespread alarm. The band had not only stopped playing, but its members were retreating down the incline with their instruments. As I passed under the portico of the house and into the vestibule, I almost collided with servants and maids on their way out.

The drawing room was to my right. It was impossible for me to enter because of the churning smoke and flame – but from the doorway I could see that fire had completely consumed that portrait of me. All that remained of it was a charred frame hanging askew on a wall left blackened where the brocade covering had been burnt away.

Calling Charlotte's name, I peered into other rooms – the dining-room, the pantry – stifling smoke rolling in ahead past me. After failing to locate her on the ground floor, I was about to mount the stairs when, through the passage to the rear courtyard, I saw the two-horse carriage which must have been waiting there to take some guests home by road. The horses were rearing and plunging, while other horses, released from the confines of their stables, raced away singly and in pairs.

One of these demented animals tried to escape by way of the passage through the house, thus obstructing me as I tried to reach the carriage – for Charlotte had appeared and had clambered up on the driver's seat and taken hold of the reins.

She thus had a start on me as she moved off around the side of the building to the driveway which wound down to the main entrance. After hauling the obstructing horse through the passageway so that it could escape by way of the vestibule, I set out after the carriage. Other horses running free crowded the driveway, but these Charlotte whipped aside. I cried out to her to stop, but she paid no heed. How my legs gave me the speed I do not know, but I managed to get close enough to the carriage to gain a hold on its side. I was endeavouring to find some way of getting myself aboard the vehicle when Charlotte saw me and used the whip to break my hold. And so I tumbled to the ground, fortunately to the grassy sward and not the driveway itself, lying there panting and helpless as Charlotte skidded the carriage around out the gate and made good her getaway, leaving me confronted with the garish spectacle now spread out over a wide area of the mirror surface of the harbour as it reflected the burning house. Turning back to the big house, I saw that the fire had rapidly gained a greater hold on it. Flame and smoke now poured from the upper storey windows and from the attics.

Using buckets which had contained ice to keep drinks cool, the bandsmen and servants formed chains from the landing-stage to pass sea water up to be thrown on the flames. Many of the guests took part in this; also the occupants of boats and the crews of ships from out in the bay. Their combined efforts resulted in a number of almost unbroken cataracts of water, but the heat from the flames was so intense that much of this water fell far short.

Near the top of these chains, Lucy Brewster stood in a stooped daze, supported by the servant who had first brought word to her of Charlotte's crazed action. As I reached this point, the men at the top of the chains were being forced to retreat.

The servant urged Mrs Brewster to do likewise – and when she ignored his pleas he began to try to drag her away. She resisted – and so I endeavoured to assist the servant in what he was trying to do.

It seemed that we were succeeding, until Lucy Brewster found the strength to break free of us and rush forward up the slope.

'My jools!' she cried. 'My jools!'

Before the servant and I could overtake her, she reached the portico and vanished into the billowing smoke. We tried to advance, but the heat drove us back. Mrs Brewster did not reappear. We saw nothing further of her. We heard nothing.

Would that I could draw a shade over the indelible pictures my memory retains of that night. The fire became an inferno, its reflection reaching to distant bays and corners of that vast harbour.

In the early dawn, when the ruins were searched, there was still no sign of Lucy Brewster – until one of the Constables discovered her body wedged in a chimney flue where she had been asphyxiated with a box of jewels clutched to her bosom, the former sooty shrimp alas grown so plump that she had been unable to escape along a route she would once have negotiated with ease, dark and perilous though it may have been.

Another of the Constables proceeded to question me as to the possible whereabouts of Charlotte who had, according to one of the grooms, secreted a saddle-bag of clothing in the stables. I could only tell the Constable that she had gone off with the carriage and two horses. He informed me that on apprehension she was to be charged with wilful arson. I had already feared that this might happen. What concerned me much more was to learn that she was also to be charged with manslaughter for the death of her foster-mother.

I therefore made no mention of where I felt the police might look. I imagined her well on her way across the coastal plain, before climbing the mountain road to meet up with Spikey Simmins and his band.

Later, I was to obtain confirmation that this was in fact what did happen; but that was not until some time after I had decided that my pilgrimage to the scene of my former benefactor's labours had continued long enough, and I was back on the other side of the world.

CHAPTER 20

Back at my hotel at last, the morning light was at full flood when I went to bed with both the inner and the balcony doors shut and locked. I slept heavily in such conditions, so therefore, when attempts were made to rouse me but a few hours later, it required prolonged knocking on the inner door before I woke. It took a little time for me to orientate myself – only to be reminded of the hideous outcome to Lucy Brewster's party.

The knocker was the landlord, but on behalf of another – a senior police officer who informed me that he must question me forthwith on certain aspects of the night's tragedy. I was obliged to make a statement which he wrote down and read to me before asking me to sign it; in it I related all I could recall of how Lucy Brewster had come to meet her death. I made no attempt to conceal anything, there was no need.

However, when he began to question me on another matter, one for which I was not asked to make a formal statement – that of the disappearance of Charlotte – I recounted how I had seen her leaving 'The Mansion' on a two-horse carriage, but volunteered no suggestion as to where she might have been going – even though I was more certain than ever in my own mind that she intended joining Spikey Simmins; and that at the staging-posts along the Western Road over the mountain range she would be able to obtain fresh horses because of her relationship to one of the part-owners of a stage-coach company. This, also, was something that was to be confirmed much later – when I was back on the other side of the world.

Since leaving Cairo I'd not had need to have recourse to any of the contents of my portable medicine chest, but I own to having had to do so at this stage. To calm my mind and my body so that I could think coherently, I took a substantial draught of that universal potion against all maladies and disorders.

If there had been a ship sailing that day, and I had been free to leave the colony, I would have sought a passage on it. But I was not free as yet. The police officer had also informed me that I would be required to give evidence at the inquest which was to be held in three days. So I occupied myself (while making sure that anyone appearing to follow me looked like an Agent of the Crown) in coming to a firm arrangement with the merchant handling the hides of cattle, sheep, kangaroos and other native animals. So much so that a preliminary consignment was loaded on the brig due to call at Suez.

This vessel was to weigh anchor for Ceylon in the first instance on the day after the inquest, so I took a gamble on not being required beyond that one day and purchased a passage from the Captain.

Meanwhile, on the day following the burning down of 'The Mansion' and the death of its owner, the *Clarion* came out bordered in black. I was reported as having valiantly attempted to dissuade Mrs Brewster when she insisted on making her fatal dash into the inferno to try to rescue her jewels. There was no mention whatsoever of Charlotte, but my landlord, who fussed over me with greater solicitude than ever, made up for this discrepancy with a number of rumours.

One such rumour had it that Charlotte, having discovered the whereabouts of the hidden Magwitch fortune and so no longer in need of Mrs Brewster's support, had set light to the big house as a parting gesture of defiance. I suggested that evidence presented at the inquest would give a rather different explanation.

That explanation caused a considerable stir in the coroner's court when I related why, as far as I knew, Charlotte put the burning flare to that portrait of me. In the course of the inquiry I gathered that the charge of manslaughter against Charlotte had been dropped – but that the arson charge still stood and that directions had been given for her arrest. As to the cause of Lucy Brewster's death, it was decided that in her anxiety to gain possession of her jewels she had greatly underestimated the danger to which she was exposing herself, and so a verdict of misadventure was recorded. No will had as yet been located.

Following all this, just when I felt I was free, I was now

informed by the police officer that I would be required to continue to make myself available until such times as Charlotte had been apprehended and brought to trial. I refused to be put in the position of having to wait around Sydney town for what could well be a period of months. In the face of my protestations, the police officer relented, and so I returned to my hotel for my last night there and gathered up my belongings and completed my packing before I retired.

In the days leading up to the inquest, there had been a steady increase in the heat. I detected a note of hysteria in the high-pitched singing of the cicadas, a growing intensification, as if each group or chorus of these curious insects was striving to inject more and more shrill sound into the air, making it another sort of parallel to the situation in the mountains when the air had been full of that gaseous vapour ready to ignite. It was as if the sound had reached such a concentration that it was ready to explode. And this, in a sense, is what came to pass the next day.

The brig was due to sail on the afternoon tide and I planned to go on board at noon. That left me with the morning on my hands, and so I set out to cover much the same route I had followed on my first day in Sydney town, looking over some of the properties that might have been mine – the cemetery, the sites of the military hospital and the cathedral, and the horse-track. The day was exceedingly sultry with the haze thickening into towering cloud, and I had not gone far before I was soaked to the skin with my own perspiration.

As expected, I was not alone. Two Agents of the Crown, one of them the man who had approached me when I had set out for Lucy Brewster's party, followed at a distance of some fifty yards. As I turned to go back in the direction of the hotel, it allowed them to catch up on me – and the same Agent was again the spokesman.

'We have been wondering, Mr Pirrip, whether you have given any consideration to our request – to be permitted to examine the two Magwitch keepsakes?'

'No,' I said, 'none whatsoever.'

'We were hoping you might have changed your mind.'

'I see no reason why I should. The matter is closed – in a few hours I will have left the colony.'

'We are aware of that, of course.' And then, after giving a small smirk, the Agent went on. 'The events of the past few days have not been without benefit to the Crown.' He noted my mystification and became more precise. 'Mrs Brewster's will has been located at the offices of one of her legal representatives. In it she bequeathed her estate in its entirety to none other than Abel Magwitch. Such being the case, that estate will be claimed by the Crown.'

If I had needed further evidence of Lucy Brewster's loyalty to my benefactor, this indeed was it.

'What about the rights of his heirs?' I asked.

'The will makes no such provision.'

'They have legal rights by law.'

'But we have no knowledge of any heirs.'

'Allow me to enlighten you.'

And so I proceeded to tell the two Agents about Estella and Charlotte, both of whom I assumed to be still alive.

After hearing me out, the spokesman Agent surprised me by saying, 'We have considered such a possibility. It may well be that each of the two women could produce proof of their paternal parentage. But to no end, since we are firmly of the opinion that the Crown would be deemed to have a prior claim.'

As if an even higher authority were endorsing this view, the sky rumbled, and thunder continued to drum and pound as I hastened to reach the hotel before the storm, which had been threatening for days now, broke upon the town. I had become weary of fortunes and claimants; now I was heartily sickened by them and anxious to board the brig forthwith.

Waiting outside the hotel in the baleful light was a covered cart hitched to a large shaggy horse. The landlord explained that he had taken the liberty of hiring it for me – at his own expense, as a sort of farewell gesture. I accepted the offer in the spirit in which it was made, loaded my effects on board the cart and sat myself on the cross bench under the canvas cover. Rain was splotching down now so I would be ensured of a dry ride as far as the wharf. I thanked the landlord for all his kindnesses and called to the driver to start.

What a start it was! At a flick of the reins the horse set off like a military charger. I was flung back off the cross bench on to the floor of the cart. The driver, whose voluminous beard made him a shaggy companion to the horse, took no heed of my predicament as I groped my way back on to the seat. The way ahead was partly obscured by sheets of rain now, but I was sufficiently well acquainted with the layout of the town to realise that we were taking a roundabout route. I tried to ascertain if this were so from the driver but he ignored my shouted inquiry which, in any event, was almost completely drowned in the roar of the rain and the crackle of thunder. Quite unaffected by the noise and the lightning flashes, the horse proceeded at the same scorching pace as if it might be heading towards some predetermined destination.

That destination certainly was not the one I had intended. My trunk and other pieces of luggage were bouncing and sliding about as I clung to the overhead ribs supporting the canvas cover and drew myself forward so that I could bend down and shout into the driver's ear. Which I did. Only to receive a violent backward swipe from his arm, which not only knocked the air out of my lungs but sent me toppling back over my effects and the cross bench. But for the raised rear boards of the cart, I might have found myself left sprawled in the downpour on the rough roadway.

Sprawled on the floor of the cart, what little strength I could summon was expended in fending off the attempts of my trunk and other pieces of luggage, including my portable medicine chest, to batter me. Suddenly the roar of the rain became less, the light dimmer, and all movement ceased as the combination of cart, horse and driver delivered me to that predetermined destination.

Rising on my hands and knees and peering over the tail of the cart, I perceived that we were in a large abandoned barn. And then, within the curved frame made by the canvas cover of the cart, there appeared a familiar trio: Tolchard, Cannibal Jack and the aborigine, Henry. As Tolchard, as if remaining within the confines of his invisible sentry-box, held the weighty pistol that had rapped on the bar of that hut in which I had been trapped, Cannibal Jack and Henry took hold of me from either side and dragged me out over the tail of the cart and stood me in front of the muzzle of the pistol.

The rain, meanwhile, seethed on the high roof of the barn and spouted through in places; lightning flashed outside and the thunder continued to clap and crackle. The driver shut the two halves of the big door, and so there I was, well and truly caught in another trap, one which, alas, it seemed that the landlord, with whom I had parted on such cordial terms, had played no small part in helping to set for me.

This was confirmed when Tolchard, who left the smirking to his two companions, informed me what had happened at the hotel when I took that last walk around the town.

'We've been through your luggage. The items we seek are not there, so you must be carrying them on your person.'

He was, of course, absolutely correct in his surmise.

'Let us have them,' he said. 'And then we'll proceed to find out what you've learnt from them – and what else you've discovered in the course of your stay in New South Wales.'

The muzzle of the pistol tilted up to aim at my heart, and Cannibal Jack and Henry tightened their holds on me. I tried to shake them off.

'I need my arms free, if you don't mind,' I said.

Tolchard used the muzzle of the pistol to wave them away from me, and so I stood alone. But what could I do other than comply? Undoubtedly it was the inborn instinct of self-preservation that motivated me in trying, even under such adverse circumstances, to strike some sort of bargain.

'My one concern is to leave New South Wales on the late afternoon tide. What guarantee can you give me of that?'

The proposal was received with stony-faced coldness by Tolchard. 'You are in no position to seek terms. Either you hand over the articles in question or they'll be taken from you,' he said; and I recalled Jock Weedin's warning: '*Ye'll be shown no mercy.*'

As Cannibal Jack and Henry prepared to put this threat into effect there was a dramatic change in the nature of the downpour. Without warning, the seething of the rain became a violent hammering and huge hailstones thrust through those overhead gaps, from which the rain had spouted, and bounced about on the bare earth barn floor before coming to rest, whereupon they could be seen to be as large as hen's eggs. The uproar was so tremendous that it rendered speech utterly impossible. Indeed, it was so terrifying that it upset the very functioning of the mind – and so, while the storm raged at this pitch, all steps to relieve me of the Testament and pack of playing cards were suspended. The size of the hailstones increased – as did the strength of their impact, so that the existing gaps in the roof were widened and other gaps appeared as the wood slats were smashed in. Even though these stones fell only from roof height, their dimensions were such that they could deliver painful and bruising blows, so that we were all forced to keep moving from side to side – not only to avoid the stones as they dropped, but also as they bounced. Tolchard managed to do this without diverting the aim of his pistol from me. The horse was least able to dodge the missiles and the animal began to rear and whinny when several large stones struck.

At my earliest acquaintance with this vast southern continent I had been introduced to the bizarre. I had seen something of the extremities in which Nature had indulged in these parts in the form of that vast shoal of jelly-fish. I had encountered fire in a most treacherous form. I could give many such instances despite my short stay in the colony; but the hailstorm outdid all else. In a matter of what could only have been a minute or two the floor of the barn was littered with jagged balls and flakes of ice up to six inches around and five in length, and the barn itself seemed in imminent danger of being rent apart under the onslaught.

Had it continued for another minute or two, I have no doubt that the roof would have collapsed leaving us exposed to a deadly deluge; but as swiftly as it had commenced, the hail stopped. Although no one could be sure that this was anything more than a brief lull. And so we all stood ready for the onslaught to resume.

It was during this lull that a plan of attack formed in my mind, one that had its origins away back when Joe Gargery and

I were indulging in playful rivalry. In the course of our walks around the marshes and to the banks of the River Thames we had taken up stones and vied with each other in trying to be the first to score a hit on a piece of driftwood waterborne out in the stream. It was a game I had repeated at a later stage in life with Herbert Pocket in another part of the world with stones of another kind. The rubble from the ruins of walls and columns outside Cairo when taking part in archaeological outings, much to the disgust of some of our more serious companions who considered our boyish frivolity a sort of desecration of hallowed relics. Having set up a target stone, we would position ourselves at a distance of, say, thirty yards and, using smaller stones, try to be first to dislodge the target. (And despite the disapproval this drew, it served us well on one occasion when we found ourselves separated from the main body of members of the expedition and threatened by a small band of native thieves who we managed to put to flight with a fusillade of stones.)

It did not worry me that the hailstones I now proposed to use could be lethal. With my eyes I marked out a number which I believed I could swiftly seize and hurl. And so, just as Tolchard and the others were deciding that the hailstorm had passed on and that they could proceed with me, I also marked my target. Tolchard, the man with that pistol.

Taking him and the others completely by surprise, I dived at the icy missiles and hurled one after another in rapid succession at Tolchard, whose invisible sentry-box proved no protection for him. He staggered back as the hailstones struck him on the chest, shoulders and arms with such force that the pistol was knocked from his hand. Seizing and hurling lumps of ice as I went, I rushed forward and managed to gain possession of the loaded weapon, and so found myself in control of a situation which had seemed utterly without hope for me.

Tolchard lay groaning on the ground while Cannibal Jack, Henry the aborigine, and the driver stood stunned at the turn of events. I did not waste time ascertaining what degree of injury their leader had suffered. I ordered the driver to open the two halves of the barn door, which he hastened to do even without the flick of the pistol muzzle which I aimed in his direction.

To all four I issued a warning. 'Lest there be any doubt in

your minds whether I am capable of using this weapon, I must inform you that the Cairo Pistol-Shooting Club ranks me as a First Class Shot.'

Then I ordered the driver up on the seat at the front of the cart and took up a position beside him. After aiming the pistol in the direction of my three would-be abductors, I jabbed the muzzle into the driver's ribs and told him to head to where he had been supposed to take me in the first place. Glancing back for a last glimpse, I saw Tolchard still prostrate and his two accomplices standing helplessly beside him (and, presumably, the shattered remains of his sentry-box).

During the ride to the wharves through streets blanketed with white ice, and past houses and cottages with smashed windows and roofs, the driver said nothing but complied instantly with my instructions. Trees had been stripped of foliage and fruit. Whole gardens lay flattened. Out in the harbour, many vessels were capsized, and a sailing barge, similar to the one on which I had journeyed to the Hawkesbury River and back, drifted with its sails in tatters. My fingers were tingling, and only now did I realise they had been numbed by the ice.

The brig on which I was due to sail had suffered nothing more serious than a violent pummelling – although the seamen, who hastened to come forward and unload my trunk and other pieces of luggage (especially when they saw I carried a pistol), informed me that never anywhere in the world had they encountered a hailstorm of such magnitude. Large stones and flakes of ice lay in the scuppers not yet melted away.

The driver was relieved to be given his freedom and the last I saw of him, the cart and his shaggy four-footed charge was their hasty retreat in the direction of where that abandoned barn was situated. Even though it seemed that Tolchard's final fling had been a failure, thanks to the combination of an Act of God and a stroke of human ingenuity, I took nothing for granted and so remained on deck with that loaded pistol until the brig had cast off from the wharf and was under sail towards the heads of Port Jackson, passing the blackened shell of Lucy Brewster's 'Mansion' wherein the skeleton shapes of the chimneys remained upright.

For several days we sailed within close proximity of the coast, so I did not feel that I had finally escaped from the perils and intrigues abounding in the colony until we were out of sight of the great island continent. Only then did I dispose of Tolchard's pistol by throwing it over the side of the ship.

As for the Magwitch keepsakes, I toyed with doing likewise with them and so severing myself from any further temptation to pursue the hidden fortune, one which I now considered best left where it was, secreted in the country which had slipped over the horizon and out of view; the country in which I had been, after having travelled so far to reach it, for only some three weeks.

Dear Joe, my blacksmith brother-in-law, had once made an observation which seemed to apply to the present occasion: *'Life is made of ever so many partings welded together.'*

CHAPTER 21

The Pockets had not expected me back in Cairo nearly so soon. One of my letters had arrived but the previous day, and others were to come in the succeeding months. But they gave me a very warm welcome nevertheless – Herbert, Clara and their children. The two girls dark and pretty, and, as their mother had been when Herbert first introduced me to her, like fairies. The two boys already showed that they were to grow into pale young gentlemen, images of their father, each with his wonderfully amiable disposition.

All were delighted with the presents I had brought them from the country they still called New Holland, purchases I had made when out seeing my merchant and bank manager. However, it was my account of what happened that interested them most; and although we settled down early in the evening for me to begin my account, it was midnight when I had finished.

They plied me with questions, most of which I was able to answer, except those which they were most eager to have satisfied. Whether I still proposed to continue to look for the hidden Magwitch fortune? The fate of the beautiful but wilful Charlotte? And my attitude to my late benefactor now that I had found out how he made his fortune in New South Wales?

It was the third of these three questions that I took to bed with me that night and pondered upon by far more than all else.

It was true that I had built up an increasing repugnance to Abel Magwitch the deeper I had delved; but now that I was at a distance from the scene of his labours, I was able to see everything in perspective. Had he not countered like with like, brutality with brutality? And even if, as Mr Jaggers had so confidently argued, his main motive was to avenge himself on those who had discriminated against him, he still laboured to fulfil a wildly romantic dream.

Without that dream, of which I was the centre, perhaps he would have despaired and gone under. I could not get out of my mind the immense despair he must have felt before our first encounter in the churchyard near our village home:

'*I was a hiding among the graves there, envying them as was in 'em and all over, when I first see my boy!*'

Indeed, I had been essential to his very survival:

'*I lived rough, that you should live smooth; I worked hard that you should be above work. What odds, dear boy? Do I tell it fur you to feel an obligation? Not a bit. I tell it, fur you to know as that there hunted dunghill dog wot you kep life in got his head so high that he could make a gentleman – and Pip, you're him!*'

The better side of Abel Magwitch – and are there not many sides to all of us? – had come out on his return, in defiance of the laws of transportation, risking his life if needs be just to see me. He had been heroically resigned:

'*I'm an old bird now as has dared all manner of traps since first he was fledged, and I'm not afeerd to perch upon a scarecrow. If there's Death hid inside of it, there is, and let him come out, and I'll face him, and then I'll believe him and not afore. And now let me have a look at my gentleman agen.*'

The pencil drawing of him had come back to Cairo with me; and when I took it out, this time I saw another side overlaid upon the lawless felon (who had once said, '*I've been done everything to, pretty well – except hanged*'); the softened and exultant fugitive after seeing the object of his life a reality; the man whose hand I had held in his dying moments. There like shadow and sunlight, when swiftly-driven clouds pass over, were the two sides to Abel Magwitch, violence and placidity, equally captured by Emma Rushmore and interwoven.

I recalled now what I had said in my earlier narrative when relating how I had been at my benefactor's bedside: my repugnance to him had all melted away, and the hunted wounded shackled creature who held my hand in his, I only saw as a man who had felt affectionately, gratefully and generously towards me with great constancy through a series of years. I can but say all that again.

For the next year, during which I heard nothing of what had become of Charlotte, life proceeded without incident, except that I couldn't throw off the feeling that I was still under a certain surveillance – and I occasionally caught a glimpse of men in pairs who had the look of Agents of the Crown about them.

The little clasped black Testament and the playing cards that had journeyed to the far side of the world remained in a locked drawer in my study. From time to time I took them out, just to look at them out of my sentimental remembrance of Abel Magwitch, for by having them in my hands I somehow felt his presence.

Once when I had them out, I turned the thin pages of the Testament, seeing the circled letters again. The sheet of my personal notepaper on which I had listed the letters in lines across the page was folded and tucked away at the back of the Testament. I removed it and opened it out.

TRSWTHTE
THEEGEAB
EHOHCOEC
TONVEEEL
ERFNAHLG
ETNMDSEW
CMED

At first the letters made as little sense to me as ever. What it was that prompted me to count the number of letters, I do not know – but I did, and I found that there were fifty-two letters in all. I counted them again. Exactly fifty-two, the same number as in a pack of playing cards from which the Joker has been removed.

Abel Magwitch had told Jock Weedin, the ostler, that the secret of the whereabouts of the hidden fortune was somehow contained between the playing cards and the Testament. He had also said: '*Patience. All it needs is patience.*'

To what did this refer? The virtue of that name? The card game of that name? Or a combination of the two?

And so I began to wonder whether the fifty-two letters might yield something were they to be laid out as Magwitch had done when playing his personal game of Patience. Using cut-up pieces of paper, I made fifty-two small cards. On each I wrote one of the letters in the list, starting with the first circled in the Testament – and again starting with this first letter, I set them out as Magwitch would have done, in four long lines, each with thirteen cards.

Lo and behold! Out of that jumble of letters, words began to emerge.

```
T E N G
R A V E
S B E T
W E E N
T H E M
H O L D
T H E S
E C R E
T O F W
H E N C
E C A M
E T H E
G O L D
```

As if by magic the words separated themselves out so that I was able to set down a couplet.

TEN GRAVES BETWEEN THEM HOLD
THE SECRET OF WHENCE CAME THE GOLD

The couplet meant nothing to me, so I brought out the other sheets of folded notepaper, those on which I had linked the indentations from the pin-holes made through the cards, making what had appeared to me to be a map of some sort.

There once again was the winding line, to which I had added further possibilities, so that in addition to being a shoreline, a boundary fence, a road, a river, a track, a stream, a lengthy marking on the ground, the edge of a lake or a cliff, trails made by sheep or goats, a reef or a shelf under the sea, it could also be a line of hills or a mountain range with settlements or buildings on the side.

Often when observing bees and butterflies, I have thought to myself that their randon flitting from bough to bough or bloom to bloom is rather like the way human thoughts are strung together. At times there seems to be no reason why one bough or bloom should be the next choice. Even so, I have wondered whether perhaps it was the mention of graves that started me along a train of thought which led me to identify the place the rough map represented.

Think of graves and you think of a graveyard. I thought of that graveyard where my parents, my baby brothers and sister were laid to rest near the village where I was born and where, had Abel Magwitch not arranged for me to be brought up as a gentleman, I would be working as a blacksmith. It was in this graveyard that I had been pounced on by Abel Magwitch when he had escaped from the prison-hulk near where I took the few items for which I was later to receive such an immense reward.

On the map spread lightly over half a dozen sheets of my notepaper was an area that could well have been a graveyard. Next moment I saw it all, and if I'd had Abel Magwitch's horn-handled jack knife as a keepsake, I'd have plunged it into the table to mark a winning score. It was, as Dear Joe had once said, '*like striking out a horse-shoe complete, in a single blow*'.

That long wavering line was the River Thames on its winding way to the sea; half way down was the outline of my home village; the old battery; the churchyard; and, by linking some of the indentations close together, I formed small oblongs which could be graves. Ten in all.

CHAPTER 22

It is at this point that my present story crosses the path of the last chapter of my previous narrative, in which I wrote that I had not been back to England for eleven years since going to the East to take a post with Clarriker and Co.

In that chapter I began by stating that I returned because of my desire to see Joe, the blacksmith to whom I had been apprenticed, and his wife, my good friend Biddy. There was, of course, as you will already have gathered, another reason – although I like to believe it was more to solve a mystery than to finally try to locate the hidden Magwitch fortune.

After reaching Portsmouth by steamer, I travelled by railway to London, and from the metropolis down the river by coach to the marsh country where I found the village unchanged. Avoiding the main street, the scene of my triumph, when I had set out for London to be turned into a gentleman, and my disgrace, when I had returned penniless after the death of Abel Magwitch, I made my way straight to the churchyard.

The cold silvery mist that lay low over the river and the marshes filled the churchyard with gloomy ghosts, but otherwise it was empty. From the rough map I had made, I had memorised the positions of the ten graves in a far corner near some yew trees – and it was at this spot that I found them. All ten of them gaping open. Ten empty graves.

Excavated earth was heaped up and around the tombstones, so that I had to scrape and brush much of it aside to be able to read the inscriptions, something I only just managed in the gathering dark. Each tombstone bore the name of a man, the date of his birth, the date of his death, his age and where he had died in New South Wales: James Cox; Samuel Peet; Robert Dennison; Matthew Mobbs; Joseph Creamer; William Twyfield; Aaron Springham; Thomas Boulton; Thomas Vickery; Seth Eagleton. From my memory of local families, almost all of these men were strangers to the locality. Their dates of birth and their ages varied markedly, but all had died within a few years of one another – and all before Abel Magwitch's departure from New South Wales.

The sexton's cottage, which was back near the village, was unchanged, except for the creeper that grew thicker over its walls; but it had a new occupant since my boyhood days, a man who eyed me with a certain suspicion before I spoke, then claimed me as a friend when I told him I was related to a whole plot of permanent residents in his domain. Being deliberately casual, I said that when wandering about the churchyard I had noticed that there were a number of empty graves close together.

'Aye,' he said, 'a mystery if ever there be. In the dead of night, around Easter it were, between sunset and sunrise, them ten graves were opened and the coffins removed. Lead-lined they were, too, all of 'em. In the lane nearby, there were deep wheelmarks of a wagon, and the marks of horses' hooves – and two dead men.'

'From the coffins?' asked I.

'No, no. Dead but a matter of hours. One shot through the heart, the other the 'ead. There had been firin' in the night. Poachers after wild fowl it was thought.'

'And these two dead men? Who were they?'

'The one shot through the heart was never identified, but the other were. Someone back from New South Wales arter servin' his time there. A master forger.'

'Not Felix Lamont?'

'Aye – 'im.'

The sexton went inside to fetch a lantern so that he could come out with me to inspect the graves; I might observe something in the vicinity that he and others had missed. As he did so, I asked myself the obvious question: had Lamont somehow extracted something from Edward Rushmore?

As I set out with the sexton and the lantern, the couplet I had made from the letters in Abel Magwitch's Testament began to run through my head once again (it had already done so many a thousand times):

'Ten graves between them hold

The secret of whence came the gold.'

If, as I now began to believe, the ten coffins had contained gold which had been brought out of the interior of New South Wales on a covered wagon hauled by two wily oxen, the scramble for Abel Magwitch's secret fortune had been a waste of time in that far-off country, since it had been hidden here in England all the time.

That Welsh water-diviner who had gone out on the covered wagon with Magwitch could have been able to locate more than water, as men with such powers frequently can. Gold, for instance. And it could well have been that it was because of the gold that Magwitch had been forced to fight for his life. While Magwitch came back cut, bruised and with broken ribs, the diviner did not return at all.

As for the ten men described by the tombstones, who were they?

The sexton, when I put this question to him, extended his hand to a distant curve of the river where in the faint starlight several antediluvian shapes could be glimpsed floating gauntly on the waters.

'Former inmates of what were then His Majesty's prison hulks. All of them transported to New South Wales, never to be permitted to return. Alive, that is. All, however, wished their mortal remains to be interred in the land of their birth, so it was arranged that they were brought back here to be buried in the earth of their Mother Country.'

'Were you here at the time?' I inquired.

'I was that,' said the sexton. 'The ten coffins as well as being monstrous 'eavy, bein' lead-lined like I said, were also sealed. Before the interments took place, I had to certify this to be so.'

'That the coffins remained sealed?'

'Which all were.'

'To whom did you certify this?'

'To the clergyman which conducted the burial service for all ten at the one time. On a paper, to be returned to someone in Australia who had arranged for the deceased to be brought home. They were in the charge of this clergyman on the voyage, on board a returning transport.'

'Tell me about the clergyman?'

'A big man in a great 'urry to have it over an' done with.'

'Was his name perchance "Chilblud"?' I asked.

'After a dozen years, I couldn't be sure. Though the name would have fitted the man. Chilblud.'

As well as a name, I gave a description, one which tallied with the sexton's recollection. For all his cunning, it seemed that the Reverend Magistrate had been completely taken in by Abel Magwitch and led into believing that the ten coffins in his charge did in fact contain mortal remains within their heavy lead linings.

The light of the lantern revealed nothing. Not that I expected it to. If Felix Lamont had been here to try to collect the gold and had been shot through the head for his trouble, who else had been here? And from where in New South Wales had all that precious yellow metal come?

I heard the couplet again in my head, but there was nothing here to tell me whence.

It was an hour or two after dark when I made my return to the village known to Joe and Biddy, and met their two children. As I have related in my earlier narrative, the following day, in the evening, I took a walk to visit the site of Miss Havisham's old house, where Estella had lived. There was no building whatever left, only the wall of the old garden.

Looking along a desolate garden-walk, I beheld that solitary figure on it, and so I was reunited with someone who had chosen this very evening to make a sentimental return to the scene of times gone by – the child Abel Magwitch had loved and lost, the same Estella who had grown to be a lady and very beautiful, and whom I had come to love, as I had told my benefactor moments before he had breathed his last.

As I have already recorded, her husband Bentley Drummle had treated her cruelly, but was now dead; and although its freshness may have crept away, her beauty remained – and her charm. As she told me, she was greatly changed; but so was I.

The evening mists began to rise and we left the ruined place hand in hand, resolved never to be parted from each other again.

CHAPTER 23

Some months after our wedding, when my partners had transferred me to manage the London branch of Clarriker and Co., so that we could settle down to live there, I was strolling in the late afternoon along Piccadilly with Estella on my arm, through a jostling tide of humanity. High on its crest a familiar item of headwear was borne towards us. A grey hat of ecclesiastical design, perhaps not as pristine as when I had seen it some two years ago in the Blue Mountains of New South Wales, but distinctive nevertheless.

Here on the pavement of Piccadilly, where it is said those from the ends of the earth are fated to meet one another, I now fully expected to come face to face with none other than the Reverend Magistrate Chilblud. I was thinking that he might well have collected the Magwitch gold after all, when I remembered that his hat had been appropriated by the bushranger Spikey Simmins, so the model now approaching must be a similar one.

It turned out to be the very same hat.

So it was that I met up again with Spikey Simmins. He also had a lady companion on his arm, someone who had not hesitated to use her horse whip to ensure at our last meeting that we parted company. It was, of course, Charlotte.

Seeing them first, I stopped – and before Estella could inquire why I had come to such an abrupt halt, she saw that another couple had done likewise. An over-dressed, vital-looking man and an expensively and most elegantly attired lady of part-coloured blood.

Across the short space of pavement between us, I glimpsed the sudden panic in Spikey's eyes as if he were about to bolt at having been recognised; but Charlotte gripped his arm tighter, quickly whispered into his ear (presumably that I could be trusted), so he relaxed a little and they came forward, as I did with Estella, to exchange greetings.

'Mr Pirrip!' he said, extending his hand.

'Mr Simmins!' said I as we shook; and then, taking his companion's gloved hand and bending to kiss it lightly, 'And Charlotte.'

'If it isn't Pip!' she said, but she was looking at Estella and not me. As was Spikey, wondering whether my companion could be trusted.

'Friends of mine from New South Wales,' I told Estella, and then I introduced them. 'I'd like you to meet my wife. Miss Charlotte Brewster – and Mr Simmins.'

Charlotte threw back her head to laugh, and Spikey fanned his hand at me, in a way that reminded me of a certain clerk who had waved a feathered quill pen.

'No, no,' Spikey said.

Entering into the fun of surprising me, Charlotte removed her left glove to show me the handsome wedding ring on her third finger.

'Perhaps yer recall the Reverend Chilblud?' Spikey said, touching his hat to help me remember.

'I don't need any reminder,' I assured Spikey; and to Estella, so that she would not feel left out of things, I added, 'Someone else I met on my trip to Australia.'

'He it was that conducted the ceremony,' Spikey went on.

'Chilblud?' I said astonished.

Giving me a wink, Spikey took my arm and led me to the outer side of the pavement, leaving the two ladies to talk – and I was delighted to see that they instantly got on well with each other, perhaps unconsciously sensing something of what they had in common.

'With a pistol in his back, o' course,' Spikey said, with another wink – and I understood. In fact, I could almost see the wedding under those circumstances.

'I wish I'd been there,' said I.

'Wish yer 'ad,' Spikey said. 'Charlotte remembers you kindly, fer all she mighta said an' done.'

I glanced back to the ladies who were talking animatedly together, the subject obviously being apparel because Estella was fingering the cloth of the other's dress as they spoke.

Returning my attention to Spikey, I said, 'So you found the gold?'

Feigning mystification with masterful aplomb, Spikey said, 'What gold?'

'Come along, now – I've seen those ten empty graves with my own eyes. I don't know how you managed it, but you got to Abel Magwitch's hidden fortune before anyone else.'

Admitting nothing as yet, Spikey said, 'We better 'ave a proper talk some time.'

'What's wrong with the present time?' I said, indicating the ladies in close conversation. 'Why don't we leave them together and meet back here in say, one hour? I am a member of an agreeable little club not a hundred yards away, in Half Moon Street.'

The ladies seized upon the suggestion; they would like nothing better than to be able to explore some of the neighbouring shops together. So Spikey Simmins, who I had last seen dressed in clothing which might have been stolen from a scarecrow, accompanied me in his new finery to the club, where I found a quiet corner in the smoking room and called a waiter to bring us some brandy.

Since I could not expect any confidences from Spikey merely on the strength of a drink or two, I decided that I must try to barter with him by telling him how I had come to be led to the village churchyard. I hoped that in exchange for such information he would reveal what had directed him to that same spot. And so, without going into the matter in detail, I said that I had made my discovery through a combination of Abel Magwitch's Testament and his old pack of playing cards.

'Now,' said I, 'what led *you* to the churchyard?'

Straight-faced, he replied, 'Yer've no proof I was ever there.'

'No,' I admitted. 'None. But all my instincts tell me that what came out of those ten graves accounts for the presence of such splendid adornments such as this on your person.'

I lightly grasped the gold fob on the gold watch chain across his exquisitely embroidered waistcoat, a heart-shaped pendant set with diamonds and rubies.

Spikey burst out laughing and slapped his thigh, which was encased in high quality doeskin.

Still not actually admitting anything, he said that Charlotte had joined him and his companions on the other side of the mountains, thus confirming what I had assumed. After escaping from 'The Mansion' with the two-horse carriage, Charlotte managed to obtain fresh horses at the staging-posts across the coastal plain and up the Western Road over the mountain range, simply because of her close relationship with Lucy Brewster. At several of the staging-posts she encountered some difficulty when it was suspected that she might be fleeing from some crisis. However, she managed to stay well ahead of the news about the fate of her foster-mother.

Since they had planned to be reunited in any event, Charlotte and Spikey had an arrangement that he would be at a certain wooded spot on the road to the Rushmore Estate every evening at sundown; and so it was that they came together again.

You will recall that Spikey and his companions were relieved of their firearms after Sam Bullwinkle had engineered their capture with the aid of his white mice. They were in need of replacements for these weapons – and Spikey now had four companions since the escaped convict I had met out in the Indian Ocean remained with him. Charlotte offered a solution. There were numerous pistols and muskets displayed above the shelves of books in Edward Rushmore's study. Why not help themselves to some of these?

Spikey undertook the raid on his own.

'No trouble at all gettin' right up ter the homestead verandah,' he said with a chuckle. 'Yer'd think all them trees an' bushes was planted just ter make it easy. The glass doors to that study was open – and that London lawyer, the one what got transported fer doin' in his 'ousekeeper, he was there readin' aloud to the owner – until 'is wife went orf in a cart to look over a new dam that was bein' built. Her an' the clerk.'

'Mrs Rushmore and Felix Lamont, the master forger,' I interpolated, closely watching Spikey for his reaction.

He betrayed neither surprise nor concern at my mention of the man who had been found dead near the open graves in the village churchyard.

'That's him – the clerk.'

But then Spikey's eyes widened of their own accord as he went on to tell me what happened once Mrs Rushmore and Lamont had left the homestead.

Mr Jaggers put down the book from which he had been reading and unwrapped the rug from around Edward Rushmore's right foot, and then proceeded to carry out a cross-examination the like of which had surely never been conducted in any legal chambers or court of law. In response to a question, Edward Rushmore could, if he so chose, give a slight wag of his right foot. Even though it was apparently little more than a tremor, in the hands of an inquisitor of Jaggers' genius it was an artifice which would have enabled him to prise out the deepest secrets from a dumb man's soul. The procedure the lawyer adopted was that Rushmore would keep his foot still if the question put called for a negative answer, but wag it if the reply was in the affirmative.

Whether the lawyer did this to appease an inborn instinct, or to satisfy a curiosity, or to try to secure a nest-egg for himself in the expectation of being granted a pardon and given permission to return to England, Spikey Simmins did not know. He postponed the main reason for his presence – the theft of weapons and accessories – and returned when Jaggers was again alone with Edward Rushmore at a time when both Mrs Rushmore and Felix Lamont were absent from the homestead. And so he had overheard Jaggers conduct a summing-up of what he had elicited from the human safe. That the hidden fortune was a hoard of gold. That it was buried in a churchyard in England. That the churchyard was near the village where one, Philip Pirrip, Abel Magwitch's former heir, had been born. And that the gold was in the graves of ten convicts whose remains had been sent back to their home country for burial.

Following the summing-up and Jaggers' return to the gate-house, Spikey carried out his raid on the study and made off with a dozen weapons – and powder, ball and cartridges to go with them.

Spikey now put a question to me.

'How was we to get to England?'

I could but shrug.

217

He laughed and told me how it had been arranged. Charlotte had again provided an answer. She knew of places in the grounds of 'The Mansion' where her foster-mother had buried boxes of coins. Lucy Brewster had done regular business in arranging passages for unpardoned felons determined to chance returning to England. Charlotte proposed that she and Spikey make use of the same channel. Which they did, leaving the four remaining members of the band with equal shares of the coins and free (but only as outlaws, of course) to explore Magwitch's old tracks in the hope of discovering where he had struck the gold.

After reaching England, Spikey had enlisted the help of relatives he could trust.

'Only as long as I rewarded 'em handsomely,' he added.

The exhumed coffins were carted to a lonely house at a point up the river nearer London. Here they were opened. The human remains returned to the land of their birth were corpses of canvas and straw, with bags of gold dust and nuggets for heads, hearts, knees, hands and feet. The 'lead linings' of the coffins were mostly gold, too. Spikey claimed to have recovered over forty thousand ounces of the yellow stuff. A solid ton and then some. A fortune indeed.

As he said, drinking his brandy as if it were creek water, 'Ole Magwitch sent ten very big men back to be planted in the land where they was born.'

What had become of the coffins and their other contents once the gold had been removed?

'Made a bonfire of 'em,' said Spikey.

'Were there any markings on the coffins – inside or out?'

'Should there 'ave been?' he asked, suddenly concerned that he may have overlooked something of importance and inadvertently destroyed it.

'I don't know. It was just a possibility that occurred to me.'

Spikey shut his eyes to help him picture the coffins and their contents. 'No,' he said. 'They was just bare wood, all of 'em, wif nothin' inside, 'cept canvas, straw – an', of course, the gold.' He opened his eyes and looked sharply into mine. 'There must be more where it all come from.'

I shook my head. I could throw no further light on the matter because, before leaving the village after I had been reunited with Estella there, I had decided that the Magwitch keepsakes had been in my care long enough. Leaving Estella in the cottage to talk to Biddy, I had gone into the forge to be with Joe; and while he was hammering out a horse-shoe, and filling the air with sparks, I had slipped the Testament and the pack of playing cards into the forge fire and had seen them swiftly consumed by flames.

And there the matter may well have rested, except that the presence of the body of a certain master forger at the church-yard had still not been accounted for.

So I put it to Spikey direct. 'Who killed Felix Lamont?'

He became all straight-faced again, but only for a few moments before convulsing with laughter.

'Didn't tell you abart 'im, did I?'

'I fear not.'

After some more laughter, Spikey filled in what he had omitted in his account of what had taken place near the study at the Rushmore homestead. When Lamont had gone off with Mrs Rushmore in the cart, it was only as far as the gate of the main homestead paddock. Here he opened the gate and shut it after she had passed through. He was to remain at this point to open the gate on her return – and he was there as instructed. But meanwhile he had slipped back through the trees and bushes to be near the study door. Spikey knew he was there, but Lamont thought he was alone. They had no dealings whatsoever with each other until in the night when Spikey and his relatives arrived at the churchyard with the cart and horses – and what then ensued must have been one of the liveliest encounters in that part of the marsh country since Abel Magwitch and his arch enemy Compeyson had come to grips. Since each of the men later found dead was out to secure the prize for himself, there were three separate contending parties involved in the shooting, in the course of which the weapons stolen from the Rushmore study played no small part, one of the results being that Lamont received a fatal ball through the forehead.

'And the man shot through the heart?' I asked. 'Who was he?'

'That were a strange thing,' Spikey answered, consulting the best gold watch that money could buy so that we would not be late meeting the two ladies, 'a very strange thing. I'll give you sumpin' ter think abart, Mr Pirrip, sir. One of my relatives once 'ad occasion to seek counsel from Jaggers the lawyer. He said as 'ow Jaggers 'ad trusted acquaintances among the criminal classes.'

Recalling my many visits to the lawyer's offices in Little Britain and the furtive and untrustworthy characters who I had seen slipping into Jaggers' sanctum to whisper information into his ear or coming out after having been through a cross-questioning as fine as a sieve, I confirmed this.

'Well then,' said Spikey. 'The man shot through the 'eart was one of them.'

Estella and Charlotte so enjoyed each other's company that they kept Spikey and me waiting for ten minutes at the side of that crowded Piccadilly pavement. The day was drawing in, the lamp-lighters reporting for duty, and cold dank airs coming up across the parks from the River.

Spikey and I shook hands, each realising that we might or might not see each other again. The two ladies also parted on friendly terms, but with no arrangement for any future meeting either. Estella had no inkling of who her father was, and I had decided against ever revealing this to her. Consequently, I would not be divulging who Charlotte was.

And so the two half-sisters, one fair, the other dusky, waved gentle goodbyes to each other as they moved off on the arms of their spouses through the evening air. Once again I heard what their father Abel Magwitch had said to me:

'*I've been a sheep-farmer, stock-breeder, and other trades besides, away in the new world, many a thousand miles of stormy water off from this.*'

I now had much more than this sketchy account of how he had come by his fortune. That is, his first fortune. For my pains, I had discovered that he had come by a second and larger fortune. I had located part of it; but its source, like the interior of the island continent of Australia until a matter of decades ago, remained veiled in mystery.

EPILOGUE

Over a decade passed, and then one morning, around about the start of the English summer of 1851, I opened *The Times* newspaper at the breakfast table and read that gold in fabulous quantities had been discovered in many parts of New South Wales, mainly just over and some distance beyond the mountain range.

The places where these discoveries were reported as having been made had familiar rings about them.

As I was due to visit Joe and Biddy again, and their children – young Pip (who was now a big Pip and working alongside his father in the forge) and their little girl (who was now quite a young lady and hoping to become a teacher as her mother had been) – I betook myself there with Estella, doing so by railway, as a line had been built to within a short walking distance of the village.

Leaving Estella with Biddy, I sauntered off on my own to the churchyard, and in that remote corner where the ten graves had been exhumed, other graves had since been dug and filled. The old tombstones were still there, in a pile nearby, thick with dirt, cracked and flaking. Nevertheless, some of the inscriptions on them remained legible – and some of the places where, according to the inscriptions, imaginary convicts were said to have died were the same as those named in the newspaper report as having been where gold had been struck.

Further newspaper reports named other places where the yellow metal had been discovered, and these also appeared on some of the tombstones. I had no feeling of having missed out on anything or of having been cheated. For had I not set out on that pilgrimage to the scene of my benefactor's labours and been brought back to the churchyard, I might never have been reunited with Estella, in whom I had something more precious to me than all the gold in Australia. No greater treasure could have been bestowed upon me by my benefactor, who was also Estella's father – '*Magwitch, chrisen'd Abel*'.

Such is the chain of Fate and Destiny which binds us all: that long chain of iron or gold, of thorns or flowers.